the idiocy of idears

L – 13 Press. London

the idiocy of idears

a skool boys tail

*being the unremarkable adventures
of gustov claudius, skool boy and dyslexic.
including his own essays, observations, and judgments.*

also including

*an account of his travels among the islands
of homer and the greeks.*

ritten by himself

privately published

L-13, London 2007

Every idea man has ever had either started with idiocy or eventually ended in it.
Jack Chatham

It is evil to give children a hard life in order to prepare them for a life that may not contain much to make them happy.
A.S. Neill, Summerhill School

To The Public

This novel, if indeed such a rapent text can be termed as such, was written by an unknown schoolboy who went by the nom de plume Gustov Claudius. At the time of writing the boy's age would appear to have been between fourteen and sixteen years, though some sections of the text suggest a wit and intelligence beyond his years.

The manuscripts came into our possession via an unemployed floor cleaner, Guillaume Amour d'Jour, (his name has been changed to protect his identity) who claims to have been a school friend of the author during the early to mid 1970s. The said floor cleaner also claimed that the author had requested on his deathbed that his memories be committed to the printed page so that 'the world shall know'. This same gentleman floor cleaner requested in turn that his own true identity must always remain hidden.

The main body of text of 'The Idiocy of Idears' was written in pencil in the school boy author's own idiosyncratic hand, contained in over twenty A5 exercise books, these ensconced in an old shoebox.

After first establishing that the text was worthy of publication our next task was collating the material into a readable chronology. It was not at all clear which notebook followed which: some chapters seem to have been misplaced, others conceivably lost and some, we would agree, deserved to be omitted all together (notably the chapter entitled 'a brief mention of moneybags' which is an obvious addendum). However, by scrupulous re-readings of the texts a sequence was established and all available chapters included, as it was considered that the violent twists and turns of the author's schoolboy mind were integral to a complete understanding of the world of a school boy of the '70s.

As to the true identity of the author, we have no clear knowledge other than clues that appear within the text. But our considered opinion is that 'Gustov Claudius' was educated somewhere in southern England, Hastings being the most likely candidate, though some academics prefer Lowestoft as the 'home nest'. Of course, it is not impossible that, following publication, some shadowy figure may step forward who believes that they can throw light on the identity of the true Gustov Claudius, though it seems more likely that he will forever remain a mystery.

But no matter what surprises the future may spring, it is unlikely that a more damning exposure of the brutality of secondary school education in the late 20th century will ever come to light or, if it does, will have a finer diarist than Gustov Claudius.

Certainly the publication of The Idiocy of Idears adds immeasurably to our understanding of the banality of our education system and the extraordinary scope of the adolescent mind. Had he lived it seems entirely plausible that Gustov Claudius would have surmounted the many traumas of his young life and gone on to write the Napoleonic sea romances he apparently loved and admired, or indeed become 'a painter of the people' as was his hero Vincent van Gogh.

As it is we can only be grateful that one who hated school so much, and claimed to be unable to read or write, could be bothered to write his own story down.

Albirt Umber and Karl Lampenschwartz, July 2006

A short note on the text of The Idiocy of Idears
Though we have standardized some spellings and corrected the more obvious grammatical errors we, the editors, have decided to leave the body of the text as written, in the apparently dyslexic hand of the school boy who shall always be known as Gustov Claudius.

NB Where no chapter titles were indicated we have appropriated an essential line from the body of the text. Likewise, chapter numbers have been added for the convenience of the lay reader and academic alike.

for Theresa

The Crucifixion of Christ.
By Gustov Claudius, Circa 1972

Book the
1st

The rite to remain ignorent

In way of a forward
by
the author himself

WHAT'S RONG with me being ignorant? We at the W- Secondery Skool for Boys pride ourselves on our ignorance. Anyway if us W-kids weren't ignorant then some other poor saps would have to be and if you think about it that wouldn't change things one single jot, would it. No, it's best that life stays exactly the way that it is, exactly the way that God intend'd, with us W- kids getting it in the neck from above and bellow. In short - carrying the can for all our parents and teachers lousey inadequacies.

Our masters grimace down at us thru the stubs of their yellowing teeth and can scarcely conceal their contempt. They pace up and down the empty corridors, flapping their big feet and grinding their back molars so hard you'd think they were chewing on gravel.

Every classroom and store cupboad is methodically serched and double check'd, making sure that none of us kids has secretly sneaked in here before morning bell for a crafty fag, or to warm our skinny arses on these clapped-out old radiators of theirs.

Apparently the fresh air is just what we need – then why do we have to come to skool in the 1st place?

Old Shawd gets down on his hands and knees and peers in under the desks looking for hidden children. He crawls about in the chalk dust down there then stands, his steel kneecap cracks back into place, the sound reverberating round the empty building like a rifle shot. Straightening up his cuffs, Shawd about turns and smartly marches back out into the corridor.

Just when you think the coast is clear and are about to put your nose out into the cold air, Shawd sticks his shrunken head back round the door frame, sniffs at the air like a horrible rat, tip-toes up to the old store cupboard and throws open the door to reveil Wingnut sat in there puffing on a snout.

Shawd starts belting him rite away. That's our signal to spring from our hiding places like gazzels and leg it down the corridor and escape out onto the icy playground, old Shawd bellowing threats after us all the way.

* * *

Yes, everybody agrees that we are ignorant and disruptive and have some rough corners that urgently need smashing off. We in the B stream, in particular, like to think of ourselves as the bane of our teachers lives. Personnaly i think that the above statement is unfair as i know myself not to be any of those bad and ignoble things, tho it is true to say that i can't read or rite.

1

A famous dictator

ALL THIS happen'd way back then, whilst i was being educated for the benefit of myself and society in one of our grand Secondery Modern Skools. I rarely smiled, my teeth ach'd and everyday became more vicious and unforgiving than the last; and everyday my manners grew more coarse, rough and obvious.

Morning times i lay in my bed til the last possible second, playing with myself and stearing up into the moth-eaten curtains; trying to find the face of a famous dictator, or prehaps the serpent-like body of a Chinese dragon.

Outside my window the echoing din of children stamping their way to skool - punching, screaming and kicking at each other - comes up off the streets.

Like them, i too have been learning how to smoke, back-chat my betters and swear like a docker. As an extra, ive learn'd to steal my fathers whisky and pornography, felch 6 pences from my mothers purse, nick my Nan's fag's, lift my brothers pocket money and spit a dockyard oyster.

Yes, it's a very special skool theyve sent me to and when i finnaly leave that dump im going to be perfectly qualifi'd.

Suddenly there's an urgent, full bludded scream as some inocent

1st year is given a horsey-bite then punch't to the ground by a towering 5th year.

I reach my hand out from the blankets, snatch a corner of the curten aside, check the sky and dive back under the covers. Judging by the gloom it must be 10 to 9 and once again my mother has neglect'd to wake me and i will be hoplessly late for skool.

If, like in the olden days my father was still at home, just about now i'd be able to hear him get hold of his hooter between both fists and start blowing on it like it was a trumpit. Next, i'd listen out for his ankles cracking as he mince'd his way down stairs, put on his small hat and my mother start'd brushing at his suit. There'd then be a short pause followed by the sound of a car horn sounding several times out on the street. You could here my father rattling the vernition blinds as he peer'd up the garden path with his blud-shot eyes to see if his taxi was waiting. This was the signel for him to sit down and have his breakfast: pecking at a small piece of burnt toast.

Only after my father was sure that the taxi driver had been waighting a good, solid half hour would he deam to wipe the butter from his wiskers with his napkin, stand, open the glass front door, kiss my mother dryly on the cheek and head up the path to his taxi; sometimes to be driven to the station, or if he so chose, all the way to his offices in London.

According to my mother, 'our father spends more a week on sodin taxi fairs than he gives her to support his own bludy children!'

"40 pounds a month he give's me, and i have to pay for everything out of that - shoe's, cloths, electricity, the lot! And then there's all the bills on top - the coal... and the food on top of that! And whats his lordship do? Fritters it all away on women, whiskey and taxis! I suppose the bus insent good enough for the likes of him! Well, i can't aford to pay for the phone bill as well, im not made of money!"

But there is no trumpit blast this morning. That silence is a sure sign that my father has left us for good. Which all in all is for the best and i lie here staring up at the curtens that hang there blud red in the morning lite.

Dreamily i allow myself to drible out of the side of my mouth and my fingers sneek benith the bed cloaths and fondle with myself. Suddenly there is a sharp pain and i wake with a start. I lift the blankets and peer down. There's a little rip in my foreskine and some fresh blud. That means that i must have been bleeding in the nite and got stuck to my knickers again. Then the old girl shouts up the stairs that it's a 1/4 to 9.

2

Amongst the mildew and damp

WHY IS it that i have to sleep in this cupboad? Priviousely i shear'd the downstairs bedroom with my big brother, then he grew pubic hair and i was order'd to leave the bedroom of my childhood and was sent up hear to sleep under the eaves with the mice and the sparrows.

Why is it me who whenever it's raining is spatter'd with ici rain water and cut thru with northern blasts? The truth is, this room is so cold that i have to sleep with all my cloths on and when i wake in the mornings my breath shows up like great plums of cigar smoke. All in all, it seams utterly unfair that i have been thrown out of my childhood bedroom and been made to sleep amongst the mildew and damp.

It was my father who, back in the ancient days of his reign, designat'd this room for the use of guests, tho as far as i can remember we've never had any guests come to stay. And anyway's, my father doesnt like guests, family, friends or people for that matter. So the whole thing was just another big sham. Besides, no kind of guest in their rite mind would want to sleep in this damp old coffin, not even if you paid them. And I am not a guest but his own son!

It's my mothers opinion that all of our sufferings are my fathers doing. His plan, so she say's, is to freeze us out of house and home so's that he can 'instate one of his mistresses in her place'.

"And if he thinks that, his got another think coming!"

Yes, im glad that my father has left us and that his pratice of pretending to be our father is now a thing of the distent past. But I am not free. Now it's my big brother who is the boss of me and he points out all of my verrious faults and inadiquesses.

No, there's no trumpit blast this morning but I still get it in the kneck. So i lie shivering in this room with no heating and it's depressing moth eaten curtens, where some mornings it is possable to see Adolf Hitlers face staring down at you, his arm flung out in a Natzi salut.

One things for sure, this bedroom is such a tight fit that if i die of the cold in my sleep it will be impossible for them to winkle me out and they may as well just nail down the lid.

If you think about it, if the old man would just give my

mother an extra 10 bob a week, then maybe she'd feel confident enough to turn the electrisity on, or maybe even chuck a lump of coal on the boiler once in a while, instead of leaving us to freeze to death on one of her economy drives.

On the cealing rite above my head is a damp patch in the shape of a vampire leaning over to bite the neck of a female dwarf with a clubfoot. Another rust stain dipicts the blud pouring out of the bite wound on her neck. Mornings, you can hear the birds scratching about on the roof up there, bringing all the pictures to life. Who'd of thort that a tiny dicky-bird could gallop like a dwarf with a club foot.

It's a shame that birds choose the mornings to start kicking up a row as the mornings are the only time i feel safe enough to finally drift off to sleep. All thru the nite i cringe here under the covers, holding my breath, listning to the silence of the nite. Then, i undo my trousers, thrust my pelvis into the farthist most corner of the bed and piss to my harts content. Who knows if my mother notices the wetness.

The reason i can't risk falling asleep during the nite is because i must be on my guard against vampires and ware wolfs. During the day i may well give the impression of a couragious skool boy, but at nite i am plagued by ghosts and fear.

Amongst the numerious ghosts that live and crawl in this house, the chief is the Messchmit pilot's sever'd hand. It's owner was shot down in a dog fight during the Battle of Britan. After the war the pilot lived here in an old shack that used to stand on this plot and his hand, which was sliced off as he bailed out, still scuttles about looking for him.

Also, there is Old Man Ghost from next door, as well as the

spirits of many disembodied animals roaming about the place.

Is it possible that the Messchmit pilot's hand is looking for the Luftwaffe ring i found in a tin on the top shelf of the garden shed? The ring is of a flying eagle clutching a swazika in it's talons and undernieth it says 'Gegen Engeland'.

Sometimes, if I strain my ears hard enough, i can hear black finger nails of the hand scurrying to-and-fro beneath the bed, looking for it's ritefull property. On these nites i cower benith the covers so's my necks not exposed to it's surching fingers.

But no matter how low i cower, or how tightly i pull the blankets over my ears, i still have to leave a small tunnel in which to breath thru and this will be how i will be molest'd. After all, It is quite proberble that one nite - if i fall to sleep and do not keep gaur'd - that the hands dead, spyderish fingers will creep up the trailing blankets, on to the bed and then, on examining my empity pillow with it's blackend fingernails, crawl down my breathing hole and lay a nest of spyders eggs in my mouth. (I am unable to breath thru my nose, this is another reason that i am mock'd).

3

An early grave

EVEN THO he has left us, everywhere are the marks of my father. On every wall, for instance, is a large, gold fram'd victorain mirror, hung there by his white, vainy hand. Also, his cloths brush - another example - is still on the hat stand waighting for him to come home unanouc'd and order my mother to brush down his suit and overcoat. Yes, all of my fathers nick-nacks and possestions are still in situ, waighting for his return; waighting for him to command them once again with his angry eyes. (I have allready ruin'd all of his high quality sabel paint brushes by neglecting to clean them after use.)

No, in many ways my father hassent left us at all and it is still quite easy to imagin the olden days when he always bully'd us.

When ever i pass down the stairs, or go thru the hallway, or walk into the front room, i am forced to look into one of those mirrors of his and against my will lift my face, look into my own eyes and see if i have somehow grown less ugly during the nite.

Shyly, i stare into my pale reflection. No, my cheeks have not miracliously fattend up to resemble my big brothers cream puffs; they are not plump and fleshy but hollow and drawn. I stand there transfix'd, wondering who i am, why i have been born and what i shall grow into.

I am vain, not thru self love, but thru self hatr'd. I put my fingers to my eyes, pull the lower lids down and peer into the pink bits. If the pink bits show white it means that you are animic and have blud cancer. Mine are very pale. My mother tells me that nanna Lewis, died of pernishess animmia. Actually, she says that my father killed her.

"How?" i ask.

"By worrying her into an early grave."

"Whats an early grave?"

My mother doesn't answer this question but just holds onto the draining board and sobs.

Also, if you have to piss a lot during the nite it's probable that you have kiddny failer, which my big brother says i most certanly have.

Also, i have bruc'd my shinns a great deal by falling over all the time and walking into things. Joanna - Susans friend who has to have sex with her own father - says that i will develop bone cancer.

Also, i have a snaggle-tooth that when im punch't in the face, causes my upper lip to rip open.

Also, all my other teeth are all rotten.

Also, it seams that althou i am still young and fresh-faced, i have somehow grown old becouse the world is too serious for somone as sensitive as me.

Is it becouse of these cursed mirrors brought by my father from cheap victorian bar-rooms that i am decaying?

Also, its true that i have learn'd to swear too much.

Also, my big brother says that my face will be ravaged by achny.

4

stop't up with boggys

BEING TREAT'D as someone of such little importance by my family, it should come as no suprise that i am also beaten and abus'd by all manner of slip-shods at skool, including my so call'd friends and our teachers. Namely, Micheal Crowsfeet and Mister Shawd.

Everyone, it seams, has time to que up in turn and smack me about the head and make lude sugestions about my sexuality. For this reason too - because i am not loved and protected by my father - i was touch'd in an unspeakable way by Susans father, Norman, who is happy to go by the title: 'a friend of the family'.

This is why i wet the bed and this is why there is a certen odour about me, which everybody passes comment about.

It is pefictly true. My big brother anounceses to anyone with ears that i am 'X' years old, still wet the bed and still can't read or rite. And i must stand there in silence and be shamed and humiliat'd by him. And now that i have been banish'd from the bedroom of my childhood, i can no longer ask him to hold my hand and protect me from the creatures of the nite, either. And so i wet the bed in fear.

It isn't just becouse my father has left us that i am bully'd. Even when my father still used to march up the garden path, gripping his tightly furl'd umbrella in his boney, white hand and sleep under the same roof as us, my life was made missrable by him ordering me to eat with my mouth shut, which, when your nose is all stop't up with boggys, is much the same thing as telling a child to go and drop dead.

I lookt at him and put my hands in my lap.

Instead of sufforcating, i refus'd to eat.

"Eat up all that is on your plate, young man!" He spoke at me, all the while dabbing his beared with his napkin "and keep your God awful mouth shut, thank you! Knowbody is interestr'd in seeing the contents of your mouth!"

And he smiled round the table at my mother and big brother, pleased as punch at his clever comments.

I tried using my nose but yet again i had to breath thru my open mouth, which he told my mother and big brother was a disguting sight. It was then that i dicided to pierrce his bulging eyes with my fork.

5

An undrinkable cup of tea

THIS BIG brother of mine is 4 years older than me and dosnt attend the local skool as i have to.

1st off, his brain is far too vast to be waist'd on Secondery Education and 2ndly, it is not his place to move amongst the 'pig-ignorent'. No, instead my big brother attends the Gramer Skool, which lies 5 miles away over the hills in G-, where he wears his smart new blazar and will take his exams and pass every last one of them with flying colours. Just as our father has proscrib'd.

Thus, load'd with glory, my big brother will go on to take his place at the forefront of socioty by becoming an estate agent, a banker, or perhaps even a teacher.

Not everything is a luxsory for my big brother. For the furthrence of his gigantic brain he has to get up at 7 o'clock each morning and catch the bus out of this 'stinking shit hole', (my fathers name for W–) and arrive at his destination ready to spark and glow.

No, unlike me, my big brother cannot aford to lie about in bed all morning playing with himself till the last possible second. Whereas i am reject'd as a retard with no prospects, my big brother is hailed as a well flesh'd genious poised for greatness. Whereas i am known for my skinny and imperfict legs, my big brother is champion'd for his shaply calfs and powerfull thighs. Where as i am a rite-off, my big brother must perform.

In the olden days, when me and my big brother were still shearing the bedroom of our childhood, my big brother was masturbating so furiously that the bed stead shook.

On another occasion he took my hand, which he was relucently holding becouse of my fear of vampires, and rubbed it into his crinckly new pubic hairs he was busy growing down there between his legs.

I was excited by this new introduction to sex in the same way as i was excited by the attention Norman gave me when abusing me as a 9 year old child.

After my brother proving his new manlyness to me i lay awake in the dark listing to my hampster running furiously round and round in his wheel and wondering if i was now a confirmed homosexual and if such exciting abuse was ever going to happen to me again.

I would be lying if i pretend'd that i was happy to leave my childhood bedroom and live alone in this empity part of the house. I am afraid and lonely and if i was braver i would kill myself.

I hug and kiss my pillow imagining that i am lying with little Joanne - little Susan's friend - benith sunlit willows on the bank of a buetiful river. How i could kiss her and let her body lie against mine.

Suddenly, there's a shrill blast on the skool whistle and i jack my head off the pillow, my hart pounding. That whistle means that it is not a 1/4 to 9 but 9 o'clock and mister Shawd, the skool proctor, will be dragging children in off the playground, cuffing them about the ears and sitting them down behind their skool desks to be beaten and educated.

My mother shouts up the stairs for me to "bludy-well get up!" and i snuggle back benith the blankets pretending to be dead. She shouts up again but still i lie here motionless trying to hold my breath.

Recently i have been putting a mixture of milk and broken biscits into a glass of orange squash, then pouring it down the toilet to show my mother that i have been sick in the nite and should not be forced to go to skool.

Next, i hear her on the stairs. She rattles the door handle and martches in.

"Your late! Come on, up you get!"

I remain motionless, peering at her thru thin cracks of my eyelids. On the floor by my bedroom door, is my homemade club. My mother picks it up and leans it against the wardrobe.

"Look, you haven't touch'd your tea, you've let it go stone cold!" I open my eyes and there really is a cup of tea stood there on the bedside cabernet.

"Ive got a stomach ache," i say feebely, "i don't feel well."

"Theres nothing rong with you, now get up. I don't want you moaping about the house all day!"

The old bag really couldn't cear less if i'd frozen to death or been stangl'd by a wear wolf in the nite.

"But im ill."

"No your not, now soddin-well get up!" and she trys to snatch the covers off me then turns and leaves the room.

I lie here looking to the door, which she has neglect'd to close properly and listen out as she stomps back down stairs.

I sit up and take a swig of the cold tea and spit it back into the cup. It seams that my mother did after all try to wake me but the tea is now stone cold and utterly undrinkable.

I put my hand under the covers, feeling for the damp patch where i pee'd the bed during the nite and sniff at it. I put my fingers to my mouth and taste them – nothing.

There are 2 digestive biscits in the sauser, which i stuff into my gob and munch to a pulp, then my mother shouts up the stairs again and i yell back down that i am already up.

I swing my feet over the side of the bed and my feet touch the ice cold floor. It is unessisary for me to dress as i have cunningly slept in my skool uniform. I just do up my fly, pull my tie over my head then pass down the stairs.

When i enter the kitchen my mother looks me up and down and tells me that i look like ive been dragg'd thru a hedge backwards.

I comb my hair with my fingers and sit down. The old girl puts a piece of burnt toast in front of me, then clentching her teeth, brushes violently at my shoulders with my fathers black, onimus cloaths brush. I have to lower my head to avoid being batt'd round the ears.

I leave her lump of old toast lying there on the plate. I have never eaten breakfast and naturaly refuse anything that my mother indevours to force me to eat.

"There! Now drink your milk - im building you up! We have to get some meat on those bones!"

And she hands me a whole pint bottle and stands there with her arms cross'd, defying me to leave so much as a single drop in the bottom.

I rip the silver lid off with my teeth and swig it back in one go, looking her straight in the eye as it gluggs down. Then i have to press my left eye with the back of my fist as the ice cold milk gives me an instant headache.

"I don't like milk" i tell her.

My mother dosnt answer me but instead turns her back, clings onto the sideboard and starts silently sobbing to herself.

I look at her sulkily. Since my father has stop't coming home my mother is so tearful and morose in the mornings that she even forgets to polish my shoes for me. She makes me sick. But i am not allow'd to cry or to be comfort'd. – No! It is me who has to comfort her - she who has neglect'd my welfare and let my boots turn into a pair of festering old rags!

I wipe my mouth, pick up my skool bag and quitely walk out into the hallway. Looking back over my shoulder i slip into the front room and pour something hot and spicy into the little hip flask which ive stolen from amongst my father's possessions. (Already i am stealing wisky from his elegant Napoleonic decanter).

I drop the flask into my skool bag, call out good bye to my mother and slam the glass front door behind me.

6

The fists of a man/boy

DESPITE THE skool being only 5 minits down the road, it is still apparently impossible for me to arrive there at the proscrib'd time. I put my nose out the front gate and peer down the empty road. There is a lady with a shopping bag, tip-toeing along the pavment. Other than her the coast is clear, all the other skool kids are now inside.

Anyway, going down the main road is pointless as the skool has a parimiter fence and there's allways a prefect station'd on the gate waighting to nab late commers. Instead, i double back down the side alley and cut over the back, which means i have to climb thru old Rollingpin's garden. I keep a weather eye open for him but there's no sign so it's an easy run.

All that's left is to dash across the farm road - Ive already cut a hole in the skool fence - then go on my stomach across the back field and slip in thru an open window without being nabb'd. Every morning it takes all of my wits just to be able to scurry into class without getting a beating.

Going to skool is no joke. Our teachers tell us that we don't know how lucky we are, that we don't know that we'er born and that life is going to get very serrious for us once we go out into the big, bad world. As if going to skool isnt serrious!

Anyway, we cow our heads and smerk between the blows, but no matter how conscientious i am in my habits, some obstinate part of my nature still refuses to allow myself to become a model skool boy.

I squeese in behind my desk, gasping for breath but still freezing my bollocks off. Tho it's rong to complain and all to easy to find fault, it still remains to be said that the heatings not been turn'd on and the classroom is like a fridge. 2ndly, we'er not allow'd to wear our coats in skool. No matter what, we all have to strip off to our shirts and jumpers and pretend that that's perfectly normal, reasonable behavior, even when the ice is like sheets across the inside of the windows.

Shawd calls out our names and we chirp up and get a tick by our name. Next, we have to make a que outside the classroom then file down the corridor into assembly, gagging at the stench of skool diners being boil'd up in the kitchens as we pass. Why is it that no matter what type of cabbage those villans get their hands on, they can allways make it reek like a load of old boiled dish rags?

We're not allow'd to sit down in asemble till our gloryius head master, Batman, shows up. Like Shawd, Batman has been drafted in from some boot camp to 'install some dissaplin in us'.

Batman comes swishing down the corridor in his cap and gown, climbs the podioum, fiddles with the stack of flesh round his kneck then call's out 'good morning skool' in a deep, theatrical voice; and we have to shout 'good morning, sir' rite back at him, in a happy little chourus.

Appartently, we don't sound quite enthusiastic enough because he cups his hand to his ear and makes us shout it all over again, 3 times in succession. Finnaly we'er allow'd to sit down cross legg'd amongst the bits of old cabbage leafs and trodden-in spuds from yesterdays dinners.

Rite off we're ordered to stand back up again and pretend to sing a hymn. The 'A' stream kids shout it out good as gold, but most of us 'B' stream kids just mouth the words when mister Mars, the music teacher, stairs cross-eyed at us.

I can't read the words in the hymn book and to tell the truth the songs quite meaningless to me. The gist of it is about 3 kings of ory and tar. I know what tar is, but what ory is is another matter. Ive certainly never heard of it befor, nor heard of the king of tar, for that matter.

We bang closed our hymn books and sit down again. Next, we're told how we are representatives of the skool, even on the way too and from skool, and must therefore behave like model citizens at all times. Old Batman then tells us about his wonderfull holliday in Switzerland, how he climbed the Alps and saw a kid get banged up for life for droping a sweet wrapper on the street.

Im sat up the back with Marshgas, by the black-out curtains. Lately, Ive become so bold in my dissregard for all authority that my mother says that im heading for 'a rude awakening'.

Batman tells us how a whole gang of uprite citizens surrounded the kid, aprehended him then handed him over to the local Gestapo, along with the offending lolly stick.

As i sit here listing to this parable something compells me to take my hip flask from my bag, duck my head inside my jacket and take a crafty swig of scotch. At that exact moment Shawd shouts out my name. He orders me to stand and come out to the front. I just have time to pass my flask to Marshgas, then start picking my way along the row of boys. Shawd shouts at me to bludy well stop dithering, which makes me step on someones hand.

When i finnaly get to the aisle he runs up, grabs me by the lapels, swings me round and bangs me up against the wall. He starts blowing up my nose, small pieces of spittle spraying in my eyes.

Shawds face is quite point'd and malevolent in it's charicter and it is true to say that he enjoys exerting his power over us little ones and rides his anger like a wild horse.

Actually, from the 1st day that Shawd was draft'd into our skool as Proctor, i could feel his hard little eyes following me about the playground, waighting to find some excuse to break me. On account of my long blond hair and artistic nature, no doubt.

Shawd puts his face rite up next to mine and questiones me as to why my breath stinks of alcohol. The thort of my drunken futcher and the waistfullness of my years to come, fills me with sudden recklessness and i start to smile.

"Ive been eating wine gums, sir!" I say, holding down the corners of my mouth.

Shawd glares at me, then holding me by the throat with one hand he starts going thru my pockets with the other. He pulls out my old snot-rag then sticks out his palm and tells me to hand over my sweeties. Quite by chance i have 2 anciant shurbert lemons stuck to the bottom of my blazer pocket. I pick them out and place them in his outstretch'd palm.

They sit there like 2 bushels of fluff, laughing up at him. Shawd sniffs at the shurbet lemons then barks at me to go and put them in the waistpaper bin. I have to walk over to the main door to do that.

I saunter off, drop them clanking into the metal fire bucket then turn back to face Shawd, who is brushing the suger off his hands like it's poision dust. He looks irratable at me then orders me to go and sit down. All of which is a dirty trick, because just as i get back to my place he calls me back out front and i have to walk the tight-rope again.

Shawd was brought into our skool as special measure, and it is in his capacity as administrator of punishment that he box's the ears of any of us boys who step out of line, have the habbit of fixing our jaws in an arogant manner, or like me, tilt our heads sarcasticly at all authority.

I arrive back in front of him awaighting my fate. Shawd examines his small, bitten nails, re-buttons his cuff then suddenly knuckles me on the head with one hand whilest simultiniously punching me, very expertly, in the upper arm with the other. I don't react, prehaps becouse i am taller than i once was, or maybe becouse i am a little drunk. Whatever, i can tell that my lack of pain displeases him as he suckes his front teeth and tells Melthrop whos sitting in the front row doing nothing to "bludy shut up jibbering."

It would be rong to call Mister Shawd completely bald as the back of his head still has some hairs left on it. Then there's his ears, which are quite bushy, and a few oily strands expertly plast'd over his pate. I wait for him to address me again but as he says nothing i turn to make my way back to my seat on the floor.

"Who told you you could sit down, Claudius? Go stand facing the wall!" Shawd likes to pretend he can see thru the back of his head but i actually saw him peering out the tail of his eye. I go over and stand by the fire bucket.

After The Lords prayer Shawd calls out the names of those boys who are to report too his office for morning punishment and i am includ'd on today's roll of honour. I whatch from under my fringe as the lesser pupules of the skool file out of the hall to go to their classes, then Shawd nabbs me again as i try to make a signal to Marshgas.

"I said face the wall, Claudius!"

When everybodys trooped out Shawd sidels over, shoves me in the shoulder and tells me to lead the way to his office. He shakes his head at me like an angry terrier, chasing me thru those desolate corridors.

As for our wonderful skool, the whole place is a disaster arear. We pass by great streaks of green mold growing up the walls from where the rain pisses in whenever there's a lite shower. Really, you can see daylite clean thru the rafters and there's a couple of pidgions up there as well, 'cooing' their harts out.

Shawd orders me to stand outside his office with the other misfits, then goes in and slams the door behind him.

We all stand there peeling chestnuts. One kid has had all his hair shav'd co's he's got nits and another kid has a babys arm which dosnt even reach down to his pocket. He can still peel the chestnuts alrite. In fact his withed hand looks quite like a squirrels paw.

One by one we all get call'd in. You listen for the swish of the cain then out they come again. Before they scamper off we peer into their faces to see if theyve been crying.

In our skool you get the choice of being cained on the hand or your arse. The arse is wurst. One trick is they ask which hand you rite with so's you havent got an excuse why you can't rite in class. That means that witherd hand has to have his squrrels paw cained.

A good half hour goes by and then it's just me stood out there on my tod. I finish off the last of my chestnuts and start playing hopscotch on the tiles.

By the time Shawd finnaly calls me in it's already break time. I hear him bark out my name, drop the shells behind the radiator, open the door and walk in. Shawd orders me to shut the door behind me, to stop slouching and to stand up straight, then carrys on marking some papers lying on the desk in front of him.

His pen slashes to the left and rite, occassionaly stabbing holes clean thru the paper. He pauses, cocks his head and bunches up his small, chapp't lips. A thort drifts across his brain like a lump of driftwood in a filthy pond then he suddenly wakes up and rushs off across the page again, doting 'i's like nobodys bissness.

Who is this small man who hates all children, hates his job and hates me? Why must i be singled out for punishment? It must also be ask't what it is that attracts such a beast to the teaching proffession? Is Shawd really of the rite charicter to be given absolute control over 700 souls when we, by virture of being children, are his natural sworn enimys? Certenly, everything about Shawd is spitfull and vindictive but is that any kind of a qualification? He stops riting, rises his head and narrows his eyes at me.

"You, Claudius are a waste of space. What are you?"

"A waste of space, sir!"

"And now not only are you a waste of space, boy, but you're a waste of time as well! You're wasting my time, your time and the skools time! I don't cear about your time, or the skools time but you are not going to waist my time. Understood?"

He's lost me there.

"Yes, sir!"

"Then why are you wasting my time?"

"You told me to come here, sir."

"Don't be impertent, Claudius, or i might have to hurt you." and he picks up his ruler and flexes it in his tight fists.

"Yes, sir….no, sir!… i mean , yes sir."

"What are you going to do with yourself when you leave this fine establishment, Claudius?"

"I don't know, sir!"

"I don't know, sir? – Well it's about time you ask't yourself some very important questions, isn't it, boy!?"

"Yes, sir!"

"Yes, sir! Becouse if i don't hear some answers and see a mark't improvement in your werk and overall behaviour, im going to be coming down on you like a ton of bricks, my lad. Understand!" And Shawd places the ruler back on his desk and cracks his knuckles at me.

"How am I going to be coming down on you, Claudius?"

"Like a ton of bricks, sir."

"Thats rite, lad. A ton of bricks!"

Behind him, just bellow his window, the skool whistle blows the end of morning break and the kids start trailing off to their useless lessons.

Shawd stands and moves slowly round his desk, a strange lite playing in his tiny eyes. I look down at his knee, which is flexing and unflexing and coming towards me out of the gloom.

Suddenly the chant of 'Fight! Fight! Fight!' comes up from below and Shawd turns on his heel, places his hands on his hips and looks down on the heads of the scum.

A large circle has form'd by the woodwerk block and a man-boy, with a real beard, is beating a small ginger boy about the face with his knuckles.

I shuffle forward and peer over Shawds shoulder. I recognise the ginger boy, he's call'd Cowsfroth and wears a hearing aid and glasses. Cowsfroth is refusing to fight, so really it is not a fight at all, just a boy with a hearing aid and glasses being punch't by an unnatureal sized thug.

The crow'd cheers as each blow strikes Cowsfroths face and an occassional 5th year emerges from the sea of legs and skillfully kicks Cowsfroth in the back befor melting back into the crowd again.

Slowly but surely Cowsfroth is being back'd up against the wall, his small, ginger hands swimming infront of him, trying to protect his face from the blows; and all the while he is shov'd, push'd and spat upon by the crowd.

If Cowsfroth trys to turn away he is shov'd back into the path of the man-boy, who again punches at him, and still the scum push in, hoping to see some blud, happy that somone is being unfairly beaten and that it is not them.

Shawd stops talking and i realise that he must have ask't me something, so i say "Yes, sir!" very smartly.

Next thing, a great roar goes up and Cowsfroth is stood over the man-boy punching his face for all he's worth. I watch the astonish't expression of this bully, who falls back shaking his head like a wounded animel.

Just as it seams that Cowsfroth is going to turn the tables and smash the man-boy for good, Shawd fumbles with the window catches, jacks his whole body out into the cold air and bellows at the top of his lungs for Cowsfroth to report to his office, 'this instant!'

Nobody takes a blind bit of notice and now the boy with the hearing aid starts to kick the face of the fallen man-boy. Shawd turns back into the room and shows me his beetroot colour'd face.

"Out! Out! Out!" And he pushes me aside and barges out the door. I have to jump sidways.

I walk back over to the window and wait for Shawd to appear below. I have to see his heroic head as it scurries across the play ground and leaps into the fray, it's past'd strands flying.

Rite off, Shawd drags the blud'd man-boy across the tarmac by his throat, with Cowsfroth still attach'd, then shakes the pair of them by the hair. The crowd is still gather'd looking maronicly on, then Shawd turns on them.

"What the hell do you lot think your bludy well looking at! Get to your lessons, at once! This instant, or ile skin the hide off the lot of you! Or if you prefer, the lot of you can queue up outside my office for a good pasteing at 4 o'clock.

Shawd suddenly swings his head round on his kneck and looks up at me, stood there in his window and i step back into the shadows.

7

A promis'd nurvis breakdown

I HAVE been praticing walking as if i have steel legs. I walk this particular way incase i should loose my legs in a car crash, flying accident or be spotted by a certan boy - Crowsfeet.

I stumble about trying not to bend my legs in the middle, my knees ridged as planks. Tho Crowsfeet is safely banged up in Borstal, i am still not certain that I am safe.

The reason Crowsfeet threatened to murder me is because i have zip boots, my father owns a car, we have a front garden, i am more likable than him and Crowsfeets family owns nothing.

Yes, Crowsfeet is my bully and has been so since he trick'd me into becoming his friend by giving me the gift of an Easter egg when i didn't even know him, which i didn't want and it wasn't even Easter.

This is how he ingrashiated himself: he ran up to me in the street when I was walking with my mother and thrust the offending egg into my hands. It was my mother who then invited him to come to our house to eat it with me and said i should become his friend. Crowsfeet scoffed most of the egg, made loud sucking noises and had chocolet smeared all round his gob. Also Crowsfeet is a thief and a lier, has stollen my familys money and made me be the look-out at his other break-ins, and so thereby turned me into an accomplice.

Even when i was tottaly obedient and gave Crowsfeet everything i own'd he still threaten'd me, beat me with a bamboo cain and made my life a living hell. In the end i grew so sick with fear that i had to pour fake sick down the toilet and beg my mother not to send me to skool. Naturally, nobody lookt out for me or stopp't the bullying and i was left to suffer.

It is my mother who makes me go to skool and so i have to limp about in this way so as to disguise my charateristic walk just in case Crowsfeet has escap't from Borstal and is 'out there' waighting for me in the fog. Now i only go out at nite times.

When i make myself ill, or rather put mush'd up food down the toilet and make loud wretching noises, i am not sinning but giving my mother the chance to show that she cears for me and really dose love me after all. My lying about being sick is an opportunity for her to save me and prove that she is a real mother.

If, when i start wretching, she doesn't run to the toilet to see if im alrite, i go out into the hallway to look for her. She is there, meeklly ironing in the kitchen so i hang limply from the door frame and tell her that ive been ill. If she is not ironing maybe she is making some toast or, if it is evening, morosely searching about the house clutching a duster, looking for our missing father, the evening sun slanting in thru the widows and a lot of tiny motes of dust floating about in it. Often as not, i find her listening to some maudlin love song by some misserable old crooner, which really does make me feel that life and all joy has come to an end.

"Dont you try telling me that youve been ill, cos your not stopping home again. Enough is enough! Ive told you - i don't want you mopping about the house all day. Ive got things to do!"

I look at her and hate her.

"But ive been sick" i wimper, holding onto my belly and letting my legs tremble a little, "Do i really have to go to skool tomorow?"

"Yes you bludy do! You have to go to skool so's you can learn to read and rite!"

"But i don't want to learn to read and rite."

"Stop your bludy whinning. God that voice!"

"But im ill!"

"No your not! You have to go to skool or i will be arrest'd and you will be put away in a remand home!"

"You can teach me here" i say flatly, looking at the laundry baskit.

My mother bashes the iron down on one of my fathers shirts (even tho he no longer lives with us my father still brings his laundry home, tho to be fair, he does tell our mother that her starching is useless and he would much prefer it to be done by a professional laundary).

"You cannot be taught at home, it isnt allow'd!"

I look at her face. She can say what she likes, i know that she is lieing.

"Look at this soddin shirt, now youve made me scorch it!"

Then she holds onto herself and starts sobbing.

No matter how much my mother threatens me, crys, or promises that she is going to have a nurvus breakdown, she can not force me to learn to read and rite.

Besides, it is hardly my fault that she marri'd my father. And after all, i am the child not her. Yet i am not allow'd to mention my fears and pain , or break down in tears at the drop of a hat. Whereas i must remain sctum about my missery, i have to listen to her harping on about the sins of my father day in and day out; about his various girlfriends, mindless extravagances, pornography and drinking.

Finally, she stands halfways uprite and asks me if ive let the cat out, which I havent.

I tell her that she is going senial and leave the room.

8

excentric and disruptive behaviour

I HAVE not allways been rude and uncearing and there was even a time when i was not ritten off as scum.

In the 2nd year of skool, for example, despite not being able to read or rite, my teachers lookt on in horror and disbelith as i inexsplicably came top of my class. In lesson after lesson i excell'd. This ment that at the end of the skool year i would automaticly assend into the 'A' stream and be allow'd to study for my 'O' Levels. I would no longer be dockyard fodder and mite even be allow'd to stay on at skool after 16, take my 'A' levels and from there go on to college.

It seam'd that despite everyones dissmissel of me as a worthless thick-o i would still somehow bloom. Nothing, it seamed, could now stop me from forfilling my destiny of becoming the greatest and most respect'd artist of the age. I was wrong.

The following September, (when the new accademic year began) i was not sent up into the 'A' stream, as was my rite, but was instead kept back in the dunces stream. From that low place i had to watch the boys who had come 2nd and 3rd to me be congratulat'd and elivat'd to my riteful postion.

Next, to double my humiliation, the boy who came 4th to me was also exault'd and sent on to mix with the elite. The reason for my disqualifcation, according to my teachers, was becouse of my 'excentric and disruptive behaviour' and their belith that i would 'not be capable of fitting in with intelligent children'.

Again no one stood up for me or came forward in my defencse. My father being absent, didn't attend the parents evening and my mother went along alone. There, Mister Shawd went to great lengths to drill into her the many reasons why i should be crushed and would not be assending into the 'A' stream but would instead be broken down and re-made into a half human being.

Despite meaning that i would be tottaly unqualifi'd when i finnaly left skool, and therefore fit only for the scrapheap, my mother, being mortally afraid of all athority, meekly nodd'd her already graying head and humberly agreed that my true destiny was with the thick.

After this trickery i vow'd never to study or follow any of the skool dictates again.

In short – i have become an idiot by design.

9

God is speaking

JUST NOW i said that i was educat'd for the benefit of myself and society, which my mother would say is downrite sarcastic. But no matter what lengths my parents and teachers may go to - with their lessons, threats and beatings, i am determind to remain blissfully ignorant and stupid and never become educat'd.

Everyday, instead of studying my lessons: trying to distinguish the difference between a 'Der' and a 'Ber', adding up a lot of pointless numbers and then taking them away from themselves again, until you no longer cear what 7 times 7 is, i draw little pictures in my exercise book and stair longingly out of the skool window as the bleek, outside world calls to me.

Occasionally, the teacher slings a wooden blackboard rubber at someones head, or there's a fist fight. Or maybe a skool desk gets set on fire, but no matter what diversions are set up the skool day still drags endlessly on, the hands of the class-room clock scearsly moving, untill you'd swear that there's no such thing as time. Finally, impossibley, the skool bell really does sound and we throw back our chairs in ecstasy and bundle for the door.

I get out into the cold air and watch the endless stream of legs heading towards the skool gate. I am jostl'd from behind but still i hang back, refusing to enter the stream. If Crowsfeet has escaped that is presisly where he will be waighting for me – the skool gate.

Instead, i cut along the side of the building, checking for teachers and prefects, then nip over the back fields. You see, i have to go home the back way so as not to be stop't and beaten by Crowsfeet.

I come out from under the hedge next to Rollingpins shed, crawl towards the house and let myself in by sticking my hand thru the letter box. The rooms are lonely and desert'd becouse my mother is afraid to turn the heating on.

I shout up the stairs but there is no answer. I check behind the sofa in the front room but she is not there.

It is possable that my mother has gone to the shops or that my father sneek't home in the afternoon and strangl'd her in the bedroom. I creep fearfully up the stairs, my hart pounding, cross the landing and listen outside the bedroom door – nothing. Even in daytime i am scear'd to enter this haunted house alone. I turn the door handle but am too afraid to go in and see her purple, gerotted face grining up at me. Sudenly the cat rushes from behind the door and i turn and run full tilt back down the stairs, jumping the bottom 5 steps and out the door into the garden.

I stand back from the house getting my breath then walk up the path backwards and climb the cheastnut tree.

Once this was a mighty tree but it's main trunk was sever'd and now there is only a small spout that has sprung up in it's place. I shinny up to the top, green stuff coming off the trunk and staining my hands and cloths.

From up here you can see thru the dying leafs all the way down to the end of the road. The last straglers from skool dash at each other, clouting each other round the ears with their skool bags. I take out my sheaf knife and finish off carveing my name in the top-most branch.

Next, old PC Leggit is creeping by with his mutt. He yanks at it's lead every time it goes to take a piss, then whipps it with his stick. 2 small children, who come cycling along the pavement, are ordered to get off their bicycles and cycle on the road. Leggit blocks the path and tells them that unless they obey him this instant he'll make a citsens arrest. The bewilder'd children are then forc'd to take their lives into their hands and cycle on the main road. They go wobbling off, almost being hit by a green lorry in the 1st seconds. No doubt old Leggit will be pleas'd as punch when they are run down and kill'd.

In the olden days, before they smash'd down the woods and built the secondery skool, there weren't any cars or lorrys smashing about and this place was just a village. Back then old Leggit was the village copper. I know this for a fact becouse one day i saw him marching up and down in the polling shed at the Hook medow, all done up in a policmans uniform that went out with the ark. He had black and white cuffs going rite up to his elbows, like a badger.

Rite now Leggit watches the kids swerve in front of a bus then congratulating himself drags his mutt down the side alley bellow. I peer down at him thru the leaves: a tiny figure draging his miniture dog behind him. Then my hart starts thumping wildly becouse i know that i am going to shout something rude at him.

"You down there" I shout. "Yes you! This is God speaking!" Old Legit peers up into the branches and i cling in close to the branch, trying to hide myself. I didn't know that i was going to shout and then suddenly i did.

"Yes you! This is God speaking!" I bellow again, trying to make my voice big and deep.

Old Legit peers around into space, his small mouth munching his gums. He really does look like some kind of old crock, fit only for the mad house, and he has no idear that i am here.

Suddenly he points his boney old knuckle. "I can see you, i know who you are and i know where you live, and i will tell your parents, you insolent wretch!"

I cling to the branch, my hart pounding. He's a lier, he can't see me at all.

He grimises up thru his small glasses.

"I no where you live and i will report you!"

I lean back round the branch and call down out thru the leeves.

"You, you old duffer! Leave those children alone or i will strike you down!" Then i somehow drop my sheaf knife. I try to grab it but it just falls from my finger tips. I lunge after it and almost lose my grip. I have to cling onto the branch, my hart banging in my throat. I listen out for a thud and a cry as it sticks into the top of old Leggits bonce, but there's only silence.

I stay hidden up in the tree, sure that ive kill'd him. No one else comes up the street, all the kids must have gone in for there tea. There really isn't a sound, not even his dog sniffing about in the leaves. I realise that sooner or later i will have to climb down and hide his body in the bushes. I try to peer down thru the folege but one things for sure, there's nothing moving down there.

After 2 more minits i climb down the trunk, hang from a branch and silently drop to the ground. I walk rite round the tree 3 times but there's no sign of old Leggit's corps, his ancient dog or my sheaf knife. Why, the dirty old twister must have nick'd it! There's a couple of chestnuts on the deck so i bust em open and fill my pockets.

Just in time i spy my mother crossing the main road with Here Boy and scamper back up the tree. She passes directly below me, totally unawares that she is being watch'd, then lets herself into the house. Here Boy grins up at me but i hush him with a stern look.

I wait a few minits then my mother comes back out and starts yelling my name. I pull off a leaf and start making a fish skellington. So, she has not been murder'd after all and has meerly been taking my stray mutt out for a walk. Now it is her turn to suffer and worry if i have been brutly murder'd and she will never see me again.

After that all's quiet till my big brother shows up. Seeings as he goes to skool 5 miles away he's always the last kid to come up the street. Not that you would ever dare call my big brother a kid, as he is 4 years older than me and is already a misearable mini grown up.

It is true to say that i admire him from the bottom of my hart and wish nothing more than to have him admire me back, tho this will never happen.

I wait till he's rite undernieth my branch then swing down on top of his head. I hang there in front of him, screaming like a monky, jump to the ground and beat my chest. My big brother merly glances irritably at me before pushing me aside and walking pompously into the house.

Why dose my big brother ignore me? Of course he believes himself to be high above myself and all others. Also, he hates me just for being born and blames me for driving our father away from home, but that's not the real reason. The real reason is that he is jellouse of me and because he knows that i can see into his scared, naked soul.

Tho i have sincerely done everything within my powers to try and emulate, and somehow become, my big brother, i also sincerely hate him.

Admittidly, i have grown my hair long and learn'd to copy his mannerisims in every detail, even listening most intently to all of his opinions and dictates, but ultimately, tho he is marked as 'special', I am in fact smarter than he will ever be.

He sounds off and I just sit back and nod. Only when he shuts up and i have chewed his nonsense over do i point out the many discrepancies and major contradictions in what he says today and what he said yesterday, last week, or even the year before.

My big brother may lord himself as a thinking man, but it seams that any attempt to disscuss the holes in his reasoning drives him to compleat and utter anger. Finnaly, he stands above me - he is 2 whole feet taller than me - looks down his nose like Hitler then viciously raps his knuckles on the top of my head. This is the signal for me to fall to the ground howling and writhing. My mother comes dashing in from the kitchen clutching her damp tea-towel, and swears at the pair of us to 'christs sake bludy shut up!' She says 'the pair of us' but her eyes are direct'd exclusively at me.

"Gustov, stop that God-awful whining! My God, that voice!" I look up at her, the tears streaming down my cheeks, waighting for her to rescue me and comfort me but she just walks away, slaming the door behind her.

Everyday, i refuse to eat anything that she cooks unless it is chips. For this reason alone i am mock'd. The true reason my brother beats me is because he is jellous of my freedom, outspokenness and charm.

10

A God-awful voice

AS IT happens, my mother tells me that i cry'd so much as a baby that she 'had to sleep at the top of the house with all the doors shut, so's that she wouldn't have to listen to that God-awful voise!'

"Maybe i was crying for a reason" i mumble.

"Well i did everything i could, but nothing was good enough for you. You just cry'd all day and all nite!"

"Maybe i was hungrey."

"Well there's nothin i could do about it, you wouldn't eat a thing."

"Maybe i still want'd brest milk" i answer. My mother eyes me malevolently.

"I brest fed you for a whole year. I was running out of milk."

"How long does brest milk last?"

"I told you, almost a year."

'You said a whole year."

"Sod you! Im going to sodding bed!" and turns her face away from me.

My mother is a short dark woman and any questioning of her mothering abilitys causes her to slam down her tea cup and sulk bitterly. The handle snaps off her cup and she takes on the expression of a tortur'd child. Actually, she cuts her finger and swears at me.

"Now look what you've sodding-well made me do."

"I didn't make you do it" i answer.

"You've got an answer for everything" she spits, "your as bad as your soddin father."

"You marri'd him" i point out. "Anyway, babies can't talk, so if they are hungry they cry, that's how they communicate." I try to explain it to her, but her eyes well up and her ears go back.

"Just you wait til you have soddin children, then you'll bludy-well see! Jesus-Christ-all-mighty! You won't learn to read or rite, you won't eat anything, you don't stop whinning and when you were a baby, my God - the sound of your voice! I had to shut the door and go to the top of the house and put a pillow over my head God-awfull voice!" She looks to my big brother who nods his head in sage-like agreement.

"You were fucking hideous!" he agrees, looking up from his book.

Whenever my big brother swears in front of our mother it frightens and excites me. I leave the kitchen and go to the bathroom to pee.

I unbutton myself quick as i can but ive already start'd to go in my trousers and some of the wet goes down the inside of my leg. I aim it in the tiolet but it doesnt go straight and i piss up the wall and over the floor instead.

I do this all by accident, as the end of my willy has been deform'd by nature, God and the doctors at the hospital.

Some of it does go in the pan and i do my best to mop the rest up with the last of the toilet paper but it all goes too soggy. I chuck it in the bog, wipe my hands on my trousers and walk back into the kitchen where the firing squad is awaighting me.

"I hope you haven't been weeing on that floor again," my mother speaks. "You're a big boy now."

"And you shouldn't still be wetting the bed like a little baby." My big brother chimes in.

And i have to stand there listening to them hurting me becouse of my childhood.

One day i will become unspeakably cruel, walk over to the sideboard, pick up the bread knife, feel it's blade with my finger tips, then step toward her.

How would you like it, mother dear, if i just plung'd this steel into your cold witches hart? How about if i just turn'd and stuck it rite in, up under your ribs? And then i could smile down at your dying face, stroke your ruffel'd hair and soothe you - 'There there, hush mother dear . . . what's that, a little tear? Ah, mother, it is you who are crying now.' Then leaving the room and closing the door carefully behind me, i would walk to the top of the house and put a pillow over my head so's that i won't have to listen to your God-awful voice!

11

In which our hero paints a crusifixtion

AFTER TEA i go upstairs and paint a picture of Jesus Christ hanging on his cross. I use my father's precious oil paints to do that and ruin the last of his most expencive brushes.

No matter that i know i must clean the brushes after use i still can't bring myself to do so. Some i leave head down in a pot of old turps so's their heads spout out uselessly, others i leave on the side of the table, smother'd in paint, there to dry out and become like iron pokers.

Mine isn't just any ordinary old crucifixion scene. In my crucifixion picture Jesus's cross doesn't just stand on a hill in a desert, nor above an olive grove, or on a hill of sculls, for that matter. No, my crusifixion doesn't even take place on dry land. My crusfixtion takes place in a sea of blud!

Also, there are no common criminals flanking our Lord and Saviour, just clouds of darkness, litening, and death. And rather than having a delicate spear wound in his side, my Jesus has a gaping great slit from which an angry great hose of intestines hangs out like a hungry cock spurting blud.

I werk on my painting very cearfully, doing his face, beard and nails. All in all, i paint it to perfection with plenty of blud dripping down into the lake bellow. Also i include a sign hanging off his arm which reads 'J C'.

When my picture is dry im going to take it round to old ma Rollingpin. You see, every Wednesday nite old ma Rollingpin holds bible lessons in her front room for the Godless kids from the council estate and soon i will show them how skillfull i am.

All last winter i hear'd childrens feet walking down the alley by our house. It was nite time and pitch dark, but i stood by a knot hole in the fence and listen'd. There were girls voices mix'd in with the boy's voices, all were high and shrill, but mostly it was girls.

It excites me to know that soon they will all be standing around me, admireing me and congratulating me, looking at my picture of Christ.

12

A brief mention of Moneybags

UP UNTILL now i have neglect'd to tell you about a girl call'd Moneybags. She has no place in our story and has nothing to add to my tail of 'my life as a skool boy'. No, there is no room for Moneybags here and actually there is nothing really to say about Moneybags. Apart from prehaps that she wants to be rich and famouse and snores like a troll!

But all that aside, no matter how aluring naked ambition may be, it would be rong to devote presious pages to someone who has so little to offer our narrative. In truth it could be highly detremental and quite simply ruin the whole tenor of our story. It is enough that you know that all that really matters to Moneybags is the money in Moneybags's pockets, and that Moneybags has enough cigarrets stuff'd in her insashable gob; and that people are respectfull of Moneybags's success, which unfortunatly i am not.

In fact, in Moneybags frank opinion, i have fail'd missrably. Or, to qoute her words in full 'I have not forfill'd my fucking potential!' Which, for somone who so shamlessly worships success - as Moneybags does - casts me guilty of the worst imaginable sin. This is the reason why Moneybags has grown to look down upon me: she is elevat'd thru art where I am lowered by it.

Looking down on people is what makes Moneybags seam so sweet and charming to Moneybags's important friends, all of whom have forfill'd their potentil marvalously – and so vulgar and witless to the scum like me who have fail'd.

According to all the papers Moneybags has now open'd her own museum in honour of herself. Last week she rang me and ask't me to visit this so call'd museum of hers, which i shall never do.

The evening that i arriv'd she was sat inside under a small desk lamp embroidering some ludicrous slippers. I had to bang on the glass to gain her attention and she sprang up and ran to the door like an excit'd kitten. I detect'd rite away that this museum of hers was not a museum at all but rather a tawdry old 60s shop front, converted from an old taxi office.

I accept'd a cup of tea and Moneybags show'd me how she'd preserv'd all my books from the old days in her filing system. Next, she ask't if i'd rite something for her forthcoming catologue (Moneybags is of course an artist).

"You can say anything about me and you can be as honest as you like."

" So I can say anything?"

"Yes, anything you like."

There was a slite hautyness in her voice, also an obvious impatents at having to explain herself to the likes of me. I ignor'd this and meekly agree'd to rite her my trueist feelings.

Moneybags gave me further instructions as to be sure not to exce'd 200 words in my essay. Again, because of my new subservents to her, i agree'd to this tiresome restriction she was imposing on my creativity. I wait'd till she was finish'd with me, then senceing an oppitunity to irritate her, told her that i must leave rite away for my train. She begged me to stay but i insisted on leaving, even tho the next train wasn't due for a full hour.

Moneybags showd me to the door. I refused to kiss her and wait'd till she'd actually bolt'd the door before i said goodbye thru the glass door. I said very sulkerly, as if it were she who had made me leave, then turn'd and walk't off down that dissmel road.

I look't back just once and Moneybags was waving to me thru the glass. I nodded slightly, as if avoiding a blow, and trudged on. Only when i was out of her site did i brighten up and put the normal spring back into my walk.

Once on the train i took my pencil from my pocket, consider'd for a long while befor ritting down the following. Vis:

'I have a friend call'd Moneybags who, acording to all the papers, has open'd her own museum. She has since ritten to me inviting me to come and visit her in this 'so call'd' museum of hers, which i shall never do. 1stly there mite be certen people there, say a young up-and-coming artist, or even somone who has already reach'd the pinicel of their career, and seeing me they mite munch their disgusting lips together and walking towards me, smiling in a hatefull manner, take my hand in theirs and give it an extra hard squeeze, just to test my metal and to see what im made of. And who knows what lies and half-truths mite spill from my dirty envious mouth, and what sort of humiliating summersalts i mite try to compleat just to be like't and adored by this puff'd-up nobody!'

I lookt down at my wonderful paragraph. Finnaly, after much consideration, i add'd a full stop. Next, I wrote it much like this: *'besides, i will never give Moneybags the satisfaction of rubbing her pathetic succsess in my face. None of her atempts at trying to apear intresting cut with me, i know that shes in the pay of the conservitives. She might want to apear aventgaurd and wreckless but in truth she hasnt got a radicel bone in her body and can't even shit without her dealers permission!'*

This, in my humble oppion, hit the nail rite on the head. When i got home i add'd one further sentence *'In truth Moneybags is just a sentimental dish-rag, whoes whole life revolves around t.v. gossip and goo, thats what makes her such a hit with the morrons, that and the fact that shes got a brain the size of a walnut.'*

I then put my comments into a brown envelope, seal'd it and sent them off to her London address.

Something else that i forgot to mention is that Moneybags dosn't accept cheecyness from people who she percieves as nobodys, even if once upon a time she us'd to come round to their house in the middle of the nite, throw stones at their bedroom window and beg them for anal sex.

Two days pass'd in silence, then on the 3rd day the phone rang. Even tho i couldn't see Moneybags's face i fanc'd that i could. Her mustash would nodoubt be twitching and her puckering lips be making a violent, downwards cresent.

1st off she tri'd to apper notcherlent, but i new full well that i had touch'd her rite where she was hiding and after a few brittle pleasntrys she breach'd the subject of my essay and my being 'as honest as i lik'd'.

"You know you can't say those things about me!" she said in her most plumy werking class drawl.

"Why not?" i ask't cheerfully, all the while enjoying the perversity of me now being the dumb one and her imagining herself to be so much smarter than me. Of course, i was trying her patentce to the absolute limit.

"Because people will think that you are ignorent!" she spat with great force.

13

Of stupid heads

WHAT'S RONG with me being ignorant? We at the W- Secondary Skool for Boy's pride ourselves on being ignorant. And if i wasn't ignorant, well, ther'd be no room at the top for all the mighty and great would there and then we'd hear some real tears.

Of course, there are some pupils at the W- Secondary Skool for Boys (notably in the 'A' stream) who will be allow'd to sit their exams and make something of themselves in life, but we in the 'B' stream don't mix with those beasts, or even dare talk of them. No, they are something like a myth that nobody's sure even really exists.

I, for one, have never sat next to an 'A' stream boy. But it is in deference to those chosen few, that we doff our caps, step aside and generally make nuisances of ourselves, thus ruining our own prospects so that our betters may fulfil their glorious destinies in the world.

And so it is that i stand in the centre of this tarmac playground freezing my little cock off, destin'd for the scrap-heap, with no one to turn to, not even sure if it is safe to go and take a shit. No, there is nothing nice about forcing children to go to skool but this skool is espesherly un-friendly and vicious.

When i was still little and my father still lov'd us, he used to listen out for me and my big brother arguing, then sneek up from behind and crack our insolent heads together. This, he explain'd, was to 'knock some damnd sence into our stupid heads!'

In my case, it diddn't quite werk, as everybody is agree'd that i am still impossably backwards. On the other hand, my big brother, with his larger and more ape-like skull, has grown astronomicaly intelligent. We are both train'd by the same master, yet one is destin'd for greatness and the other for obscurity.

Maybe the reason that i have fallen so far behind in my lessons is becouse my father has left us and it has instead fallen to my mother to do her best to try and educate me and force me to read and rite.

Every nite befor bed i have to repeat lists of words out of a little red spelling book that she brought with her from the war. How i hate to see the cover of that book appear in mothers dreary old hands, and how i hate to see her knobby old knuckles pointing out the stupid words that lie therein.

Each collumn of those words has it's own special letter with which the words start and each letter is follow'd by another letter and another and yet another. The list is endless. Apart from the opening letter all the words are quite different and have their own sperssific sounds and meanings that go with them.

After wasting half an houre going over and over the same 2 lines, trying to make me learn the diffrence between a 'th' and a 'fer', my mother throws the book down and shouts "Bludy well sod you!" stands, walks out the room, then comes straight back in and lists all of the things that i wont be able to do when i grow up.

My 1st problem, according to her, is that i wont be able to understand the diffrence between the letter 'D' and the letter 'B'. Or the letter 'Q' and the letter 'P' for that matter.

"If you can't read or rite no one will want to marry you, espersherly with your teeth! And you wont be able to travel on buses, catch trains, read road signs, go to the toilet either!" she reassures me.

"You could come with me and then you could tell me what the signs say," I suggest.

"Im not trapsing around after you for the rest of my soddin life!"

"I could ask a policeman then."

"You wont be able to read the paper."

"I could listen to the radio."

"Your'll not be able to get a job. Besides, no one will employ you."

"I don't want a job."

"You wont have any money."

"You could give me some."

"I havent got any. Anyway, your not living off me. If you think that, you've got another think coming!"

"I could ask dad."

"Your father isnt going to give you anything!"

"I could sign on the dole."

My mother stairs at me with her mouth slitely open. I can hear her breathing, which has grown raspy of late.

There is quite a lot of silence as she surveys me, her face now quite flat and expressionless.

"You know what the problem with you is?" she asks quite violently, "you're argumentative and have an answer for bludy everything, just like your soding father!"

I have to try not to smerk.

"Life isn't a picknic you know, it's a matter of servival!" she shouts.

She is quite rite, becouse everybody who agrees with her helps makes the world be just that way.

"Ive surviv'd, no thanks to your father! If it wasn't for me ther'd be nothing. Nothing! Nothing! Nothing! You'd be in care if it wasn't for me and don't you forget it! His lordship would have fritt'd it all away, every last penny. I have to pay all the bills – everything! Ive brought you up single hand'd whilest that bludy skunk wines and dines his mistresses! And what bluddy thanks do i get for it? You will go to skool and you will learn to read and rite, or sod you!"

Yes, i can assure you that i didnt come to the W- Secondery Skool for Boys of my own free voilition, none of us kids do. Tho our parents and instructors assure us that we are here for our sole benefit and certainly not theirs. Which is another fucking fairy tail.

14

In which we meet creeping Jesus

WHILST I am forc'd to go to this skool against my will, my mother is allow'd to stay at home enjoying herself. Whenever she wishes she can go to the shops, or even go for a walk over the backfields with the mutt, if she so chooses.

How is her life worse than mine? Yet she complains to me constantly as if it is me who has control over her. And meanwhile my father lives the life of Rielly up London, has 18 pairs of shoes, his suits hand taylor'd by Newcombs of C-, Shirt Makers to the King and all in all dresses like an Edwardian spook.

It is true. Whilst i shamble into skool in my brothers hand-me-down trousers and drink my fathers water'd down whisky, my father drinks bottles of fine Champainge, eat's 50 guinnea lunchons at Clarrages of London and sleeps with high priced prostituets. Whereas my father has a Rolls Royce Silver Cloud, which we are not alow'd to even sit in, i only have one pair of miss shapen zip boots that cost 2 pounds 50, and are festering like old dish rags.

If you see my father get out of his taxi and walk down our garden path (on one of his rare vists) you will notice that he also wears a blond beard, a small hat, a starch coller with stud and eligent little side buckle shoes.

Apparently, my father has a flat somwhere in London where he lives with a woman call'd Anne, the woman who my mother mysteriously refers to as 'his mistress'. My mother tells me she went up to London on the train one afternoon, found 'his misstresses' flat and peered in thru the letter box. There she saw a large dog that barked at her, 'and he dosnt even like dogs!' she shouted, exsasperated.

Is it becouse my father has left us that my brother beats me? Certainly a son, without his fathers protection, is an open target for the angriness of teachers, sodomites and the world. But dose it also follow that my big brother should beat me? Strangly, i prefer being on this scrap-heap to being a brite, shinning star. To be held up as a pillar of virtue when one knows that inside a devil is laughing and your boots are covered in shit, well that would be lying.

When i say that my father has left us, this isnt entirly true either. Becouse, as ive already hinted, some weekends it is still possible to see his large, wobbly nose coming down the garden path, his boney old hand clasping his brollie in it's claw and his eyes peering from over the top of his bags.

He apears out of the ether and makes our lives a living hell. Just befor tea time he rings our mother and anounces that he'll be home on the 6 o'clock train. Next up he calls at 7:30 and says that he has been involv'd in a terrible car accedent, somone has been kill'd and that he is going to be arrest'd.

After that it's silence and we don't hear a dicky bird for a good month or 2. But no matter, we are kept on tenderhooks by our mother beause there is allways the chance that he mite just show up and this is the hope that she clings to. Every time she falls for it, hook, line and sinker.

The fact that we are happier without him has never occurred to our mother. Our father never visits us because he likes us, or cears for us. It is purely to catch us out disobeying his orders. Maybe sniffing the air to see if we've been liting the paraffin heater to keep warm, or using the word 'aint', or perhaps painting a picture or having a pice of litter blow it's way into the garden. Just the thort that he might one day come home and discover our world is not pristine keeps my mother in a state of constant worry and agitation.

So in turn our mother makes our lives unlivable by cleaning, sobbing and telling us that our father is going to give her a nervous breakdown.

And it's true, every once in a while a car door really dose slam out there in the drive way and a man, known as our father, comes floating up the garden path like a ghosty.

Quick as a flash my mother rushes to the front door clutching at the skin of her throat.

When our father visits us in this manner he does not enter the room, say hello, or acknowlege us in any way but imeadiatly assends the stairway to the 'masters bedroom', where he locks himself away until he decides to go to the bathroom and boil his flesh in a scolding hot bath.

Any messages about our behaviour are related to us by our mother who scurreys up the stairs trying to find ways to temt and please him.

Me and my big brother look to the ceiling and listen to his small feet mincing about and then our mother comes back into the room hissing to us in exaggerat'd wispers that our father 'wants a cup of tea and a biscit but he wants digestive biscuits and she's only got rich tea!' All in all she creeps about the house like a fucking zombie.

Then, in the morning, after his trumpit blast, our father again vanishes and it is possible to at least try and breath again till his next visit of the futcher.

In this way our lifes are ruind by him even in his absence. Our mother is his gutless agent. In this way also, we are constantly remind'd that we are not free human beings at all but small, broken children, to be seen and done with as he see's fit.

Tho i say that my father vanishes, this is not strickly the case. Sometimes i wake on Saturday morning, look out of my bedroom widow, and there he is - examining his lawn for disobedient stems.

All morning he trundles up and down with the lawn mower, manicuring and preening and pointing out wind blown sweet wrappers to my mother, who follows in his wake like some kind of gannit on a string.

Later, i am lectur'd about the sweet wrappers. I am told not to drop them in the garden but to put them away tidaly in the bin. I point out that the wrappers my fathers holding up are not mine, that i don't eat those type of sweets and that the wrapper must have blown there off the street.

My father holds me with his cold eyes.

"That's all very well, Gustov, but it is possible that you may have drop't them so just make sure you don't do it again in the futcher."

Nothing about me is quite rite. Even my feet, according to my father, have grown to big. My father also says that my teeth are 'worse than my mothers.' It has also been noted that my speech is imperfect.

It is because of my father's indelible presence that my mother is trying to force me to speak correctly, tho in truth her own accent is as rough as a badgers arse.

"You need to learn to speak The Queens English, so's that everybody can understand you clearly and you can get on in life."

"Surly," i reason, "the Queen can speak her English and i can speak mine."

This, my mother says, is further proof of my sarcastic nature.

Silently i glow with pride. Later, it's my fathers turn to interigate me.

He really is at home and is down there sharping his sheers. I go outside and try to sloap off down the alley when he comes round the corner wearing his gardening sandles.

"Ah, just the villan I was looking for. Follow me, young man!" and he marches off round to the front of the house. I have to run just to keep up.

He pulls up in front of the chiminy breast and points with his boney finger. I look. There is nothing there, just a gleaming white chiminy brest.

"There!" he speaks. And I walk over and peer at it close up. Admittedly, if you really studdy it you can just make out some brown oil stains which have been badly paint'd over with some cheap white emulsion paint, but otherwise it's clean as a whistle.

"Explain!" he snaps.

I shrug my shoulders.

"These are stains, creasote stains!" he speaks.

I look at the greasy brown spatters that rise in a high ark above his head.

To all intence and purposes you could argue that my fathers once imaculatley paint'd chiminy breast has been ruin'd. On the other hand, what is rong with the colour oily-brown? Also benieth his feet is a large stretch of dieing lawn, which he hasn't yet notic'd. I look away quickly and try not to glance at his small feet stood there amongst the blackened grass.

"So?" barks my father.

I scratch my chin thortfully, trying to understand what it is that i am supposed to be looking at. If i remember correctly, this is where me and Crowsfeet fill'd a plastic bucket half and half with creasoat and petrol and set it alight, just to see if the mixture would be flammable. I drop't the match and a jet of flame shot up taking off most my fringe and eyelashes. The plastic bucket, which was a precaution against such an occurrence, instantly start'd to melt and it seamed to Crowsfeet that the blazing mixture was about to spill out over the ground so with quick thinking he kick'd the bucket up the wall, setting lite to the chimney brest and his foot in the process. So really the whole thing was nothing but a harmless accident and i certainly was not personally responsable.

"Are you responsible for this?" My father demands.

"No." i reply quietly.

"You've kill'd my bludy lawn!" he shouts.

So he has notic'd the dead grass after all.

"If you didn't do this then who did, may i ask - the bludy fairys?!"

I shake my head. "I dunno."

"Not 'I dunno!' I do not know, father."

I look again at the freakish brown stains. When you look at them in this lite, with your eyes half closed, they make up the shape of a charging bull tossing a bull fighter.

"So all this happen'd by it's self, did it? A can of creoasote pour'd itself into a plastic bucket, took a walk round the front of the house set itself on fire and then flung itself up my chimney breast?" he asks, bulging his blue, sacky eyes. Luckerly he hasn't found out about the petrol yet.

"I spose so." I reply quietly.

"Then you're a lier as well as thief and a vandel!" he pronounces. "And 'spose' is not a word! It's not in the dictionary, so it is not a word!"

Then he leads me back round the side of the house, in thru the front door and presents me to my mother, who is stood there timidly clutching at the skin of her own arms.

"I don't want this child playing with those kids from over the council estate again. They are a bunch of bludy hooligans!"

My father can be rude as he likes about the kids from over on the council estate, but he can't then be surppriz'd if they refer to him as 'creeping Jesus' on account of his floating about the garden in his sandles and wearing a blond beard.

My mother goes to the sidebord and pours my father a cup of tea, the spout nocking against the cup like a casternet. I ask if i can go ouside to play. My mother looks to my father who just holds me in his cold gaze.

"You are not to go into my garage and steal my petrol. Do you understand me?" I nod, very slightly, studying the great soft bags of skin gathered under pale blue eyes. "My things are not bludy play things! You've been up in that studio again, haven't you? He's been up their, Juny, and ruin'd all my paint brushes! Now tuck your shirt in, stand up straight and stop running about like a bludy savage!"

Next, i am told to 'comb my hair, clean my ears out and Christ's sake to talk bludy properly!'

"Dont let me here that you've been over on that council estate, hanging around with those damn'd yobs again. Do I make myself clear?"

I look at him. "Do you mean those bludy hooligans?" i correct him.

Altho i am obedient by nature i have to look away and try not to smerk. On the side board, behind my father, is a little statue of a rampant silver horse. It is my fathers silver horse and unbeknownst to him, it's back leg has been snap'd clean off and is now only hanging on by a bit of spit and a matchstick.

"Look at me whilest im talking too you. And you can whipe that insolent sneer off of your face or ile wipe it off for you!"

He then lets me know that i am ill manner'd, that my teeth are appalling, that i am bludy thick, that my feet are too big and that i wear out my shoes and scuff them because i am arrogant.

"Its about time that you pulled your bludy socks up, and start'd to behave like a young gentleman, not a common pig. And pick your feet up when you walk! You do know how to walk i suppose? And learn to anouciate. Speak the Queens English, not 'aint' and 'i dunno'. You need to think ahead to what your going to do with your life. Get a few exam results under your belt. Get a commission in the Royal Navi. That's what i wished i'd done instead of settling down and waisting my life on bludy kids!" He then walks over to the side board, picks up his silver horse and leaves the room. I listen to his small feet going upstairs.

Really, to start trying to teach me the Queens English now is a bit rich. If my father really want'd me to be 'a young gentleman' or 'joing the Royal Navi' as he claims, then why did he allow me to be sent to the W- Secondery Skool for Boys in the 1st place? And how am i ment to learn elercution, or good manners for that matter, from parents and teachers who can't get to the end of a sentence without swearing like troopers themselfs?

Yes, us kids already talk like a bunch of dockyard chavies, and that's just as well, co's that's exactly where our destinys lie: in the dockyard or the dole queue!

Looking about me, at my job prospects and the verrious forcasts of a missrable life ahead of me, i will aim for the dole queue with all my hart.

15

A sacred alleyway

MY MOTHER says that my father has the gift of the gab, is a born lyer and that i am a chip off the old block. In short – in being my father's son, i am as much to blame for her misery as he is.

Seeing's that i am cursed, and have apparently already fail'd in life, it would seem to be a bit of a waist of time for me to bother getting up for skool in the morning or bothering to learn to read and rite. Which is the reason that i lay here in my warm pit playing with myself until the last possible second.

Yet, despite my familys best efforts to make me see myself as worthless and less than everybody else, i still somehow see myself as superior. This they reffer to as 'my attitude problem' and is, so i am assur'd, going to get my teeth smash'd in for me. It has been said befor: my face is petulant and sarcastic.

In my bedside cabinet i have some of my father's pornography, stollen from his brief case by my big brother then stollen from my big brother by me. I peer unbelivingly into the strange, contort'd pictures. So, this is what my parents did to each other to make me and what people have always been doing to each other and this is how they look at each others faces as they are doing it.

I here my mother coming up stairs, quickly stuff the books under my pillow and pretend to be dead. I will refuse to get up and instead lie here under the sheets and let her stupid tea go cold. Next, old Shawd, the skool proctor, starts blowing on his whistle and then all hell breaks loose. Only then, when i am on the edge of danger, do i scurry from under my covers, stamp my feet into my scuff'd shoes and scamper off to skool.

Like i say, the quickest way is to cut down the back ally, nip over the back and your there. Ive already cut a hole in the skool fence with my father's hack-saw, the only other obstacle is old Rollingpin hiding in his garrage waiting to nab me.

The way that old man Rollingpin has got his teeth into that alleyway you'd think he own'd the place. Mainly, he says that i have no business climbing thru his back garden - something which i wouldn't have to do if he hadn't erected a barakad to stop anyone getting into the back field. And that's not all, the rest of the time he dosn't like me going thru his orchard, either.

Even if you creep down the ally, quiet as you like, old Rollingpin still manages to detect your presence and steps out of his shed with his hands up ready to grab you. He peers down at me thru his thick glasses like someone studdying an insect thru a pair of jam-jars.

"You go round the long way!" he shouts, and he waves his big, dirty finger thru the air. "This is my property and if you don't keep out ile tell your father."

"My father isn't home."

"Well ile tell your mother, then."

"Why don't you call the police?" I look up at him, shading my eyes and squinting in the harsh morning sunlite.

"I will if i hear anymore of your damn'd cheek my lad. Now you just turn round and go back the way you came."

"It's our alley 'n' all."

Old Rollingpin straightens his skelington. "This is not your alley. It is my personal rite of way."

"But we can use it 'n' all."

"Oh no you cant. This is a private driveway."

"It goes over the back to the woods" i correct him, "'n' how can we get to the big beech tree if we don't come down here?"

"You can go the long way round."

"But it takes for ages, that'd be stupid."

"Stupid or not, ile have words with your father."

"My father dosnt live with us anymore."

"Thats not my concern. I don't want you trespassing in my alley and thats finnal."

"I only want to go down the alley to get over the back."

"It is not 'the' alley, it's 'my' alley."

"My dad's car has to come in and out as well."

"From what i here thats not all of your fathers that goes in and out."

I look at old Rollingpin hard becouse i know that what he is saying is dirty and rude and he shouldnt be saying it, what with his fat, ugly wife being a Christain 'n' all. I keep stairing till he takes off his jam-jars and rubs nurvisely at his eyes. Next, he polishes his glasses up with his shirt tail then pushes them back on to his nose with his forefinger.

According to Mrs. Moffit - the old dear who lives in one of the houses just befor the skool - even in the olden day's Rollingpin was a rite misery guts and used to boss old Stuker Joe, just because he only had one hand and used to like to take a strole in the evening and smoke a harmless cigarette without Gods permission.

"Alltho my house and your fathers house at present shear the same alleyway," and he rises his eyebrows at me, "it is only the top part of the alley that is allocat'd for his usage."

"And what if we said you weren't allow'd to use the top bit?" i point out and get ready to run.

I see he's big hands come out of his pockets and i expertly duck under his arm, jump his garden fence and sprint off across the fields. My hart races with glee and i run much faster than i really need to, my whole chest pounding with wonderfull fear.

If you really get down to the bones of it, who that drive belongs too, is the ghost of old Pole.

Back in the olden days, befor my father left home, old Pole was still alive and kicking and he was even more obss'd with who went up and down that stinking drive than Rollingpin. Whats more increadable is that the entrance to old Poles house was out on the road and he had no claim to the alleyway what-so-ever, but no matter, he was forever dragging his gammy old leg up and down that drive, waving his stick at us kids and shouting at us to stop antagonising his pack of huskys. Ile give him that, as we did used to goad them thru the fence, pushing sticks in their faces and snarling back at them.

Then there was the Christmas when it snow'd and old man Pole died in bed as we threw snowballs up at his bedroom window.

Yes, there can be no doubt that old Poles ghost is the true owner of that drive and Rollingpin is walking on thin ice. Must be that he fears nothing of the dead, or he'd be a bit more humble about boasting.

I have try'd to point this out to old man Rollingpin but he says that i have no business being rude about the memory of mister Pole and no business going thru his garden either, for that matter.

Why should i be put on detention when it's only old Rollingpin's obsession with the ownership of the alley that makes me late in the 2nd place? Without Rollingpin holding me up with a lot of foolish talk about ghosts and what not i could lie in bed till gone 9 and still be on time for lessons and not be beaten by Mister Shawd.

The battle for suppremissy of the alleyway delites and excites me. Sometimes, when i know old Rollingpin is layin in wait for me - hiding there in his wrickity old shed, or perhaps crouching behind his hedge - i have the urge to let him capture me. Then i have to tease him with my extra fast running.

The best thing was when we explod'd a fertilizer bomb on the roof of Rollingpins shed and his fat wife peer'd fearfully out from behind her net curtains and crossed herself. Must be that she thort it was a thunderbolt sent from God, or that perhaps an angel had land'd in her orchard proclaiming that the alleyway was now recognis'd, bless'd, holy and sacred, and belong'd only to them there Rollingpins.

16

Taint'd goods

IF THE kids over the council estate are all yobs, robbers and thiefs, as my father claims they are, then why did he choose to make his family home in such a nest of vipers? Of course, he can come and go as he chosses, also, my big brother escapes everyday; it is only me who has to make friends with the snakes, to lean their ways or be eaten up.

Say what you like about the the boys at the W– Secondary Skool but it is the girls who are the most vicious and cruel. Of all the people who hate me, it is they who i most fear. After all, it is girls who have the greatest power to scorn, ridicule and humiliate a young artist.

Fortunatly we are forbidden to mix with them and are infact seperat'd by a tall, wire fence. This fence runs rite around the entire perimiter and then disects us into 2 distinkt skools. What can be the reason for this rigerious segregation?

The girls have their own playground, teachers and skool buildings and the only time we actually get to see their bare legs is in the mornings, for a short spell at dinner time, and then in the evening as we all troop home.

If i have to walk to skool down the road i keep my head down, my legs stiff as iron pokers and peer from benith my fringe at their cold, corn'd-beef looking legs. Occasionly there is a red knee, or a bloated thigh cramm'd into white skool socks all fleck'd with mud.

I want these girl-women to worship me and adore me but instead they just ridicule my awkward manner and spit in my face. Is it becouse of my unaturaly long hair and my refusel to follow the dictates of fashion that they dispise me? Or maybe it's becouse of my snaggl'd tooth and shabby appearance? Or pehaps it is becouse they see that i smile in an apologetic and unatural way and have shy eyes? But since when have sensitive eyes been consider'd the mark of the devil?

It is true, i have been mark'd. When i was 9 years old we went away on holiday to S— and there a man who term'd himself as 'a friend of the family' did an unspeakable thing to me.

Already my father was absent and was unable to protect me as he was bissy in London fucking his mistress; and my mother was to preoccupi'd with her 'nurvious brackdown' to notrice my plight. This is what happen'd. Viz:

We stay in a small shack by the sea and every morning i wake at 5, get out of bed, pad across the cold linolium floor, lift the cotton print curtens and look out of the small windows at the gray sea and sky. My mother is already up, staggering across the shingle to empty the shit tank into the sea. A flock of seagulls goes up then lands around her, pecking at the shit.

My big brother is lying asleep on the couch. Now i must go back to the bedroom with brown, fury, nak'd Norman lying in it. There is also a large, ominus wardrobe with woodworm holes in it's door and the smell of old furniture polish.

Nite times my mother sleeps in the rear bedroom with

Norman's 11 year old daughter, Sue. My big brother sleeps out here and i have to sleep in the big bed with Norman.

I wonder if my mother is instructing Sue in the ways of sex in the same way that her father Norman is instructing me? Is this some strange inishation into the world of adult sex? Could this be the mysterious 'facts of life' that my mother has told me i need to learn whenever threating me with predictions of my dismal futcher? Is all this nite time groping taking place by some special, unspoken, agreement amongst the grown up's? Maybe my father has hired Norman to have me broken-in in his absence.

I knew that i was bad for letting Norman touch me and for enjoying it, but it was wonderfull having an adult noticing me when i had no father to speak of.

I look to my mother each morning over the breakfast table for a sign that she is going to marry Norman, that he is breaking me in and that everything is allrite. But she just butter's her toast, tells me that i am a fussy eater and looks away.

It must be a secret initiation, i decided.

No, no one speaks of the nite times and what happen's when i go to that room, not even Norman. Only at nite does he speak to me in hot wispers, his toung rite in my ear. 'Can you keep a secret?' he keeps asking, thrusting his hips at me. I had to agree dutifully and then he pull'd my knickers down.

In the daytime Norman pats me on my bottom and buys me an ice cream.

From then on Norman call'd me Fred and whenever i heard his voice or he tri'd to touch me in public with his hairy fists, i duck'd or sped away from him.

Becouse i have been touch'd by a man, does that automaticly

mean that i am to be forever mark'd as a homosexual? That i can never be love'd by a girl or a woman? That i must forever be unclean?

It was shortly after this defilement that i tried on my mothers dresses and started expossing myself on the streets. I shav'd off my eyebrows, hik'd up my skirts to passing buses and start'd having sex with my stray dog, Here-Boy.

Then i start'd hating my stray dog, Here-Boy - who i had formaly found it easy to love - and practic'd strangling the disgusting beast. Next, i commenc'd my regime of pissing the bed every nite to spite my mother for giving birth to me, and now my mother has to change my bed sheets every morning and has to take Here-Boy for walks due to my neglect and dislike of my pet. Maybe this will finally teach her a lesson.

Later, Norman, who is a woodwerk teacher, sent me a wooden crusifix he had made out of wood and brass. Now i have to stand that cross on my bedside cabbernet to protect me from wearwolfs and vampires. Which is crazyness as the damned cross itself was made by a vampire!

Norman also told me that the swastica is evil. I have spat on his cross.

Is it becouse Norman actually spoke to me that i let him ruin me? Is this why i look everywhere for recognition? After all, to be aknowleg'd and regard'd as somone who is auctually alive must be wonderfull. Yes, it is true to say that now, in my pathetic attempts to be like't, i will smile at almost any beast.

17

A little friend

ME AND my worthless companions stare felornly out thru the rain-fleck'd windows to the distant road beyond the perimeter fence. A lone car goes past and a lady with elephantinetitas hops about putting her red umbrella up.

Why am i afraid of her? Just looking at her makes me sceared that i am going to somehow catch her disgusting disease, but is that any kind of reason to loath and despise her? What ever has happen'd to the simple, gentle child i remember myself to be? It seems that i am getting more and more vicious by the second. In fact, i have never felt so spiteful in my entire life and can positively feel the anger crawling across the backs of my hands like a lot of poisons red ants.

The teacher calls out something and i look back up to the blackboard and the clacking of the chalk as he screatches out the letters to some ridiclious word that means nothing to me.

So, now it seams that i can't even stand to see a perfectly ordinary woman putting up a red umbrella without wishing her to drop dead on the street, or for some passing plane to fall from the skys and smash her to smitherines, and all because i am afraid of catching something off of her disgusting old legs.

Must i always do rong and make the world hate me, just so's i can be cleans'd in hells firey flames? My mother says that i am sarcastic and argumentative by nature and Mister Shawd says that i am 'a prize speciman' and for this I am beaten.

Every day a dozen of us boys are singl'd out for correction at his hands. Naturaly, i long for the attention that is to be gain'd by these beatings. And it is not just Shawd, our skool proctor who disciplines us. No, all of our masters, with the exception of Miss Hart (the assistant music teacher), has a special 'little friend' - either a vicious bamboo, or perhaps an especially ancient and pliable slipper - which is kept on the desk in front of them within easy reach so as to whip our buttocks - or sometimes, if they are a little more shy, he or she, (for all of their weapons have sexes) is kept in a drawer, or perhaps in the store cupboard, which in many of our classrooms doubles as the punishement room. There are no windows in those dungons and the teachers can do what they will with you once they get you in there.

Any of us who are chosen for punishment - whether it be for our disobedient natures, or merely at the passing whim of one of our glorius masters, refuse to cry out in pain and are proud of our scars and our heroes names being enter'd into the hallow'd pages of the punishment book.

Yes, all of our teachers are instruments for our purification and we goad that gang of criminals to new heights of anger, just to marvel at there bulging eyes and spluttering faces. No act of cruelty surprises us anymore, already we have been humiliat'd in every conceiveable fashion and firmly believe that we deserve to be spoken to sarcasticly, hammer'd with boot and fist, then made to apologise and be thrown on to the rubbish heap.

One of the funnier aspects of our situation is that if we are indeed the lowest of the low and nothing more than a bunch of worthless cretins - as we are assur'd - then what does that make our gloryious teachers and masters?

The answer to this question cheers me no end and i smile a particular little smile - which i am assur'd will be wip'd clean off my dirty kisser once and for all.

Yes, despite how amusing i find the whole thing, it really is true that i am going to be made to pay, not only for my own faults, but for all the faults of my perents, teachers and betters in general. Then, if i take my punishment like a man, i will be allow'd to crawl benith the lowest piece of dung and live out my life as a worthless, stinking louse.

18

A military knee cap

AFTER SKOOL monday, we don't go home as usual but instead stay behind to watch mister Goldfinch, the deputy head master, being chas'd round the skool field by a flick knife wealding 5th year.

The whole skool crowds round to get a better view, like as if it was sports day. Even some of our student teachers pull up a seat on their way home. Underpaid and timid by nature they do not dare trying to intervine.

Mister Goldfinch is one of the old skool who fought thru the last war but his glory days are in the past. No longer can he box the ears of Natzis, now he is fat and slow and can only just manage a wheezing trot, zig zaging about in front of the knife thrower like a tir'd old donkey. We all cheer as he does several laps of the silver birch tree befor collapsing in a heap.

The kid with the knife is just playing cat and mouse, he walks over and prods Goldfinch who springs to his knees, clasps his hand to his hart and beseechs the skool boy, in Gods name, not to cut his throat. The kid doesn't stab Goldfinch outrite but instead pretends to knight him. He makes a whole show for us with Goldfinch knelt there before him praying for his life. Suddenly Goldfinch lunges at the boys legs and hangs on for dear life. The boy trys kicking him off but Goldfinch wont let go; and all the while he is sobbing and wetting the boys thighs with he's tears.

The boy backs away, dragging Goldfinch along after him, like he's wading thru mud. Goldfinch implores the kid again, who raises his knife arm and for a moment it looks like he's going to stick him one in the guts but just then the cavalry rolls up, 2 of them pushing thru the crowd.

The 1st policeman distrackts the kid whilest the 2nd sneeks up behind him, grabs him round the throat and slings him to the deck. The 1st policeman then stamps on the kids hand and kicks his knife away, next they unhook Goldfinch from his lap and drag the kid away.

Just then old Shawd comes sculking out from behind the science lab, runs bravely across the field and sneeks in a crafty kidney punch before the old bill stuff the kid in the back of their blue Marya. Thats the end of Monday and thats the last we see of the knife thrower.

Tuesday we have Biology with Swain. Swain is small with a rat-like moustache and a Canadian accent. Swain also thinks that all of us pupils are pathetically stupid, with me being king of the pile. Naturally, he believes himself to be incredibley smart, which is why he is our teacher and not vice versa.

Swains job is to beat me across the buttocks with his size 12 slipper, on account of my cheekiness. Who knows if he gets a 'hard-on' as he beats us poor wretches in his care.

Needless to say Mister Shawd, the skool proctor, has no need of such pathetic means of correction as the cane or slipper, because he is a military man with a military knee-cap made of British steel.

This is his main weapon against us insobordinant children. Oh yes, when Shawd is making love to you (and in truth he really is nothing but a bald midget) with his toad-like tongue whispering threateningly into your skool boy ear, then you know for sure that you are about to be shown the error of your childish ways.

Yes, when Shawd starts blowing you kisses like that it means that in the not to distant future you are going to feel his steel knee-cap come smashing into your skool boy thigh as he delivers one of his famous dead-legs. Whereupon the happy recipient falls howling to the feet of his Lord and Master.

"Am i hurting you, Claudius?" he whispers.

"No, sir!" i reply most truthfully and honestly.

"Well i should be, because im standing on your hair, boy!"

This is one of Shawds little jokes and really, in some ways, i think that i am suppos'd to laugh but im not sure which will bring me the most pain: to smile with him, or to stand rigidly to attention as, in his military fashion, he has taught us all to do.

"Do you think i am hurting the boy, Mister Dog-Jaw?" Shawd

turns to Dog-Jaw, the physics teacher. Dog-Jaw, who stands head and shoulders above Shawd, is his constant shadow. Dog-Jaw smiles down from his big doggy face and shakes his jowls.

"Aowe downt know wroughtly Muster Shward. Boot Aowe fink der luds in need off un air coot!" Dog-jaw has 2 pink, plastic hearing aids wired to his huge dome and speaks like a barking dog.

Shawd smiles anticipatingly, nodding his small head and licking his thin, dry lips.

The point is, is that i have long butiful blond hair, the exquisite face of a cherub and Shawd hates my beauty and natural grace. I glance into his hard little eyes, looking for some warmth and compassion that might be lying hidden there and thereby spare myself but there is none. I bite my tongue and go down.

"Did i tell you that you could lie about on the floor, Claudius? What do you think this is, a bludy holiday camp!" Shawd turns to Dog-Jaw as he delivers his hilarious joke. Dog-Jaw smiles uncomprehendingly so Shawd turns instead to the class. The class takes it's cue and goes boggle eyed with laughter, everybody busting a gut to show their appreciation of such wit. And even i have to laugh, lying there on the floor; my feet kicking on the tarmac; my face contort'd by the sharp, stabbing spasms that shoot up and down my paralys'd leg.

Shawd leans his little face over mine as i riggle in the grit grimacing.

"Say 'thank you', Claudius."

I am in too much pain to speak.

"I said, say 'thank you, sir', Claudius!"

"Fuck you, sir" i whisper it thru my clench'd teeth, my eyes smarting on account of the cold. But he hasn't heard me properly, i say my naughty word in secret.

"Speak up, Claudius, so everybody can hear you" and he licks his thin lips again. "Say 'thank you my dear teacher, sir.' Say 'thank you' Claudius."

I try to get up, but he easily pushes me back down onto the cold ground before i can find my balance.

"You want to decide whether you want to get up or lie down, Claudius!" He turns triumphantly to the class, which hands everybody another good laugh. They stand around puffing out their stupid cheeks, grateful, because in truth they love Shawd and his brutality. Then suddenly he turns on them.

"So you think that Master Claudius is a comedian, do you?" Shawd scans the little circle of malnurished faces. They imeditaly stop laughing and instead hang there heads, shrinking their necks into their shirt collars.

"Is Master Claudius an endless source of amusement for you? Would anyone like to come out front and swap places with him?"

A hush falls over the little group and they look demurely down at their scuff'd shoes. I pull a face at them from my resting place at Shawd's feet.

"You, Grimthorpe, would you like to come out here and swop places with Master Claudius?"

Grimthorp shakes his head. Shawd re-pastes the little strands of hair that flap insolently in the icy wind. He glues them back in place like as if he's a small kitten fixing it's whiskers. It really is comical to see that idiot trying to arrange his pathetic strands in that defiant wind. Finally he slaps them down with a thick lick of his disgusting spit and defies us all with his quick, rodent-like eyes.

"Get up Claudius and rejoin the class. And get your hair cut, this isn't a bludy girls chorus!"

I climb from the tarmac and hobble over to stand with my classmates. Even compar'd to a skool boy Shawd really is quite small. And Dog-jaw stood there towering behind him like the village idiot.

Tho brutel it is never-the-less comforting, and reassuring, for us to be remind'd of our station in life and to know that we should expect nothing from the future other than a good duffing.

19

An unask'd for duffing

ON MY 1st day at this skool i stood timid and alone on the cold, harsh playground, toeing the bust'd tarmac. Misserly weeds push'd up into the cold September sunlite and i realis'd that i was like one of them. The skin of my cheeks smart'd and i put my hands numbly in my short pockets.

My blue blazer, which my mother had bought 2 sizes too big for me as an economy measure, drew a gang of elder boys who surround'd me and taunt'd me for having a new jacket.

One boy, a great lout of a lad with a hiddious cold-sore covering his entier chin, ask't me where my mummy was, whilst another sneek'd up behind me, knelt down on all 4's then cold-sore shov'd me backwards over him and i came crashing down, my head rebounding on the tarmack.

As soon as i was down they all leered their jeering faces into mine, mocking me for wearing shorts, having a new blazer and being a rich kid.

I wait'd till they left, then pick'd myself up from the ground and lookt down at my bruis'd, goose-flesh'd legs, trying to comfort myself against the cold and the loneliness. Also, my head was pounding from where it had hit the deck.

So this is the brave new world where i have been condem'd to live for the rest of my childhood.

There was already a tear in my new blazer and lots of little pieces of black grit stuck into my shaking, white knees. Then I realis'd with fear that i really needed to take a shit.

I hobbl'd over to the main building, following a little river of piss that trickl'd out thru an open doorway and snaked across the playground. Cat calls of the 5th formers echo out from inside that dark cavern and a 4th year gobbs down my back as i duck inside.

The 1st thing that hits you in that place is the stench of piss. It rises up like a fog, stinging your eyes. I pick my way along in the half lite checking all the cubicles, trying to find one that's empty, still has some bog paper left in it and where someone hasn't shitt'd all over the toilet seat.

They only have the hardest, shinnyst bogpaper in those stables, the type that skids rite off your arse and the shit ends up under your finger nails. And all the while a gang of 5th years is swinging between the cubicles, kicking in the bog doors and howling like a lot of monkeys looking for 1st year cock. I sit hovering over the cold bust'd seat, trying to hide my small, nude penis.

What i wanted most desperately was to somehow become older

straight away, to be free of my hiddious childhood; so as to be able to leave this place and be free of skool, teachers and bullys forever.

Whatever great advancements may have been made in the skooling of the masses, it has to be said that brutality still rules the roost. Every face in here is either blank or excessively aggressive. You will never see a kid who is genuinely happy or smiling. If we can swear, drink, smoke and smash things up in the manner of our fathers and teachers, only then is there any learing merryment.

The reason us human beings are such a lousey lot, in my humble opion, is because we are a bunch of theifing, murderous, chimpanzees with no respect for God or his universe. If you don't want to become one of them: wear their fashions, listen to their music or to fit into their disgusting world then . . . well, they will hate you, never let you rest and set out to destroy you.

After my shit it's assembly time, then off to lessons where we have to sit at our desks and copy up the skool timetable. At break time Crowsfeet shouts that he's going to get me after skool and that im to meet him on the Hook Medow for a fight. And thats how my life continues, day in, day out. Lesson after lesson week after week, month after month and then add some years.

And being made to run round the skool field in the sleet and snow, take ice cold showers while the games teacher screams blue murder at us if we don't get rite in under the icy jets. And all the while i have to try to hide my self, because i am asham'd of my poor underdevelop'd body. Because i have been touch'd by the hand of a man.

20

Imogin Hudson

At 4 o'clock the skool bell goes. I scrape up my skool books, shove them in my bag and barge my way out of the classroom. I keep my head down as we stream along the screaming corridors.

Once outside i run like the clappers across the skool field, not only to escape Crowsfeet but also in case any of the skool girls spot me, ridicule me, or hold me down and expose me. 2 boys from the 2nd year have already been pinn'd down and had their nude cocks shown to the cold air and jeering crowds.

The girls skool classrooms show behind a very tall fence. Stepping onto the grass, or going anywhere near that fence, is 'strictly out of bounds'. When the girls come out to play, put their wet fingers to the rusty wire and call out to us across the damp grass, i pretend not to be able to hear them and instead look very hard at a lolly-stick dug into the bust'd tarmac.

When i say that i ignore them, i should add that one of the girls i do actually recognise. Her name is Imogin Hudson and she already has large, woman-like breasts. Some of the 5th year boys say that they have felt them and suck'd on them.

When i hear their boasts and the strange guzzling sounds they make in their throats, a buzzing noise fills the inside of my head and i have to turn away. It is me who loves Imogin Hudson, not they. They have no rite to utter her name, let alone bost of touching her and Imogin Hudson has no bissness pushing her body up against the wire fence and making lude gestures with her mouth and toung.

In my early life at this skool i stupidly boast'd that once, when i was a mear child back in Junior skool, i was in the same class as Imogin Hudson. For a moment my skool mates lookt up and i could feel that they were actualy listening to what i said, then they lookt away again.

"I kiss'd her" I quickly add'd, which in some ways is true. This brought them to look scepticly at me once again and also seal'd my fate.

In juniors skool we were not segregat'd, as we are here, but had mix'd classes and were allow'd to talk with the girls, even taking gym together.

There was no wire fence seperating us in those days and in the spring and summer we went running on the skool field, playing kiss-chase and rolling in the grass. In short - behaving like real children.

Of course, all of this has now been stopp't, we have been stripp't of our inosence and are instead being beaten and prepar'd for our hard lives in the adult world.

It may have been rong of me to boast, but saying that i once kiss'd Imogin Hudson is not exactly lying.

When we had gym on Thursday mornings we boys troop'd out into the playground in our shorts and vests and the girls lined up beside us in their vests and blue knickers. As we stood there in the freezing air i would take longing, side-ways glances at Imogin

Hudson, willing her to look at me. When would she finnaly make the sign that she knew that i lov'd her and that i was as unique and as special to her as she was to me?

I stood on my tiptoes and peek'd down at the beginnings of her wonderful, girl-brests, her nipples pushing rudely against her white skool vest. None of the other girls yet had breasts but Imogin Hudson did. What would it be like to kiss her, suck her lower lip, then put my toung in her mouth? - which is call'd French kissing.

In all of these childish notebooks you can discount anything you like but it is important to understand that Imogin Hudson was not like any of the other girls in that skool. No, Imogin Hudson was different in every respect. Just the way she push'd the hair from her eyes was unlike any other girl, and there are a hundr'd other things i could list that made her stand out like a flower in winter time.

Imogin Hudson was special and had been sent for me to love and me alone.

And so i lookt upon my vision, then i would look up and find myself surround'd by the shrill, hard voices of my playmates and i would run and shout in anger, stamping my feet on the damp ashfelt.

There was a huge map of the world hanging down alongside the blackboard in our classroom. Over on the left hand corner was America, and rite above America was Canada and at the top of Canada was ritten Hudson Bay, in large black letters.

Even tho i couldn't read or rite as such i knew that it said Hudson Bay, becouse Mister Hendy had point'd out the letters with his stick and told us to repeat it after him and my ears had blush'd.

I stair'd at the map and memoriz'd the 1st letter – a letter 'H' i repeat'd it under my breath and every time i came into class i would look up to that alter and see Imogin Hudsons name written up there on the map of the world and my hart would flutter in my throat.

It seam'd amazing, yet only naturel, that my loves name should be ritten like that, rite across an ici sea. And once, after skool, i came back into the classroom, pull'd up a chair, stood on it and kissd the letter 'H' of Hudson bay. And that spring i really did kiss Imogin Hudson and not just a map either but the real Imogin Hudson.

Even tho i couldn't read or rite, Imogin, i learn'd to spell your name and once, during a game of kiss-chase, i caught you round your skool girl waist, and no matter how despretly you tri'd to get away and shake me off, you couldn't. And the more you struck out at me the tighter i clung on. Oh yes, Imogin, i am amongst other things a wonderful runner, and as i lent in to claim my prize, my lips looking for your sweet cheek you pull'd violently away, and not in fun but with real disgust on your mouth. And so i let you escape and you ran off whilest i was left standing, stairing after you and as i turn'd a boy, who in this history i will simply refer to as the Vicas son, laugh't in my face.

Next day that same boy comes up to me and says that he is going to bring flowers into skool to give to Imogin Hudson and i look at him and think that it is the most wonderful idear that i have ever heard. Yes, to bring flowers into skool for Imogin Hudson!

The Vicas son has delicate frecles on his nose, where as i have just a small mole on my upper lip. The Vicas son's hair is a brite cheastnut brown, whereas mine is a dull straw colour. Also, my ears stick out and i have a snagl'd tooth.

"Yes, and i know where we can get the flowers." i tell him.

"Where?"

"From the woods over the back, there's loads of flowers growing in the woods, i could pick them on my way into skool!"

The Vicas son nods slyly at me and brushes his brown fringe from his eyes.

Of course, i don't want to share Imogin Huddson with the Vicas son but this way i will at least have a companion, someone who understands my trueist feeling, and at least i wont have to approach Imogin Hudson alone. Besides, how could i let the Vicas son bring Imogin Hudson wild flowers, whilest i stood by and brought none?

I tell him that we should meet up the next morning and pick blue-bells in the woods together but the Vicas son says that we'll have to pick our flowers sepperatly as he's father drives him to skool. I nod thoughtfully. Very well, we will pick our own flowers then present them to Imogin Hudson together, when we get into skool in the morning. And so our plan is agreed.

In those days i had to walk 2 miles to skool, rite thru the woods and beyond. My mother used to walk halfways with me, then the last bit i'd go on on my own.

Once we get to the woods i go to werk. It's not the easiest thing to find flowers that will adequately show the true depth of my love for Imogin Hudson. Most importantly, my blue-bells must be better than anything that the Vicas son might find by the roadside.

In the 1st woods there's nothing doing, then in a little wood by the old style i find not only blue-bells but some white-bells as well. I dissapear in amongst the trees, there seams to be loads more growing over by the old bomb hole. I just start picking the 1st, most important blue-bell when my mother shouts out for me to hurry up and stop dawdling! I rip the stalks from the ground in great fist fulls, then run back out onto the path.

I look around but my mothers already half way up the field. Then Here-Boy comes lolloping up, going sidways like a crab, then we both run and catch her up.

In skool i don't hang my coat on my peg as we have been directed to but instead chuck it on the bench and go straight into the classroom. I march rite up to Imogin Hudson's desk and hold out my blue-bells in my fist.

I can feel the other children stairing at me, my ears go hot and the hairs prickle up on the back of my skull but i don't look round, i only look to her - my beautiful Imogin Hudson; at her small nose and blond-brown hair tied back in a ponytail. Today, she is wearing her blue strippy dress and her small brests show thru the gloryious matirial.

Imogin Hudson tilts her chin at me as i hold out my flowers and mumble that they are for her. I say it very quietly, under my breath and i don't look in her eyes, which are too sceary. But Imogin Hudson doesn't reach out and take my flowers then kiss me like in my dream. Instead she just calmly folds her hands in her lap and turns her face sharply away.

I stand there waiting then here sniggering coming from behind me. In fact there is sniggering coming from all around me and i feel the blud filling my ears. I try to force myself to look up and smile into Imogin Hudsons gray eyes but i carnt, and then the Vicas son is there, leaning his face into mine and it's all too late - it's all over and everyone is openly laughing at me.

Of course, the Vicas son has no flowers, he was never going to bring flowers because the Vicas son is not open and knightly like me but is instead mean, clever and gaurd'd. I see his nose close to, it is small and freckl'd. No, that charlatan dosnt really love Imogin Hudson, a boy with a nose like that doesn't even know what love really is.

Some readers will no doubt say that my history stinks and that meer sckool boys should never think or speak in terms of love. Well, may i just say that life is more full of poetry than any of you so call'd artists, poets and teachers will ever be able to grasp and in truth skool boys are a lot closer to God than every single one of you.

I look around me in fear and want to tell my classmates that it was the Vicas son's idear to pick the flowers, not mine. That he surgest'd it, not me. That i have been set up by a villan of the church.

I want to tell them all the truth but no one is the least bit interested. All they will ever listen to is lies and slander until the day they die. They prefer it becouse of their inherent, spitfull natures. But i assure you it was he - the Vicas son - who surgest'd we pick flowers for Imogin Hudson, yet now it is he who is pointing his finger rite into my hart and holding his yellow belly'd stomack and laughing. Becouse never has there been anything so funny in all the whole wide world as me stood here holding out flowers for a girl who is disgust'd by me.

I go to my desk and stair hard at the blackbor'd. All morning my buetifull bouqet of wild blue-bells lies there dying on Imogin Hudsons desk. Then at at break time she stands, picks them up, walks to the front of the class - i watch her butiful skool girl legs from under my lashes - then turns, smiles sarcasticly at me and very purposely, drops them into the waist paper bin.

21

In which our hero has a narrow escape

REALLY, BOASTING is a sin and i should never of told those roughs that once, in the olden days, Imogin Hudson let me kiss her in a game of kiss chase. Espersherly as one of those roughs was none other than the Vicas son, and he remembers me well, is now a prefect and continues to mock me to this day.

Once again i have left myself open to be swiftly beaten and publicly humiliat'd. This is how it happens:

After skool on thursday, Shawd sends 2 prefects out early to patrol the backfield. Luckerly i spy them before i am nabb'd and go home the front way instead.

I scuttle across the tarmac, heading for the skool gate. I have already lerned to never look anyone in the eyes and always look at the ground, but halfways across the field someone calls my name out and when i peek from beneith my fringe Imogin Hudson is stood there, her arms fold'd across her large breasts. Her skool blouse is open wide, each tit hanging there like the nose of a large dog.

No, Imogin Hudson is not the sweet girl that i once knew and lov'd from afar. Her once impish face has now grown pinch'd and sour looking and she is dragging on a cigarett, gobbing and chewing gum.

A gang of laughing faces - also sucking on cigarettes - surround her like a body gaurd. They leer in at Imogin Hudson like hyenas and i want to march over, snatch the cigarette from Imogin Hudson's ugly mouth and tell her to spit out her gum and act like a real girl.

Naturally the Vicas son is stood there and i turn my shoulder away, looking down at my feet and hoping to sidle past unnotic'd, but it's not possible.

Instead i decide to cut back across the grass (which is forbidden) climb the skool fence and make my escape that way.

Quickly, i sprint across their precious lawn, run and jump up (im a very good climber) and in 2 shakes im at the top.

It seems that i really am free and have escap't their vile clutches. Im just about to pull my feet over and jump down the other side when 3 boys rush me from behind, grab my legs and put all of their wait on me. I cling onto the top of the wire with my fingertips but one of them, the Vicas son, pulls off my shoe and throws it into the bushes.

"Where do you think your going, lover boy!"

"Ive got to get home, my mothers waighting for me."

"You know your not allow'd on the grass, it's out of bounds!"

"Your on it to!"

"We'er prefects and somone wants to see you."

"Im late, ive got to go home now."

"Imogin, Claudius wants to go out with you!" He shouts it, so that eveybody can here. Then turns to me again. "She says that she'd never go out with you because you're a fucking hippy!"

I stare to the shabby grass that has been worn down by the feet of generations of disobedient skool boys.

"But i never said that i want'd to go out with her," i whisper, "i never said that. I just said i knew her once, thats all." My face purples up, the tears already pushing up behind my eyes.

The 3 of them force me down onto the ground and pin me there by my shoulders. I beg with my captives: the Vicas son and 2 other lackys from the 'A' stream, to let me go, but they are all of them just a bunch of lying, fawning, stinking rats!

One of the prefects goes and fetches Imogin Hudson. I crain my neck and can just see her face as she looks over to us, throws down her cigarette and slouches over, her large nipples - saucer shap'd - moving beneath her skool blouse. As she comes nearer i look pleadingly to her frozen face for mercy, but she just blows a large pink bubble at me, which she pops with her tongue and then sucks back into her cavernous mouth.

Imogin Hudson's breasts loom over me and i screw my eyes up tight like fists. My Captives turn their faces admiringly towards their Queen and i feel their grip lesson ever so slitely. With a sudden yell i yank my arms free, spring to my feet and run.

At 1st i can't believe that i really have escap't and i do some expert swerves to put them off my sent. A shout goes up and they come galloping after me but i can see that i will get to the skool gate before they can cut me off.

The Vicas son try's to scale the fence but he will never be able to climb as well as me and i can outsprint all of them.

I tear out the gate and dash up the road, my breath coming in hot gasps.

There are many liers and changers of the truth in the world and no one says anything to defend the holders of real spirit, which i think is unfair.

22

A religious meeting

WEDNESDAY NITE i take my painting round to Rollingpins.

It takes a great deal of courage to approach that front door. 1st off, the alleyway is in inky blackness and the ghosts are out. Next, you have to pick your way along the windy path and thru the rose bushes that stand up like the shadowy figures of people. Also, old man Rollingpin has never forgiven me for going thru his hedge.

When i finnaly get there i stand oustside the door for several minits listening to the shrill voices of girls on the inside.

Looking down at my broken plimsoles, i debate weather to just go back home. It is only the fear of setting off into the black nite that forces me to knock on the door and face my fate. I hold my painting away from my chest as it is still a little wet.

At 1st no one comes so i knock again. The voices on the inside go quite and a shadow walks down the hall and the door opens just a crack. A small kid with freckles pokes his head out looks up at me and tells me that Mrs Rollingpin is in a prayer meeting. I push open the door and walk in past him.

The hallway has a strong smell of boil'd cauliflowers and there's a stairway with a blud red carpet leading up into total darkness. I lean my shoulder against the bottom of the banister and peer up into that nite but it is impossible to see anything, or guess what they might have hidden up there. I climb up onto the 1st step and am wondering weather to investigate further when I hear old ma Rollingpins voice call out from the front room.

"Who's there, Jimi?" There is a doorway in the hallway and the voice comes from behind there. Jimi goes to speak but i make angry eyes at him, open the door and push him inside. I follow behind with my picture held away from my legs.

A whole gang of skool girls is sat on the floor in there, crowd'd round old ma Rollingpin, who lay's on an old couch in the bay window wearing a real beard and looking just like Henry the 8th, her fat little legs sticking out infront of her like a pair of bandag'd risoles.

I look to the faces of the skool girls who surround her but cannot bring myself to say hello and look away again quickly.

"Oh, look what the cats drag'd in, Waffels. It's that nasty little boy from next door. What can he want with us, dens?"

Old ma Rollingpin tugs at her goaty, all the while feeding little tit-bits to a spitful looking lapdog clamped under her gargantuain boosom.

"I brought you this" and i hold out my picture.

"Oh, whats the naughty boy got in his hands, Waffels?"

I look down at her fat, swollen legs. "It's an oil painting," i tell her blankly.

"Oh, the naughty little boy's made us a picture, Waffels. What can it be of?"

Even tho she is asking the dog i presume she expects me to answer in it's place.

"It's a crusifixion sean," i say flatly.

She turns her small, marble-like eyes on me. "Oh, it's the crusifixtion, Waffels! . . . Of our savoir? . . . Well, hold it up for the world to see. He doesn't want to go hidding his lite under a bushel, does he children?"

And she looks smugly round the room, nodding at the childrens pale, luminous faces. I hold my picture up so that all of the children can get a good butchers.

"Now isn't that nice, children? Isn't that clever? Yes, now look, Waffels, isn't he a clever little boy, dens."

I stand there but judging by the confused faces nobody seams to like my picture at all.

The silence goes on and on. Just then, one of old ma Rollingpin's daughters - who is actulay some sort of grown up cuckoo - stands, takes my picture from me and studies it at arms length. She has one boggly eye, which roves all over my painting, and her head nodds and jerks a great deal, as if she really dose understand something.

"It's very good, mother" and she looks at me and smiles. I reach over and take my picture back off her. She has scarlet paint all over her fingers.

Old ma Rollingpin asks me to sit down and makes little Jimi offer me a glass of tepid lemonade and a tin appears from somewhere and i am offer'd a slightly soft biscit. Then we have to pray. I put the lemonade down behind an aspedester plant and secretly crumble the biscit in my coat pocket. None of the girls in the bible class talks to me and im prity much left to amuse myself.

The wallpaper in there is quite ratty looking and several lumps of it are coming off in the corner by a spreading damp patch. Basicly, it has a pattern made up of brown leafs with red berrys and some sparrows, that look more like vultures, drawn on it.

Old ma Rollingpin comes to the end of her sermon and i stand up and tell her that i have to leave on account that my mother is ill. I collect up my painting and start making a move towards the door. Quick as a flash, old ma Rollingpin starts rolling back and forth, trying to haul herself up onto her bandag'd legs. She sticks out her short, thick arm and calls for her grown up cuckoo daughter to help her to her feet. She really rolls from side to side like a walrus, then with a grunt she's up, and still clutching Raffels to her giant tits, hobbles towards me like shes on stilts.

"Let me see that!" she says reaching out her puffy hand towards my wonderfull painting. I try to hang onto it but Raffels growls at me and she snatches it.

"He knows that your the enimy!" she says triumpantly, "and we know what his nasty fathers like, don't we, Waffels! Yes, we do! We all know about his father, don't we children." The children look up at me with their mouths hanging open like a lot of zombies. All you can hear is the sound of the clock on the mantal.

"And whats that?" i ask defiantly, still holding onto a corner of my picture.

"Whats what, dear?"

"What do you all know about my father?"

"Well, i think we all know," she says smiling under her beard.

"We all know what?" i ask again.

She holds me with her marbl'd eye. "That he drinks! That his a womanizer! That he dosnt no rite from rong! That he defies the Lord. That his children run around like Godless savages! That there isn't really a man in the house, at all!"

She looks down and chucks Raffels under his small doggys

chin. "And we knows that the naughty little boys been climbing thru our garden again, don't we Waffels? Yes we do!"

And she looks back up at me, dearing me to contradict her, but i prefer to say nothing.

"Everyone who's ever liv'd on that land has been Godless," she suddenly exclaims. "That German, whats his name?... Stuka Jack, or Joe, or whatever it was. My word, the rows Malcom had with him - smoking cigarettes in the alley and what not. And as to that terrible woman he lived in sin with - the language! You wouldn't belive the words that came out of that harlots mouth! And all in front of her own little ones as well! I said to her 'Mind your langague woman or ile come round there and wash your mouth out with soap! And i meant it. Dirty disgusting woman! A harlot as God is my wittness!" And with that old ma Rollingpin clutches Raffels so hard between her breasts that he yelps out in pain. "We should all pray for her. And your father."

"I have to go . . . my mother . . . " i explain.

"Listen to the silly boy, children. He doesnt have to leave, does he! No, of course not. Look, he hasn't even finish'd his leomonaid yet. Jimi, give the naughty boy another biscit and then we can all pray for his father."

I am given another glass of Lemonade which i set down on the mantle pice next to the old one.

"I really do have to go," i explain, "I told my mum i'd come straight home."

Old ma Rollingpin serches for something in my face, then still holding onto Raffels, leads me out into the hallway, pulls the door clos'd behind her and asks me in a hush'd voise what is rong with my mother. I edge round her, get the front door open and step out into the porch. Once outside i allow myself to breath again.

"Its cancer" i tell her, avoiding her searching eyes.

"Cancer!" She whispers, "God bless the poor soul." And her hand crosses her mamouth brest twise and Raffels barks at her and she has to tell it to shut up. She looks up and studies me with a very concern'd look on her face, which makes me want to smile.

"And where has she got . . . it, child?" she rasps hotly.

I look at the hairs sprouting out of her mustash and think hard.

"In her lungs" i tell her.

"In her lungs" she repeats.

"In both of them" i add.

I notice that all 10 of Old Rollingpins fingers are stuff'd into impossably tight rings. In fact, it is only just possible to see the tiny diamonds and rubies glittering out from between her fat knuckles, like stones sinking in mud.

"Your poor mother" she rasps, "she hasn't said a thing to me." Then she holds me with a questioning gaze.

"Ive got to go now" i say looking away, and leaning my painting against the porch, turn and scamper down the garden path.

Old ma Rollingpin calls after me.

"What about this picture?"

"You can keep it" i shout and keep on running. I stop by the gate and look back at her. She is stood there under the porch lite, studdying my still wet painting with a look of disgust on her face. Then shaking her head and telling Raffles that it is a lot of silly rubbish, hobbles back in doors.

23

A rude awakening

IF IT is our job to learn absolutely nothing, then it is Shawds job to install total, absolute fear within us: to make us dread skool, dread life and dread him. But i do not.

Actually, there is nothing that amuses me more than provokeing my teachers to anger. To see their face looming towards me amuses me.

For instance, i have drawn a likeness of one master, Mister Gorf, metimophosizing from frogs spawn into a tadpole, then into a frog. I drew my picture in clear view of the class so as to attract the curiosity of the other children and there by the attention of Mister Shawd.

Gorf play'd rite into my trap and had no alternative but to call me out in front and make an example of me. The whole point of the exersice was to to be punish'd and become centre stage.

After holding up my masterpiece and fully understanding it's implications: that i was squarly ridiculing his office and all that righteousnss stand for, Gorf sent me to Mister Shawds office to collect the cain and the punishment book.

Naturally, when i reported to Shawd he sent me crashing to the deck with one of his famous dead-legs then sent me back to Gorf with the cane and punishment book. I hobbled up to Gorfs desk and was then soundly beaten in front of the class and my name enter'd into those hallow'd pages.

No teachers hold fear for me. It is only skool bullys who terrify me. They are the true masters of aggression (I am of course aluding to Crowsfeet). Shawd is a meer amiture by comparison.

1st off, Shawd doesn't come round your house and make you steal coins from your own mother so as to buy him ciggerets then puff those same ciggerets in your face then say he is going to fuck my mum then threaten to kill you. Even my big brother can't bully me properly, not compair'd to Crowsfeet.

Yes, when Crowsfeet beats me across the thighs with a bamboo cain then makes me beg for forgivness in front of my playmates my whole life streatches out in front of me and seams hatefull and meaningless. Every day i am bullied and tormented in some new and sickening way. I am forst to steal, rob and lie, when it is quite against my nature.

If, on the other hand, my big brother rises his fist to me i don't wait for the blow but fall imediatly to the floor and i lie there screaming untill my mother rushes into rescue me. And when she tells me to 'soddin-well-shut-up!' i cry out even louder in mock agony. My big brother may aim another kick at me but all the while i am smirking to myself.

To hear my mother swear at me is strangely thrilling. When, for example, she tells me to 'soddin-well-shut-up', i have to pull down the corners of my mouth to keep from laughing.

All in all, i think that my teachers and family having to hit me is proof that i have autonomy in the world; that they admit that i am in charge and that they cannot fully control me. It is only my skool bully that can ultimately humilate me, him and the skool girl slags.

It is true that i am afraid of my father but not as afraid of him as my big brother is. But none is more afraid of him than our worried, trembling mother.

It is she who manicly hovers and tidys the house, week in week out, in her vain bid to please him and win him back. All of our fathers suits are press'd till the creases are scortch'd clean thru. Next, his shirts are starch'd like iron and the garden pick'd over for wind-blown litter. In short – everything is made ship-shape and Bristol fashion by our fearfull mother.

6 oclock, he rings from London and say's he will be on the 7.30 train. Our mother asks if he would like anything to eat when he gets in.

"Yes, Juny. Roast beef and yorkshire pudding for supper!" And she puts down the reciver and frets because shes only got cheese on toast.

Every evening she cooks him a meal, waits for the last train to roll in, then chucks it all in the bin. For my tea i like egg and chips and sometimes some bacon. If there is any fat, i refuse to eat it. Also i refuse vegetables.

Me 'n' my big brother sit in the small room, huddl'd over the parrafin stove waighting for the old girl to finish frying up the grub.

After talking to our fathers mother on the blower for a decayed she finally surves it up on these little tables that sit between our knees. I have to get up to get the salt and pepper and accidently knock my table over. My egg and chips goes face down across the carpet.

My big brother raises his fist at me and such a terrible fear grips my hart that i have to run from the room. I dash out thru the kitchen, past my mother, out thru the back door and over the back fields. My mother chases after me, screaming and waving her teatowel.

Yes, i am a villain. So i am hat'd and lift'd to the same pedistal as my father. Acordingly, there are many lists and lessons that have yet to penitrate my thick scull. It seams that as an adult i won't be able to travel on trains, go to the toilet or ever have a proper job. Neither will i be able to read road signs, drive a car or read a book. Also no one will want to marry me. And i am assur'd that by the time i reach the age of 20 i will have false teeth, becouse all of my real one's will have rott'd clean away, due to the fact that i eat nothing but chocolet.

It should be not'd that my family call me 'Smell 'and have taught me that my legs are too thin and that i am ugly and unlovable. And lastly, and most importantly, that i am in for a rude awakning.

24

My Bully

THE THING to know about Crowsfeet and his trip to Borstal is that he had it coming. Like me he is the runt of the litter in his family, only his father beat him with a steal brush.

The trouble is Crowsfeet ask'd his father to many 'damnd silly questions'. Like he always had to ask his parents permission to go out and play and his mother always said that she didn't know and that he had to go ask his father.

Crowsfeets father was always werking under some wrecked old motor and didn't like being asked anything by any of his 7 children, least of all 'Weed', as they called him. So Weed's father comes out from under the car, black as a sweep, and lands one on Weeds bare calf with a wire brush, hard as you like, then just jeers at him when he starts crying.

I stand silently to the side, knowing that it is me who will be made to pay for this attack on Weeds leg by his short, bald, red faced father.

Crowsfeet is 1 year older than me but still pretty scrawny. If i wanted i could beat Weed. Only i do not fight because there is no fight within me. Plus Weed uses his ugliness as his weapon. It's like this: Weed is out for revenge on anyone he sees' as having a weak spot.

Im not afraid of Weed but of the idear of Weed. Not the living, breathing Weed but Weed's ugly face. Weed's resentment, Weed's worty old fists and his artistry of fear.

Yes, i am terrified of Weed and have become his dog because i have been trained to see myself as less. As my mother has lower'd herself to creep benith my father, so i have lowered myself to creep benieth Weed. In short – i cannot vanquish Weed becouse my mother is too afraid to devorse my father.

Before Weed was banged up and he told me i must give him my pocket money, i gave Weed my pocket money. When Weed told me i must steal my nanna's ciggerets, i stole my nanna's ciggerets and hand'd them over to him. When I spy'd the hiding place where my mother keep't the misserly 40 pounds a month my father gives her to pay the bill's and feed us kids, i duely ran and reported my discovery to Weed, and so he stole her money and every month we went without. And likewise, when Weed told me i had to be the look-out for his house breaking, so i again obayed orders without question and stood in the rain as he robbed the poor and the inocent. Even when Weed told me to wait outside his gran's house as he went inside to 'rob the old whitch', i duly stayed at my station a full 4 hours, till he emerged having eaten his fill and fleeced her of her hidden savings. When Weed told me to give him my zip-up boots, so's he could go on holliday with the Ratton Twins and pretend that he had brought them new, i gave him my zip-up boots and lie'd to my mother that they'd been lost. And when Weed brought them home, all streatch'd out, the zip's busted and polish'd the rong colour, i said nothing and again lie'd to my mother that i'd broken the zips myself. When Weed told me to paint him a picture so's he could take it into skool, show Catweasel and be lorded as a great new artist, i duly painted that picture and also told his mother that i thort Weed show'd exceptional talent. And when ask't by Catweasel if i'd help't him, i deni'd it even tho Catweasel new that i was lieing.

No, a bully isn't known for his eligance and ferness. When Crowsfeet bullys me he rolls his eye's into the top of his skinny scull, his mouth puckers up like a baby rats and he belts me. So i lower my eye's and bow to him.

I make myself less to acomidate the world, to not upset my teachers, to not shine. I talk'd Weed up to his face but all the while i secreatly pray'd for his death, along with the death of my father and my big brother. Thats why i am evil: because i am not brave.

How i longe'd for Weed to leave me alone, to the point of planing to kill myself. God finally helped me when he put Crowsfeet in the Borstal, tho of course one day he will escape and return.

25

Applecakes

BEATINGS OF one kind or another are regular as clock werk at our skool, either from teacher to pupel, or pupel to pupel, or pupel to teacher and the most valued thing, amongst us kids, is to not be surpris'd by any act of violence; to never be a spliter and to never show fear.

To never be faz'd or bother learning, to have no respect for rules or authority and to have no mercy in the face of weakness is also highly valu'd.

The names of the boy's who held me down so's i could be expos'd by Imogin Hudson are as follows: the Badger and Applecakes.

I have stood near them and listen'd to their dirty hyena laughs but it is impossible for me to join in and become their friends. This is because i have the rong type of hair, the rong make of shirt, the rong type of trousers, the rong shoes and the rong type of face.

Like them i can go thru the motions of smoking ciggarets but the taste makes me sick. Also, i can pretend to not care and to swear and spit, but i could never pretend as brilliantly as they do, nor hide my hart half as well. In short - i disobay the rules of skool boy fashion. This is not thru choice but by instinkt.

Oh, yes, in this prison it is very important to dress like the tribe. But on this score alone i could be hung. Truly, there is no forgiveness or sentimentality allow'd at the W– Skool for Boys, so it's just as well that we are all hard, uncearing children.

In class i sit away from the others and pretend to be ritting, but really i am listening very intently. It seams that the Badger and Applecakes were playing football over on the estate last Saturday, when one of their nabours kids, a baby girl, crawl'd out thru an open front door, up the garden path, across the verge and into the gutter. Where at, it was crush'd to death benith the wheels of a dust cart.

Acording to Applecakes it was the funnyist thing he ever saw in his life. I watched him and The Badger clinging onto each other, genuinely crying and shuddering with laughter.

"Then the mother runs into the street calling her name - Simone! Simone! Simone! - ha ha ha! Then she see's the crowd and the bluds spread rite up the road - ha ha ha! 'n' then she starts screaming – Simone! Simone! Simone! - ha ha ha! Her gobs wide open, like this, but no noise comes out – ha ha ha! 'n' then the old cow starts pullin her own hair out – ha ha ha! Next, the old man rolls up. Only now, thers blud running down the gutter – ha ha ha! - and he stands and stairs at it then runs round 'n' trys to grab the lorry driver by the throat 'n' nut him one. He chases him clean round the truck - ha ha ha! But the lorry driver locks himself in his cab 'n' the father can't get in 'n' the other dustmen have to pull him away – ha ha ha! Then he see's us, just rolling there on the grass laughing our heads off – ha ha ha! - We'er fucking crees'd up, - ha ha ha! Then the fucking nutter trys to punch us, for doing fuckin' nothing and we leg it, but i shout back at him, 'you touch one fucking hair on my fuckin' head you cunt 'n' my old man will fucking kill you, you fuckin' nutter!' Then the old bill rolls up 'n' arrests him, so's we go back and watch. We tell the old bill they should lock the cunt up, but they just ignore us and tell us to get lost. Anyway, then this fire engine rolls up 'n' fetchs the kiddies body out from under the weels with a spade 'n' they lay down a ton of sand, to soak up all the blud, like – ha ha ha! It was fuckin 'annskomb!"

Apparently, it was just the sight of the little child being toss'd about benith the back weels that amus'd them so much.

The other kids stand around looking at the Badger and Applecakes with open admeration, whilst i stand and pretend to be examining the buckle on my skool bag.

Applecakes has longish, blond hair and strange dark eyebrows. My hair is longer than Applecakess but my eyebrows are fair not dark. Naturally, i wish my eyebrows were darker, but they quite simply aren't and that is an end to it.

It is because of my long blond hair that Mister Shawd drags me out from my desk, humilitates me in front of the entire class and tells his hellerious joke:

"Am i hurting you, Claudius?"

"No, sir," i reply boldly "how could you possobly hurt one of your belov'd puples?" Shawd holds me with his small eyes trying to judge my sarcasm and i staire dumbly ahead, trying not to flinch as he clentches and unclentches his jaw mussels.

It is possible, if you listen most intently, to hear Shawds steel knee creeking as he shifts his wait from foot to foot, really i was not smirking in the least.

"Well i should be hurting you Claudius, becouse im standing

on your hair!" Then instead of giving me a dead leg he raps me sharply on the top of the head with his knuckles and i stagger sideways with a feeling like hot lead being pour'd into my skull.

Shawd then simply straightens his cuffs and orders me to return to my desk. Next, the bell goes and i have to grab my bag and scurry off to be beaten by Mister Mars, who takes music.

It is not just our hair length that's regulat'd at this skool, there are strick codes regarding all aspects of our dress and behaviour.

According to the Shawd 'we are representatives of our skool, even on the way too and from home, and by that measure we can even be punish'd for misdemeanors that take place on the weekends.'

To dress like identical little solders, so we are told, is good for our rotten charicters and will set us in good stead for our lives beyond the perimata fence.

There are also many regulations in regard to our not walking on the grass, not running down corridoors, not picking our noses, not spitting, not smoking, not answering back and not talking in assembly. In short - keeping our foul traps shut at all times.

Tho we are all class'd as retards of one stripe or another, there is one boy in this skool who Shawd loves above all others. This boy's hair comes down almost to the top of his collor, and tho blond he's eyebrows are quite dark, and when you see this boy running amongst us it becomes quite clear that he dosnt belong here becouse he is a racehorse amongst donkys. I am of course again referring to Applecakes.

What i find hardist to swallow is that Mister Shawd has never once rebuck'd Applecakes for the length of his hair. No, where as i am singled out for punishment at the drop of a hat, Applecakes, who is far more rude and viciouse than me, is smiled upon by Shawd.

In fact, Shawd has never even said a cross word to Applecakes. This is becouse Shawd is in love with Applecakes and he is not the only one. Even the the girls like to stop Applecakes on the way home from skool and crowd round him brushing their bodys against his blazer.

And they don't cackle out loud, or jeer at him either. No, they just love to be near him, with his small nose, dark lashes and smiling body.

Yes, Applecakes is accept'd by all and sundry but i don't allow myself to feel anything for him, becouse in our skool it is a sin for a boy to feel love for another boy, or to desire him even in thought.

Is it not possable that i look upon Applecakes and his dark eyebrows only out of a sence of curiosity? Not because i am jellouse or a homosexual, but becouse of what Norman has done to me?

26

Gurtie Bunions lude memorial mirror

This is the story i have riten for my English homework:

Enchant'd by Gurtie Bunions Lude Memorial Mirror
By G. Claudius. Form 4B1

DURING THE 19th centuary a breed of chicken was develop'd peculiar to the M- area. The Buff Medway, now extinct, was a table bird for the London hotel market. Until the mass production of battery hens became common after the 2nd world war, chicken was a luxury item, afordable only to the middle classes and as a treat at Christmas.

The Buff M- linage includ'd 3 other breeds, the Buff Orpington, develop'd in North K- during the 19th century, the Buff Cochin, and the Faverolls.

Information is not yet forthcoming concerning the actual date of creation of the Buff M-, but the last of these chickens is believ'd to have died out around about the time of the 2nd World War. This is the story of the last of the Buff Medways, C'- s only known chicken.

On the November nite that a 2176 lb aerial land mine, type C, took out 4 blocks of houses on O- street, C-, one thousand headless chickens descended upon the town centre, swarming like hungry mice down M- Road and out onto the High street; their vocal chords uselessly trying to cluck thru the thick clots of blud that hiccup'd in the vulva-like openings of their ragedy old necks.

It seems likely that that land-mine not only destroy'd the life and limb of many a good towns person but also levell'd a humble chicken farm as well. And even if this isnt the case may i just remind the esteem'd reader that it was quite common for the people of this particular town to keep all manner of exotic fowl in their backyards, before and after the war years, thus explaining the prescence of so many chickens.

At approximately 7.30 on that dismal nite my grandfather, Reginald Alexander Lewis wash'd up his tin mug, slipp'd into his greatcoat and dart'd out across the narrow rat run that seperated the Dockyard Werkers Friendly Society and the Nissan hut which hous'd the HQ of the Dockyard Home Guard.

Banging the door shut behind him, Reg cross'd the room and warm'd his mitts on the pot bellied stove. Without looking up from his copy of The War Illustrat'd, the little desk Sergeant, Blackberry Bob, puff't on his pipe and spoke.

"Whatch'yer Reg, there's one mark'd 'Urgent' to be bik'd over to West Malling."

Reg glanced at the blackberry birthmark that blott'd out half of Bob's face, walk't over to the desk, lift'd a small brown package and read it with his blunt fingertips - Captain Jeff Scully, Home Guard, RAF, West Malling, Urgent!

The little Sergeant (Blackberry Bob), who every nite had to

walk a gauntlet of screaming skool children that ran along the pavement behind him chanting 'Blackberry Bob, give us a bob, so's me mother can go blackberrying in the morning', stood, tapp'd out his pipe on his heel, retriev'd a pair of singed longjohns from behind the stove, put his nose to the crutch and took a deep wiff.

"It's a bastard of a nite out there, Reg but i promis'd they'd get that package before 18.00 hours."

Reg lookt at Blackberry Bob's purple left ear and Bob self consciously brought up his left hand and pulled at it. "You'd better be putting some fire under your arse as well!"

Reg nodded, slipped the package in his coat pocket and left the building. Closing the black-out screen behind him he stepp'd back out into the nite, mounted his motorbike, kick'd it into life and sped off in the direction of The Long Bar PH. C-.

Once out the gates he open'd her up to 75 down Dock Road, touching 80 as he pass'd Kitchener's statue, then decelerating, he lean'd the machine round the steep bend and swoop'd down to the Town Hall.

There was a slite hold up when a beard'd matelot in a silk nite dress dash'd out in front of him follow'd by a fat lady in nothing but her rollers.

Weaving between the tram lines, Reg took a rite up M- Rd, then left onto the High Street and pull'd up outside the pub.

Gunning the engin twice a sudden dread pass'd over him. A feeling like as if a large object was about to drop out of the skys and smash him.

Looking up into swirling clouds Reg heav'd his bike up onto it's stand and, still looking skywards, duck't in thru the butiful green and gold doors of The Long Bar.

There in, Reg order'd his usual pint of mild, said a civil hello to old Harry - who at 109 still manag'd to stagger the 200 yards from his rooms above the slaughter house so as to wash the taste of blud from his mouth - and picked up a copy of the C- Standard from the bar.

Old Harry nodd'd his head at Reg 6 times in quick succession, then chuckling to himself about some hilarious joke, start'd blowing kisses into his glass of poker beer.

Reg mosey'd on down to the back of the pub and sat himself down beneath a vast and extravagant mirror that had been hung there in memorium of one Gertrude Bunion, actress and prostitute.

Miss Bunion, or Gertie, as her more intimate acquaintances had known her, had had occasion to replace the original mirror, which had hung there since the diamond jubilee of the late Queen, after flinging a completely full and perfectly drinkable bottle of dry Gin at the noble head of our 'Bastard Lord Mayor'. The mirror was smashed to smithereens but the Lord Mayors nobel head was left perfectly intact, his fat face still grining like an idiot.

Shortly after resiving the bill for damages Gertie was tragically taken from the world by what was referr'd to in the local papers as 'tuberculosis of the lower extremities'.

Once the death notice's had been duly post'd and the venerable woman laid to rest the 'Bastard Lord Mayor', and his uprite friends of the local lodge, call'd an extraordinary general meeting of the Towns Council where it was decided behind clos'd doors to cut off Gertie's one and only surviving heir, a certain Timothy Bunion of Cooling, and donate the entirety of Miss Bunions estate towards the installation of such a gothic horror of a mirror that the gentler souls of the parish would flinch whenever they beheld it.

And so the town came to have a terifying monument to the nite that Gertie Bunion trashed The Long Bar.

When the air raid siren sound'd at approximately 8.05 p.m. my grandfather Lewis, and the stalewarts of The Long Bar, lookt thoughtfully up to the ceiling, toward the door and then back to the butiful row of gleinting bottles that lined the bar like so many manly soldiers.

A full one and a half hours later the all clear had sound'd and The Long Bar was a scene of quite contentment, the otherwise hard and imbitted men nursing their warm beers as if babes to the bosom.

At this moment, cruising at 5000 feet and running thru scudding cloud, Staffelführer Paul Steinmetz, the pilot of the Heinkel He111 that dropp't the parachute mine that took out 4 blocks of houses behind O- Street, C –, there by releasing a plague of headless chickens to desend on the town centre, was already dreaming of his snug billet in the commandeer'd Belgian chateau he now call'd home.

As Reg order'd his 4th glass of mild, put his hand in his pocket and pull'd out the still undeliver'd package mark'd 'Capt Scully Urgent!' the Heinkel He111 releas'd it's deadly cargo and Herr Steinmetz's hart buoy'd. A little cheer went up in the cabin and Staffelführer Steinmetz bank'd the plane for home; his German lips already sampling a mouthfull of fine claret and the delicious breasts of the Belgium servant girl, Moneek, who shav'd his Nazi chin every morning befor kissing his German eyes, "Im coming for you, my little schnecke!" he call'd.

Reg turned the packet over in his big hands, before placing it cearfully on the bar, the land-mine now majestically swinging on it's silken parachute bearly 3000 feet above his head, drifting inexorably towards it's fated target.

If one of the ever watchful hero's of Observer Corps had quit gassing about the amount of sawdust that Harrisons and Harrisons 'butchers to the gentry,' were now stuffing into their inedible sausages and had glanced skywards for just one moment, he would have seen the dark silhouette of a Heinkel bomber slither over the grassland of the Great Lines, crossing Lower G- then out over the estuary and to Belgium beyond.

It only remains to be said that the ensuing explosion rattl'd old Harry's skull so violently that his last remaining tooth - one which had surviv'd both the Crimea and the Boer War, slipp'd from his gum, rattl'd out across the bar and plopp't into the slops tray beneath the foaming bitter tap.

From this innocuous resting place the tooth set out on a wild and mischievous journey: from the slops tray to the slops barrel, from the slops barrel to an exciting ride on the back of the brewery dray. From racing round the streets like a red Indian, to being poured into the vast vat of filthy slops that the brewery had the gall to re-sell as dark mild. In short – from one stink to the next.

Here the trail of the tooth goes cold and it's extact location for the remaining war years was a mystery. Old Harry resigned himself to the fact that he would never see his beloved tooth ever again - the very tooth that he had used to nibble on a bit of raw turnip at the relief of Mafaking. But then VE Day 1945, whilest old Harry was celibrating his 110th bithday, he took a last gulp of his Style & Winch Dark Mild and the intrepid incisor tinkl'd from the bottom of the glass and roll'd back into the very same lifeless socket from whence it had 1st sprung.

Some sceptics have suggest'd that this is not quite the miracle purport'd and that this so-call'd 'Hinkel tooth' was never anything more than a 3rd set of teeth that old Harry had start'd sprouting thru extream old age, or pure idiocy. Other ingrates have surgested that it was not a tooth at all but more likely some old piece of bakon rind that Harry had tucked in his cheek from breakfast.

But whatever the truth of the matter, it is known for certain that once the reverberations of the exploshon had subsid'd my grandfather Lewis, holding his glass of mild in one hand and shielding it from falling plaster with the other, walk't to the door, lift'd the latch and peer'd out into that blazzing nite.

"Don't go out there old son" whistl'd old Harry "or you might fall down the 'ole."

It is at this point that our story takes another mighty twist and some readers may ask just how much stock can be put in a tail recounted by a dislexcic skool boy. May i just politly remind the esteamed reader that the more unbelievable and outlandish a story appears, then the more likely it is the whole, unadulterat'd truth; where as the mundain and common place is often patched up and embedded with nothing but lies and hear-says. So, with our harts at rest on that score, let us continue.

It seems that some 2 or 3 minutes elaps'd before the terrible gurgling of upwards of 2 hundred headless chickens descend'd upon the High Street, inciting rumors that the invasion had at long last begun.

The bell's of St Johns church were sounded and mass panic was only avert'd due to the quick thinking of the C- Home Guard who's Captiain, Horatio Perrywinkle, had his men throw up a barb'd wire cordon across the bottom of M- Road, thus protecting The Dockyard from these hostile, and possibly Nazi, fowl.

All these events unfold'd compleatley un-be-knownst to the men of the Long Bar, who were still ensconsed in their cosey womb supping ale, even my Grandfather Reg being entic'd back to his seat by the offer of a free drink by the publican, in celibration of their all still being alive.

However, despite the Home Guards most gallent defense one of those headless fowl, a prize cockerel by the name of Burlington Bertie, slipp'd beneath the barricade, surreptitiously hopp'd along the High Street leaving a thick trail of scarlet blud-clots in his wake and arrived non the worse for wear outside the green doors of Long Bar. The said chicken (Burlington Bertie) then side-stepp'd the boot of a young ARP officer before squezzing in, unnoticed, between the doorfame and Reg's leg.

After gathering his witts for several moments Burlington Bertie then flapp't he's wings, sprung up onto an empty barstool and from there onto the bar, from where he danc'd what can only be describ'd as a sailors horn pipe to the tuneless whistle of old Harry's toothless gob.

Here on in our story becomes vague and muddl'd, but according to local history the headless cockerel then bow'd slitely to the left, skidded in a puddle of Guiness before zig-zagging off down towards my grandfather Lewis, as if enchant'd by the ostentatious decorations of Gertie Bunions lude, memorial mirror.

Dodging blows from the barman, 2 blazing cigarettes and numerous glasses of half-consum'd ale, Burlington Bertie duely arriv'd before my grandfather, the back of who's head was magnificently reflect'd in the mirror of a whore who was lov'd by all who bed'd her (Gertie Bunnion).

At this precise moment Reg rais'd his eyes from the clue 'to strike' 4 letters, in the C- Standard crossword puzzel and came face to face, as they say, with the headless fowl; where upon the hapless cockeral ruffl'd his magnifecent tail feathers one last time, scratch'd twice at a stain'd beer mat between his desheveld feet, and quivering with estercy, collaps'd into my grandfathers glass of mild, his neck stump pumping blossoms of black, clarety, colour'd blud.

Hear it ends.

After word

Of what became of Burlington Bertie on that black and dismal nite we can be quite certain: That prize cockeral was at once wrapp'd into that evenings edition of the C- Standard, plac'd inside my grandfather Lewis's great coat and whisk'd off on his Panther motor cycle to the back of beyond (Wigmore), where he was duely pluck'd and roast'd by Granny Minnie.

But as to the fate of those other wild and headless chickens no one quite knows, but it seems likely that after they were herd'd off the High Street by Captain Perrywinkle and the bravehearts of the C- Home Guard a terrible calamity befell them.

A diary kept by Captain Perrywinkle sheds lite on the question why not one of those headless chickens survived to tell the tail.

The reason, Captain Perrywinkle explains, lay in the chickens shock'd and headless state. Rather than turning rite up onto H– Hill and safety - as directed - it seams that the confused fowl inadvertently took a left and ended up swarming towards Sun Pier and the river. From there-on-in there fate was sealed.

One can only imagin the crush, termult and fear as the headless chickens flock'd down M– Street, the wait of the chickens in the rear of the file driving themselves and their fellow fowl inexorably towards disarster. In short - there would have been no turning back.

Thus it is assumed that the last of this noble breed lept blindly (or were push'd) to their deaths in the icy waters of the river M- .

NB The package address'd to Captain Jeff Scully, Home Guard, RAF, West Malling, Urgent! remaind in my grandfather lewis's bureau unopen'd untill his death. It's current whereabouts and contents are not known.

The Longbar Public house has since been demollished and it's exact location is hotly disputed.

On studying the electoral register the author found no evidence that Gertie Bunion had ever been resident in this parish, or indeed that there ever was such a person. Her lude memorial mirror is presumed destroyed.

* * *

I have read my story to my mother who tells me that I shouldn't try to be clever and 'must learn not to antagonise people'

"Who am i antogonising?" i ask her.

"You shouldn't draw attention to your self."

But she doesn't deni that a headless chicken did once jump out of grandfather Lewis's holdall and march the entire length of the R- tram, before dropping dead.

27

A skool full of perversion

WEATHER IT be sex with children or simply seduction with the rod, the teachers in this skool are all perverts of one stripe or another.

I am now refuring to Mister Russel who, in the interests of science, locks his classroom door, orders all the black out curtens pulled, then selects a quiet, unassuming lad to climb up onto his desk, pull his trousers down and part his buttocks. At this point Mister Russel inserts a thermomiter up his rectum, all under the pretext of 'assitaining the lad's tempreture'.

After lesson Mister Russel calls me back into the classroom and asks me to come to his 'special after skool sience club', which convenes in the back fields beyond the perimiter fence . . .

Its funny that everything in this life is so full of sex yet our teachers and parents pretend that it isn't. If some dogs start fucking on the skool field, for intance, many of the courser children shout and jeer with delite but our teachers just frown darkly, even whilst planning to touch up one of the children in the store cupboard.

Likewise, if the farmers horse teloscopes it's giant cock into the dust down by it's hoofs us kids feel that the day hasn't been entirly waist'd, yet our teachers, who are so full of sex themselves, pretend that nothing at all is happening. Only slyly do they finger their flys and eye us.

Acording to Crowsfeets big brother there is a boy in the 5th year who wears a rubber johnny on his cock at all times and keeps a hole ready in his pocket so's that he can be wank'd off instantly if any of the teachers get horny.

I have feelings about sex but am to shy to speak of them. When another boy in form B4 got a hard on in the showers, i lookt but pretend'd that i wasn't. His name begins with a G. He wav'd his cock at us, the hot, soapy water dripping off it's purple end and he proudly lookt down at himself. His balls were nak'd and pink and i marvel'd at his lack of shame.

Why am i alone in my fear of nakedness? Could it be that when i was 9 years old something happend to me that i cannot talk off, involving a grown man touching me? I thort Norman was going to teach me the facts of life and possibley marry my mother and become my father. This hasn't happend.

All that can be said is that i now know for certain that sex with adults is rong and waving your cock about in the showers is next to the devil.

Even as i rite my skool boy testiment, i know that no one must come to know of these words ritten here, or of this wound in my soul. This is why i walk in shame of my nude penis and why i must always remain different and seperate in the classroom. Now i will never speak of it again.

Marshgas has a large fat cock where as mine is small and imature. Where as he already has a coating of course, manly hairs crinkling all up his belly, i have none.

Just becouse i have been made into a homosexuel by that 'friend of the family' it doesn't nessiseraly follow that i am in love with other boys or am indeed a homosexual. If i admire Applecake, it is not becouse of his dark eyebrows and eyelashes, but becouse he is surgestive and lude to Miss Hart, who in turn incourages him.

Crowsfeet was also full of sex before he disappear'd to Borstal. He often told me that he want'd to fuck my mother and that one of these fine days he was going to do just that. He puffed on a ciggeret (that i had paid for with money he made me steel from my mothers purse) and then spat a big, yellow, grollie down my leg. And all the while i had to listen to his indescent talk and sucking noises.

"She's fuck'n up for it, it's ritten rite across her fuck'n face. Your mothers fuck'in gagging for it!"

And he leer'd at me, the edges of his teeth coated with yellow scum, rite round the red gums.

"I'd fuckin give her one - any fuckin day of the fuckin week!" Then he spits juce on me and patts his rancid crutch.

Crowsfeet has a tattoo of a black panther drawn on his arm. It hangs there by it's claws, wriggling and scratching blud from his bicep and often as not he flex's it at me.

Before his arrest, Weed came round my fathers house, nock'd on the front door and asked my mother for a ciggeret, rite to her face. Of course my mother meekly ran and got him one and even lite it up for him and he blew the smoke rite in her eyes. Rather than gobbing on the step, out of respect he wip'd his dirty mouth with the back of his hand and all the while a hiddious smerk play'd on his lips, his sand colour'd eyes yellow as a wolfs.

"Ile be round to see you one of these day's." He leer'd, rummeging in his pockets and winking indesently.

Who would belive that such a beast is only a skool kid? In my oppinon the eye-lashes of ginger hair'd people are as hiddious as those of rabbits.

Our teachers are not the only one's desperate to shoot their bolts. My father espersherly is infect'd by sex. Always there is a secret in his brief case, and not just pictures of men and woman either, sometimes there's photos of men rideing men as well.

Like me, my mother has also cracked the coad to the combernation locks on my fathers brief case and she also steals his money. When i borrow one of my fathers magazines i sit and read it in the toilet, touching myself.

Afterwards, if the coast is clear, i return the offending magazines to my fathers breif case. My big brother, on the other hand, keeps the books he steels from the old man and hides them in a shoebox behind the old tree stump in his bedroom.

It is true that i will sometimes re-steal books that my brother has previously stollen and these i keep.

* * *

There are many unpleasant feelings and thoughts that plague me. 1stly, i am afraid of my mother dying and leaving me. 2ndly, i am afraid of pain and skool, and 3rdly, i believe that there are hidden cameras in the toilet at home, watching me and studying me.

Could it be that every act i commit is watched by the people in charge? By some control centre somewhere?

Also, could it really be true that nobody in the world has an arse crack but me and my family?

Also, it seams certain that the whole invisible world is populat'd by ghosts, werewolves and vampires.

None of these thoughts are ment to be funny, they are the

true and honest fears of a skool boy and shouldn't be mocked or laugh't at.

28

A strange and impoverish'd nobility

THERE IS one girl who lives over on the council estate who is not hard, cackling, and vicious. She is 2 years younger than me, has short blond hair that curles slitely at the ends and i love her. Will she, like Imogin Hudson, turn into a vile harpy? I hope not.

When i say that i love her this is not strictly true. What i should say is that i like her and in my broken way do love her, but of course i don't look directly at her and i have never spoken to her.

Yesterday, i stood benieth one of the large oak trees that grows there over on the green and watch't my princess from benith my eye brows. She only talks with girls and plays only girl's games. The hardest thing is to pretend that i am not looking at her. I back't round the oak tree then follow'd her from a short distance. I found it hard to breath as my breath caught in the top of my chest.

She walk't to her garden wall, picked up her skipping roap and talk't with one of her little friends. Quietly, i sneek't round the side of the wall to see the shape of the bottom and strange feelings ran thru me: my thighs shook and i had to stop myself from reaching out and touching it.

In my dreams, whilest lying in bed in the mornings before

skool, i get down upon my knees and start kissing the split. Her name is Elspeth.

Elspeths father is a fireman and he rides to werk each shift on an old bone-shaker, his knees sticking out either side as he peddles along. He is quite mysterious and has a mustash like a knite of old. In fact, his whole bearing is dignifi'd, not cheep and violent, as is the manner with other fathers on the estate.

Is it possable that Elspeths family are desendents of some strange and impoverish'd nobility? His daughter, Elspeth is certenly a princess.

All my thoughts are ridiclious, any fool can see that they live in a mear council house, but in the mornings i wish i was lying with her and could show her that i have the hart of a true poet, but the world is not made that way and again i am too shy.

29

Miss hart

THE CORRIDOORS in here are loud and unfriendly and Miss Hart, the music teachers assistent, is often follow'd. Miss Hart is in love with the boy call'd Applecakes. I know this becouse every lesson Miss Hart singles Applecakes out to perform some special task for her.

After Applecakes has fetch't the board rubber and plac'd it

cearfully in Miss Harts outstreatch't hand she looks hard and longingly at him. It is Applecakes who goes to the store cupboad with 'Miss' and Applecakes who hands out the woodblocks, triangles and tamberines for 'Miss'.

"I do not choose Applecakes above anyone else. There is no favoritism in my classroom." She tells us, lying.

"You fancy him, miss." A voice calls from the back of the class.

"Who said that?" She stares around the room but no one owns up. "Well, it's a stupid and ridiculous thing to say."

We all sit staring at her, not swallowing a word of it.

"You do miss." Calls the same voice again.

"No i do not!" She says shrilly.

"Oh yes you do, Miss." We all shout back at her in a chorous. Only Applecakes says nothing.

"Don't be ridiclious!" says, Miss Hart, blushing, "Applecakes is only a skool boy." But we look at her knowingly, sat their on her desk with her big legs and large sexual buttocks.

Is it rite that a femal member of staff be allow'd to wear such overtly tight fiting trousers? Apparently so.

Again, sex is beckoning to us but we must pretend that it isn't and ignore it. I rite in my notebook and stare at Miss Hart thru my fringe. After lesson i have to stay in and rite lines.

All the other kids have been dismissed and Miss Hart sits bashing the ivorys whilest i copy out 'i am not the class clown', 100 times off the blackbord. Next, she calls me over and i have to go and stand in front of her.

She carries on tinkling then absently reaches out her left hand and guides me close to her.

"You know it is a very silly thing the other children were saying in class today, Claudius." And she stops playing and looks at me.

"Yes, Miss."

"I have no favorites."

"No, Miss."

"And your not to join in with them, or look at me in that . . . way."

"What way, Miss?"

"You know very well what way, Claudius." And she pouts her stawberry lips a little.

I decide that it is best not to contradict her and just nod slightly and look down at her breasts.

Miss Hart turns, bashes one of the black notes then cearfully lowers the lid.

"You know, you've grown, Claudius" and she looks me up and down. "You've changed, somehow. Your not like these othere little boys, are you?"

"Ive been away walking in the mountains, Miss."

"Really?"

"Yes, Miss, in north Wales, Miss. The Llanbaris Pass".

"So that's how you've grown, theres lots of fresh air up in Wales, that's good for a boy."

"Yes, Miss."

"You seem to have ... fill'd out."

" Yes, Miss. Last year my chest size was 32 and now it's already nearly 36."

"And you rite things down, don't you Claudius?"

"A little bit, Miss"

"And you draw pictures. I hope you haven't drawn any nasty pictures of me. Have you Claudius?"

"No, Miss."

"Well, your'll have to come round to my house one evening and show me so's that i can cheque."

"Yes, Miss."

"So what are you going to do once you leave skool, Claudius, be a mountain climber?"

"No, im going to be an artist, miss. Like Vincent van Gogh, Miss."

Miss hart looks into my eyes and i want to grab her and kiss her. To reach my hands down her jumper and feel her tits; for her to stop pretending, for all this talk and nonsence to end; for her to just lift up her skirt, bend over the piano stall, stick her arse up in the air so's i can lick between the cheeks, one on each side of my face and then she can fart on my tongue.

Book the
2nd
Against England

30

A bed of Bludy Roses

IN A thousand imperceptable ways my childhood is slowly being eaten away.

Already in my short life ive been defiled by the hand of a grown man and i now know that there is no wild wood beyond the distant hills. No, the land behind the H- meadow is not a wilderness leading to the edge of the world but just an empty hill hiding a stinking motorway. I know this for certan as ive seen that great road with my own 2 eyes. And even tho a fox can eat a goose, it can't eat me because it's to small and sceard.

I am safe, yet not safe. There are no longer any wolfs or bears loose in merry England but that dosnt account for wearwolfs or ghosts.

* * *

In the olden, olden days, before i even went to skool, all my time was spent with mummy. I remember finding a hedgehog in the back garden and mummy put it in a cardboard box for me and i sat out in the yard and drank my milk drink. Then, intent on playing with my new found friend, i put down my drink and peer'd into it's box and accidently tipp't the hedgehog out. I shout'd for mummy but still the hedgehog escap't.

Next, i was told that animals don't really talk to each other, don't have names for each other and aren't friends with each other. Even parrots, according to my father, doesn't know what their talking about and it's just another form of squaking.

It seam's that the grown ups i am with need me to be grown up super fast.

After my milk drink me and mummy used to leave the house and go to the shops and i'd trail behind to see if mummy would notice if she'd lost me; to see if she would bother coming back to fetch me or even notice that i was missing. I stood behind an oak tree and waight'd, but she didn't come and fetch me or comfort me, instead she shout'd at me to 'blud'y hurry up and stop dawdling' and then threaten'd to pull down my trousers and spank me.

"Do you want me to pull your trousers down in public and smack you!" where her presice words. Everyday i fell on the concreat and graz'd my knees.

Then the day came when i was dragged into skool screaming and kicking and now my childhood is all but finish'd and i am being made ready for werk. Naturally, as someone who is as weak and easily bully'd as herself, my mother is very keen that i too should accept a low position in life.

Ive allways prefer'd not to exert myself, or do houshold chores, and have resist'd every attempt of my parents to try and force me to do so, even declineing bribes of money. My mother tells me that this attitude of mine is to no longer be consider'd acceptable and to this end she has arrange with Marshgas's mother that i do his paper round for him whilest he goes away on his hollidays.

"I have spoken with his mother and you are to do his round untill his return."

How is it that my mother is so forcefull when it comes to making me werk yet so pathetic when it comes to standing up for me and protecting me from the teachers and bully's?

It is not just my mother who wants me to stop enjoying life, when my father was still here he also try'd to force me into servitude.

He wasn't just fernicity about mowing the lawn into perfict parralal lines (something i couldn't do) he was also obsess'd with massarging his car, and likewise thort that i should enjoy cleaning it just as much as he did.

At 1st i admit i very much like't the buckets of water, but then i was told that i was splashing too much and that my waxing wasn't perfict enough. So i lost interest in car cleaning and my big brother took over that duty as well.

Although i paint a slightly dark picture of my father, it would be rong to susppose that he was only interested in lawns, litter picking and car massage. He also had a passion for polishing his shoes as well. 1st the uppers we're attacked with great vigour, then he'd turn the shoe over and give the soles a violent brushing, his face turning quite red.

Again, my shoe polishing infusasim was not of a suficiant enough level and i was told that i was recalcitrant and need'd to 'buck my bludy idears up'. A phrase that i try'd to invision but could never understand.

All their catch phrases are meaningless. My mothers 'you need to learn some facts of life' never involves her telling me about sex, but is just another illusian to life giving you a good doffing.

My father's maxim 'it's the presentation that counts' and 'money dosn't grow on trees' are also too strange and silly. It seam'd that all he was really trying to say was that who i was and what i felt were of no interest to him, and i have never claimed there was any such a thing as a 5 pound note tree.

Being constantly told i was useless in this way, i soon learn't that uselessness was freedom. From then on, whenever my family went out into the garden to fight nature, or polish things that only got dirty again and try'd to cajole me into joining them, i'd feebley fail; and they'd be happy i was so useless, 'cos they could mock me and i'd be happy i was so useless 'cos i could sit in doors and watch them from out of the window.

In those ancient summers i'd sit behind the safty of the bedroom curtens as my big brother labour'd behind the lawnmower in the blinding sun, going up and down the garden, striving to get the exact straight lines that his father decree'd.

Next, my big brother's instructions were to cut all the blades of grass that the mower had miss'd with a pair of blunt sheers, after which, my father would come and check his workmanship; bending his thin, straight body in the middle, moving his beard'd face down closer to the ground, cheecking if any stalks had escap't exicution.

When he look't up to the window, i stepp't back into the shadows. Striving is something that i shall never do.

31

The greatful position of an admiring doormat

MONDAY, MY mother gets me up at 6 and i have to go and report to Smelly Al's to do Marshgas's paper round.

Actually, mother insists on getting up a whole hour before so she can fuss about. She makes my breakfast, not becouse i make her do it, but becouse it is her nature to surve; becouse she belives that her lot in life must be harder and more unplesnt than that of anyone elses; becouse life has train'd her to take the greatful position of an admiring doormat; because she wishes to surve me so's she can resent me along with all men and my father in particular.

Naturally, she belives that as her youngest son, i will wish to join her in her marterdome and peer up happily as the world scrapes it's dirty boots across my face.

Yes, she is glad that i have at last been call'd to account and will be made to join the ranks of the unhappy employed, and if she can get up just that bit earlyer than me and suffer just that bit more, then she considers that her life hasn't entirly been wast'd.

After forcing me to drink a pint of milk my mother leads me to the door and, smiling contentedly, sends me off into the darkness and damp fog.

I see her blurry face at the window, willing me to see myself as nothing, or at most, perhaps as a tiny broken cog which should be greatfull to be smash'd with a hammer befor being thrown away.

"I couldn't wait to get out to werk when i was a girl. I left skool when i was 14 and started werk the same week at La Fevers department store. I earn'd 7/10 a week as an apprentice. Of course, i was a bit of a rebel myself in those days but i soon learn'd not to antagonise people. Now you hurry along, don't be late and don't answer back."

I get down Smelly Al's, peer in thru the darken'd window and bang on the door. I stamp my feet co's of the cold. Finally, Sally, Smelly Al's grown up daughter, peers out from behind the blind and lets me in. The stink nearly drops me dead. It really is as if a 1000 rats have curl'd up and died under the counter.

I stand shivering and trying not to breath thru my nose. One thing's for certan: the only person getting any warmth in that place is old Smelly Al himself, sat out in the back parlour with his gangerious legs roasting away on top of the fire, all 3 bars banging out. – No kidding, that's what's making the stink, his cooking his old legs back there.

As im here 1st i have to help Sally bring in the milk crates and bundles of papers from out front, then wait about whilst she sorts thru her book for the list of addresses for my paper round.

I peep around the dusty shelfs, stack't with boxes of breakfast cereals and tins of spam that went out with the ark. Most must have been sitting there since before rationing.

The bell goes and some other kids bundle in. They're regulars and bag up their papers quick as you like and head straight back out on to their rounds. In the end it's only me left.

It takes longer to get me ready as i can't really read or rite propperly + my numbers aren't too good either. Sally has to go and surve her father his porridge, when she comes back im still there on my hands and knees trying to werk out which pile is which.

Sally 'tut-tuts' me but once she's cottoned on that i really am thick she gets out her pencil and helps me.

1st she rite's all the house numbers along the top of the papers then folds them into the sack so's i can still read them off as i walk along. Sally has glass's like old Rollingpin, the type which make your eyes look like they'er peering out the bottom of a pair of jam jars.

I watch her giant eyeballs roving about all over the pages as she stands over me, her pencil moving really quick. Occasionally i nod, trying to listen to what shes telling me but it is difficult to concentrate, what with it being so boring and old Smelly Al sat out back, whezzing his way thru his porrige.

Every time you come in the shop he's sat in that chair and you start to wondering if he ever moves, or goes to bed at nite or visits the toilet, or anything. You can allways see just one part of him thru the half open door: his shoulder and a big, old man's ear. Also, he's got his 1st war cardigan on, with a hole at the elbo and a potatoe sticking out.

The other kids say that he's leg's are rotting on account of them still being full of shrapnal that he brought home from the Somme.

After numbering my papers for me Sally sell's me a single ciggeret, a bit of strike and 3 matches, which is Smelly Al's special for us skool kids who can't afford a whole pack of fag's. I spark up outside and stagger off into the cold fog.

As it happens, i only get across the road to the H- Meadow befor i have to throw the ciggeret away. I change shoulders 'n' drag the sack all the way up past the bus shelter, to the bottom of King Georges Avinue then sit down on the little wall oustide the library to have a breather.

I look up that impossably long road. You can just see the street lites fading out half way's up then everything dissapears into green fog and then blackness. And i don't even start my deliverys till i get rite the way to the top of that road, cross the estate - which is about another mile - and then it's all the way up Tonbury Avenue to my 1st address.

A bus loomes out of the fog and wizzes past me. It go's round the corner and picks up a couple of old lag's and off they go to the Dockyard. My mother says that the Dockyard is the only place where you go into werk then sit down to have a tea break.

Just on the oppersite side of the road there's a house with a tall hedge round it. I wait till those dockers are all on board and the bus is pulling away then, checking up and down the street, pick up my sack, drag it over the road and sling it over the hedge. I look about but no one's seen me. The sack goes 'woosh' and that's the last i see of it. After this adventure, i walk back home.

Coming thru the trees the house is still in darkness. My mother must have gone back to bed. I jam my arm in thru the letterbox, lift the latch and let myself in. Silently, i walk up the stairs and climb into bed fully cloath'd. It will soon be time for my brother to get up and leave for skool.

32

Laugh't at by adults

Ive allways want'd my mother to feel pity for me and for her to guess exactly what is rong with me and fix it for me without me having to tell her anything but instead i have to comfort her.

After Norman touch'd me i wait'd for my mother to rescue me but nothing happen'd, then i smash'd my head against the bathroom wall and told my mother, my big brother and my nan that i want'd to die, but they all just laugh't at me. So then i smash'd my head against the bathroom wall again, just to spite them, but still they just laugh't.

When my father 1st left home and my mother sat sobbing on her bed, i put my small arm round her and clumserly stroked her hair but i new that it was rong and in many ways it was part 2 of my abuse.

I cannot kill myself because i am too scear'd of death. Death is like space but without stars. It is an infinitly, a nothingness that goes on forever and ever and i must be awake to always watch it and wait for the breath of a wearwolf.

I have run away from home before. I walked the 2 miles up to the motorway bridge and start'd off towards London.

I tryd to thumb a lift but the car's were going too fast and one swerved in at me on purpose, so i climbed down the embankment and started hiking thru the fields instead.

It had been raining the nite before and rite away my trousers got soaked thru on account of the long grass.

I kept at it for half an houre, my feet sloshing about in my shoes but when i looked back i could still see the bridge scearsly a mile away.

It was getting cold and dark and i had no food or money so decided to return home, steal some money from my mothers purse and catch the train instead. I climbed back up onto the hard shoulder and run back onlong towards the bridge crying.

When i got home i sneeked round the back and let myself in. No one had notic'd my absesnce and i took off my wet cloths and climb'd into bed.

There was no way i could sleep so i made a model or 'living dummy' of Elspeth. She is made out of my old cloaths and has no face as i lack the necessary time or materials. I stuff'd the rest of her very thoughly - so as to be realistic about the shape of her buetiful bottom - and then lick'd the deep split, pushing my tounge agaist the cold denim. All the kissing dry'd the spit out of my mouth.

I love you Elspeth. I wounder if i will have sex soon? I hope so.

I say a lot of things that may sound like jokes to but they are not jokes, they are my most truthfull and painfull feelings of a child and are not to be laugh't at by adults.

33

a 1/4 of Sherbert lemons

JUST BECOUSE Vincent van Gogh is my favorite artist, it dosn't atomaticly follow that i like all of his paintings. Infact i disslike many of them.

This morning i lay on my bed and cry'd when i realis'd that Vincent has now been dead for exactly 84 years, then went down stairs, lift'd 50p from my mother's purse and run away for good.

After walking all the way down to the end of the main road and missing 2 busses on the way, i manage to catch a bus at the bottom of the W-Werks hill. Theres only an old lady in there and she gets off at the Co-op laundry. My stop is C- railway station. I go to the wooden ticket kiosk and buy a pink ticket from the hunchback who sits there.

The hunchback peers suspiciouslly out at me from his rock shap'd head, curles his lip as he examins my money and i creep past him and down the stairs into the cool damp shade of the platform.

Nobody minds or cares if i run away from home and altho i should be pleas'd to resive an education, im not. Even if i were to die, it would make little or no difference to any one.

Suppose, for example, i had gone to the woods with Norman, as he ask't me to, and he kill'd me. Well, my father wouldn't even of been able to find the time to get off werk, come down from London and attend my funeral. As was the case when Nanna Lewis died, his business commitments wouldn't of allow'd him the flexability.

Plus, if i had of let Norman rape and murder me, all of the efforts that they have made to make me learn to read and rite would have been waist'd and then my grave been forgotten within 3 years. No one has thort of that.

The train rattles in from the smoke and i climb on board. The carriages are all the old sort without corridors, so once your in your in for life. Also, there is no toilet.

I walk along the platform til i find an empty compartment, jump in and bang the heavy door shut behind me.

Inside the compartment stinks of old smoke and strange dust. There are black streaks of greese on the backs of the seats from years and years of old men rubbing the heads against them. I sit down, press my cheek against the corrugat'd surfiss and sniff at it. There is a staleness which feels cold, then the whistle goes and we clank out of the station and into the tunnel.

Theres no lite bulbs as they've all been unscrew'd and chuck'd out the window at passing traffic, so it's pretty dark. I pull the window down and dare myself to stick my hand out and touch the speeding wall. I reach fearfully into the darkness, till my arm is stuck out to my shoulder. A dull lite from the next carriage reflects off the tunnel wall, encrust'd with soot and years of grime. Little cubby-holes rush past, made for rail werkers to jump in in emergancys, i should reckon.

Suddenly my arm is jerk'd and i snach it back in. When we come out of the tunnel i open my fist. It is full of blud and my middle fingernail is missing. Next, we go over L – Arches and then one more tunnel and we'er in G-.

I keep my poor hand in my pocket and hot tears stream down my cheeks.

I bite my trembling lip and try to watch the countryside go by. We stop at 4 more stations but no one gets on, then there's some sheep, then the sea and then we'er at W- . I climb out onto the platform, hobbling about with my finger throbbing unbearably.

Anyway, all the other people dissapear quick as you like and i am stood alone waiting. Nothing happens so i walk out front of the station and look up at the sign there. It definitely begins with a 'Wer'. A lady comes along with a fox on a lead and i follow them down the road untill we come to the shops.

Once we hit the High Street there's some traffic and the fox scampers up the lady's leg and sits on her shoulders. How is it that all the small dogs of the world belong to old women and visa-versa?

The lady and the fox go into a sweet shop with jars and jars of sweets lined up in the windows. I slip in before the door closes and stand behind the lady as she buys some bon-bons. She lets her fox down onto the ground and it looks at me then licks a drop of blud that drips to the floor from my damaged finger. I wait until they have been serv'd then i buy a 1/4 of sherbert lemons.

When i come out the lady and the fox are already gone, swallowed up by the traffic. I hear some sea gulls and decide to follow them instead. The sound is coming from the end of the street.

I climb up over a wall and there's a whole flock of them screaming at each other. Their black heads and orange beeks pecking at a dead cod and behind them is the sea.

I walk along the top of the wall and eat one of my sherbert lemons, there are some yachts and i throw some stones at the small waves. Already i am lonely and my finger is still bleeding into my pocket. Maybe they've miss'd me at home and have already call'd out the police to search for me. With this in mind i decide that it is best to return home immediately rather than be arrest'd for vagrancy. I have another sherbert lemon and crack it open with my teeth. It is very easy to cut your toung and the sherbert takes the skin off the top of your mouth.

Back at the station there's a very old porter sweeping up sweet wrappers and the platform is covered in some sandy looking dust. I ask the porter how long till the next train and he tells me it is due in at 3.55. I sit on the bench and wait.

My damag'd finger has turn'd blue and start'd throbbing so hard that i have to squint and hold it between my thighs. To comfort myself i eat 2 more of my sherbert lemons but now the skin on the roof of my mouth is coming off in strips.

What if Elspeth has gone on holiday with her family and happens to be on the train when it comes in? But not knowing that she secreatly loves me i get on the rong carrage and miss this chance to be with her? Then my whole life would be ruin'd by the simple accident of getting on the rong part of a train. I jump up and rush off up the far end of the platform, peering into the distance for the train that will change my life forever.

When it finally pulls into the station i try to see in thru each grubby window, to spy if Elspeth isnt sitting there waiting for me. But the train is moving too fast to tell.

Luckerly the London train has connecting corridors, so i climb on boad and walk it's entire length, checking all the carriages.

The 1st section has 2 old people sat in there but the rest of the train is pretty much empty. I check every compartment and Elspeth is definitely not on board.

I walk back to the 1st carrage for company and sit down oppersit the old couple, who are eating their sandwiches and drinking cold tea from a lemonade bottle. I put my damag'd finger in my mouth and the man tells me to take my feet down off the seat. Actually, they are not even really on the seat, but i do as he tells me.

As we pull into the next station i jump up and go back out into the corridor. I try to pull the window down but it james half way. I can just get my head out sidways and peer up the platform to see if the girl who could love me isn't getting off of the unchequ'd carrage at the rear. I twist my body round and also check to see if she isnt boarding one of the 1st class carriages at the front of the train.

Indeed, a family does comes along. They are looking for the gaurds carrage but instead of a daughter they have a son lieing in a wheelchair. He has an increadably long head, which is propp'd sideways on a pillow so's that his watery eyes have to squint up at the sun. I force myself look at him, despite the fear that i might suddenly become him.

It is becouse off this distraction that i miss somone who runs onto the platform and jumps aboard at the last second. Now i will have to go rite back up the front of the train and re-check the carrages all over again. I head off immediately but all my efforts are for nothing. All i find is a father and his small daughter, and she really is only a little girl of about 6, so i walk back along the corridor, rocking with the train and wondering how God could of made me as i am and force't me to miss the only girl who could really love me.

In all probability Elspeth has miss'd her train altogether and is actually back in W- or even been abducted by a sex beast. Other than that, maybe she caught the train last week on a wedneday afternoon at 2.55 instead and now there is absolutly no chance of me meeting her ever again.

I go and sit in an empty compartment and the train slows and we come to a stop in the open countryside. Opposite is the coast bound train, also at a standstill and inside the compartment are 2 skool girls with their mother. Instinctively i un-button myself and as our train starts to move forward again, i lower my shorts and expose my nude penis to them.

There appears to be nowhere where i can live and nobody who will look after me. I brought my sherbert lemons, return'd to the train station and did this rong thing.

* * *

Mister Shawd has again ask't me for my homework and told me that it is now 2 weeks over due.

34

Catweasel and the cartoon faces

I HAVE painted a portrate of myself wearing my Royal West Kents, Colour Sargents jacket. It is painted in oil paints on hardboard and it took most of the Christmas Hollidays to finish.

In my painting i am looking out into the world with an heroic defience. The jacket is paint'd blud red and my hair is long and yellow colour'd, mixing into the red. My face is young looking but i have added a large handle bar mustash - which is also blond but with a slightly redish tint added - to show how i will apear in the futcher.

On the 1st day back at skool i bring my painting in to show our art teacher, Catweasel.

Unlike the other teachers at the W- Secondary Skool for Boys, Catweasel doesnt wear a suit and tie, nor even a cordery jacket. No, Catweasel sits there behind his clutted desk wearing a dirty old track suit and a beard.

In many ways it seams that Catweasel would of preffer'd to have been a gym teacher than an art teacher. This mite explain his manner of dress and his dislike of us. I am one of the hardest werking puples in the art class yet no matter how much i sharpen my pencils and how many expert drawings i make, it is still impossible to please Catweasel.

I try to ingage him in conversations about Vincent van Gogh, Pablo Piccaso, and the Serilist, Salvador Dali, yet in every lesson i am slippered for dissobedence with his very hard and heavy training shoe.

Tuesdays art is our 2nd lesson and i bring in my wonderfull self portrate. I am very excited at how pleased Catweasel is going to be with me. It is quite grown up for a seconday skool boy to be painting in oils, and i should think that no kid in the 'B' stream has ever done so before.

Tho my father is not interested in me or my young life, nor able to recognise any of my talents, im sure that Catweasel - as my art teacher - will appreciate all the hard werk i have put into my painting and no doubt cogratulate me in front of the entire class.

Even before assembly some kids in the playground ask to see my picture, and when i show them just a corner of it out of the bag they say that im easily the best drawer in the whole skool. To be able to draw in skool means something, even to a bully.

I force myself to wait until Catweasel has done the register before i stand, step forward and produce my self-portrate from out of it's black, plastic carrier bag; like as if i am a magician at a fair ground. I stand there holding it up for all to see.

But rather than being awe-struck and congratulating me on my master piece, Catweasel is dismissive and irrateated. He dosnt mention my choice of colours or even pass comment on the realistic way i have painted my nose and eyes.

"I hav't time for this now, Claudius. Besides, you need to learn to draw befor you can paint, walk befor you can run, crawl befor you can walk! Now sit down, put it away and shut up!"

And i have to return to my seat as Catweasel instruckts us on how to draw cartoon faces.

35

Class 4B

AS EVERY year is devid'd up into terms - which in turn are devided up into months and weeks - so the days to are devid'd up into periods. Assembly follows registration, followed by classes and break time and more classes and dinner time and more classes and break time and still more classes then home time.

Slowly but surely we are being regiment'd and render'd down into sludge. Soon, we will all be pretend grown ups and everybody can pretend to be happy. It is presumed that to be obedient and fear'd of life will make us perfict adults. Yes, we are being polish'd like stones in our teachers pockets, but we are not stones, we are dirty, playground grit.

Mornings, we tramp our way into skool, go to registration, sit and wait for the late comers to show up, then 'sir' calls out our names and we call 'here, sir' rite back. Sometimes no one ansewers, then 'sir' asks if any one has seen Milkthrop this morning. No one has seen Milkthrop, so a red cross goes by his name.

Once were all accounted for 'sir' closes the registar and we all sit and wait for the bell to go. Bang on 9.15 we bundle out into the corridor, sneeking kidney punches as we get into line.

'Sir' shouts at us to bludy shutup, then stands to attention in front of us with the register tucked under his arm. He tells us all to shush and we all straightn our ties and file into assembly to be lectur'd on our many shortfalls.

After assembly, we split up into the spersific classes deemed fit for our individual abilitys, or for those like myself and my classmates, our lack of any abilities.

Yes, it is me who is force't to become ingnorant; me who in my 2nd year was disqualifi'd from entering the ranks of the elite because of my so-call'd 'excentrik behaviour', me who, despite - or rather because of my shining star - has gain'd the attenion of all of my masters in their gallent attempts to extinguish me.

We cross the tarmac and enter our dismal classroom and sit contemplating the empty blackboard. It is good to sit here at peace, where nothing is taught and nothing is lern'd; where a kid can while away his skool days and no one pretends that he is even worth regarding, let alone teaching, because he has already been ritten off as a retard.

A usual class lasts half an hour, but a double lasts 1 hour. This morning we have a double English with Ball-Scratcher.

We sit waiting for him to show then Crumb-bum jumps up and rites 'SHAWDS A CUNT' on the blackboard and the reast of the class start screaming and smashing the lids down on their desk like machine gun fire.

Another kid, with shit marks on his shirt tail, climbs up onto his chair, pulls his trousers down and parts his buttock at us. Next up we turn round and Shawd is standing in the doorway. Silence falls like an axe.

Skidmarks jumps off his desk and sits down, tucking in his shirt. Apparently Ball-Scratcher is off sick, so we have Shawd instead. Rather than relaxing ourselves for an hour, we will now be beaten and bully'd in all manner of ways til the bell finnaly sounds the end of our missery.

Befor the class can even begin Shawd has to grab the boy who was airing his arse and repeatedly smash his fingers with the edge of a wooden ruller. Then, grabing him by the back of the neck, Shawd thrusts his head into a metal bin and makes him spit out his chewing gum. Skidmark is then order'd to clean the blackboard with an old duster. Onece his got all the letters wiped out he has to stand to attention so that Shawd can knock him to the ground with a swift dead leg.

We, as a class, are direct'd to find all of this highly amusing and laugh our lungs out as Skidmark writhes on the floor in agony. Rite up we are order'd to shut up, sit up straight, not slouch and sing out 'good morning, sir' 6 different times, untill Shawd is convinc'd of our zeal and enfusiazim. Finnerly, we have to open our exersise books and read out our English homework.

Shawds plesure is to make every aspect of our skool boys lives as uncomfortably and unnessisaraly painfull as possable. For Shawd, and people of Shawds stripe, life must be at best a drudgery and ideally a torcherious, never ending ordeal, punctuat'd with explosions of controll'd but sadistic violence.

The 1st boy has forgotten his exersise book, and the next 2 haven't even bother'd doing their home werk at all. But rather than disciplining them, Shawd forgives them with a meer wave of his hand, as if he is tottaly unconcerned weather a child does his homework or not. Then it's my turn.

I stand and look at Shawd for several moments, waiting for his signal to begin. If i start reading before he says 'begin' he will tell me to shut up. He stairs irriatably at me, trying to catch me out then barks "bludy well get on with it then, Claudius. I havent got all bludy day!"

I begin to read out my story about Grandfather Lewis and the headless chickens. The whole time that im reading, Shawd stands there tossing a piece of chalk from fist to fist with great agitation. Just as im getting to the wonderfull climax, Shawd marches over, snatches my exercise book from my hands and throws it into the bin.

"Audatious clap-trap, master Claudius! Claudius thinks he is a comidian, class, but i am the only comidian here. Claudius should know that 'fowl' langage is not permit'd in my classroom!" And Shawd stands there with his teeth gritt'd, in what he imagines to be a smile but no one understands his hellerious 'joke'. I look about me, then cautiously go to sit down.

"Did anyone tell you that you could sit down, Claudius?"

"No, sir."

"No, sir! Then stand still boy!"

I stand with my waight on one leg and scratch my head.

"Now go to the bin and fetch your 'story'!"

I go grab it and knock off the bit of gum that got stuck to the cover.

"Put it on my desk, boy!"

I place it there and Shawd unfolds my exercise book, smoothing the pages flat, his thin lips reading my words. The simple truth is that my story is beyond him.

Shawd takes up his red biro and slashes at the pages with it like a dagger. In short - my best efforts are brand'd as 'inane' and 'ridiclious'. Also the word vulva is cross't thru in deep red gouges by Shawd.

"Dose anyone know why i have mark'd Claudius's fancyfull story down with a C minus ? ... no? ... Smileson?" Smileson dosnt know either. "Is it, perhaps a 'C' for chicken?" Again Shawd waits for laughter but there is none.

"Well, i have mark'd this vulgar attempt at humour down with a C minus becouse of Claudius's appaling spelling. Coupl'd with his need to see himself as remarkable and special when in fact, as im sure you already know, Claudius is neither of these things becouse Claudius is a prize idiot. What is Claudius, Cowsfroth?"

"A price idiot, sir" replys Cowsfroth. There is a little ripple of laughter and Shawd tells them to all shut up.

Shawd go's on to say that my invention shows a perverse mind and that in his opinion, i am destin'd for the mad house and in need of psychiatric help. Again everyone laughs and Shawd slaps me round the back of the head with my exercise book and tells me to go and sit down.

"You need to concentrate on the basics, boy! On gramer and punctuation, not fancyfull rubish about the origens of extinckt breeds of chicken!" He looks round the class again inviting them to laugh then scowling at them when they do. I put up my hand to speak.

"What is it now, Claudius?"

I stand to answer him. "It's not about the origin of the chickens, sir."

"What?"

"It's not about the origin of the chickens, sir."

"I fail to see what point you are making, Claudius."

"It's the story of the chickens extintion, sir."

"It appears that Claudius has a case of verble diarrhea, class. Sit down, and belt up before i box your bludy ears, boy! Hindly, read your story out to the class."

Hindly says that his dog ate his home werk. Shawd dosent dissaplin him but mechanicly moves on to the next boy. Wagstaff has also neglect'd to do his home werk.

Neither Wagstaff or Hindly are singl'd out for punishment. It seams that Shawd respects genuine lazyness, it is only children who think and haven't quite been smash'd that he cannot abide.

There is an inch of chalk dust benith the blackboard, compleat with footprints from some mouse that has walk't thru it in the nite.

The next kid who has actually ritten a story is Cowsfroth. His hair is red, close cropp't and full of fish scales, like the body of a cod.

According to Cowsfroth his grandad once grew a marrow on his alotment and his favorite food is fish 'n' chips. This story really seams to strike a chord with old Shawd, who places his peice of chalk cearfully on his desk, walks up the isle between the desks and plants one rite between Cowsfroths fish scales. Crowsfroth screams in agony then Shawd absently admires the view out thru the window, straightens his cuff and ambls back to the blackboard where he orders the next boy to 'read out his masterpiece'.

There are 7 more storys, all of which are less than half a page. Despit there lack of substance Shawd marks all of them with 'B' or a 'B+'.

Mister Shawd can say what he likes, but i know that my story is the best by far and all the others attempts are distinkly 3rd rate.

Finnerly, it is Applecakes turn. Applecakes scrappes his chair back and stands to read his monologe. He is only just stammering out the 1st line when Shawd stops him mid sentence and invites him to come out front to read his story to the class. Applecakes duly picks up his exercise book and walks up to Shawd.

Shawd tells Applecakes to about turn, stand up straight and read out his story. Applecakes begins to read and Shawd moves rite up next to him, pressing his body against Applecakes flank, still with his manic grin cracking his mug.

Applecakes's voice is high, like a girls. His lips are also girl-like and his story is very silly. It's about how his Grandfather Pooker won the battle of the Somme single hand'd. There is also a cat in there call'd Calico Cat.

Aparently, Calico Cat stole the last of grandfather Pooka's choclet ration, (which had been personally given to him by Queen Victoria, during The Boer War) and Grandfather Pooker gets wildly angry, disowns Calico Cat and refuses to carry him about in his kitbag anymore.

He never see's that thiefing cat again, that is until one cold, lonely nite Grandfather Pooker is on sentry duty in a forward sap out in No Mans land when everything comes to fruition.

1st off nothings sterring and Grandfather Pooker thinks he's in for a quite nite. He makes a cup of tea, smokes about 40 fags and is just nodding off when a thumping great hun looms out of the darkness and trys to stab him thru the neck with his butchers bayonet.

The blade is just about to split open Grandfather Pookers gizard when Calico Cat leaps from the ramparts and scratches the dirty hun's eyes out. Grandfather Pooker finishes him off with his bayonette and sounds the alarm.

The long and short of it is that the Hun trench raid is kyboshed and Grandfather Pooker is given a medal and Calico Cat gets a whole bar of choclet out of Grandfather Pookers Christmas ration tin. Later on in the story Calico Cat gets his tail shot clean off in a gas attack, which is the bit i like't best.

Finnally, the wars done and dust'd and Grandfather Pooker and Calico Cat return home to a hero's welcom only now Calico Cat is a Manx cat and Grandfather Pooker is a General.

Applecakes finishes his story. There's a long silence and nobody knows where to look. Shawd is still grinning like in a trance, then a kid up the back coughs and Shawd wakes up. We all wait to see how hard Shawd is going to thump Applecakes between the ears. He has already shown his distast for animel storys and for certen, Applecakes is for the high jump. Yet Shawd doesn't beat Applecakes. Not for his idotic cat story, nor his silly, girl-like voice and rather than marking him down with a C- Applecakes recives a glowing A+.

No, after re-reading Applecakes story and bowing his head slitely, Shawd roundly congratulats Applecakes for his obsevational skills, puntuation, imagination and overall grammer. In fact he sings Applecakes praises to high heven.

I look on in dissbelith as Shawd tells Applecakes to return to his seat then tries to induce the rest of the class to applaud him, which we don't. Shawd barks at us and a few hands clap insolently together. But apparently, we are not cheering with enough enfusasim and he threatens to put us all on detention.

"Applecakes has surpass'd himself, gentlemen and you will show your appreciation." He underlines his complement with a dark smile for Applecakes and a fierce grimace towards the rest of us.

Shawd then turns, picks up his chalk and rites: 'Class B4 are all morons' in great gothic letters across the blackboard and we are direct'd to copy this statment 100 times into our exercise books.

36

Some repeat information

IN THE course of this short history of an anominus skool boy i have already spoken too much about the liers who fix'd me up. Also, that at the end of the 1st year of my time here at the W- secondery skool for boys, my mother attend'd a parents evening where a Mister Shawd, our skool proctor, inform'd her that despite my coming top of the form that year i would not be going up into the 'A' stream, as was the normal prosedure, but that the boys who came 2nd and 3rd to me would be reward'd instead. This dissision, he explain'd, was taken on account of my 'eccentric behaviour' and becouse, in mister Shawd's personal estermation, i would not 'get along with boys of a higher caliber'. My mother duelly knod'd and appologis'd on my behalf, bowing slitely as he rebuked her.

For this reason: my mothers humble abdigation, i was not allow'd to join the 'A' stream boys and thereby forfitt'd the rite to sit 'O'levels and get any job that would afford me a station in life.

It was after this revelation and my mothers timidity, that i desid'd to become doubly stupid and thwart all attempts to educate me.

My mother believes teachers and doctors to be high and mighty beings that must be honour'd and obay'd at all costs. I, on the other hand, believe that they are a bunch of liars and thiefs.

I repeat this information at this point in our narrative becouse, as mister Shawd himself has said on many occasions, one cannot repeat things to often for the dull witted, stupid and ignorent. So, if any of my old masters are reading this, by now the information may slowly be penitrating their thick sculls.

Since my refusel to become educat'd my skool werk and general abilities have plumited.

Even in junior skool i could make complicated calculations in fractions, then i was molested and my mother up'd her threats about me being headed for 'a rude awakening'; and my big brother shout'd at me that i would suffer terrible acne as a teenager. My father (who was on one of his rare vists home), look't piercingly at me, plac'd his large, white handkechife over his nose and blew it like a slide trombone.

Acording to the doctors my mother dosn't have cancer after all but instead has TB. Dr Craig says that she must go into hospital immedeatly and that we all must have tests to see if we are incubating the disease. Even Crowsfeet will have to be tested seeings as he lunged down so many of her dog-ends.

This means that our father is going to have to return home and look after us.

Before the ambulence takes her off my mother confid's in me that our father wants her dead.

"You mark my words, he's trying to worry me into an early grave, just like he did my mother! All because he owed her money! And now he wants to install one of his mistresses in my house whilest im laid out in hospital!"

37

A dose of TB

MY MOTHER is gone and i don't have a key to the house. My father has not come down from London to look after us as my mother said he would and my big brother hasnt come home from skool, so im fors't to break in. There's a letter on the kitchen table with my name on it but i have to wait for my big brother to be able to read it.

Theres no money in the house and very little food. I go thru all the draws and cupboards but everything is pretty much stone cold. Basicly, Crowsfeet removed most of the stuff that wasn't nail'd down. Also there's no coal for the heating.

Later, my big brother shows. He comes in and ignores me, cooks up some instant mash potatoes out of a tub and im allowed one bowl. This is our new dinner. After dinner he reads the letter and tells me that i have to report to the hospitle for my TB test next wendsday. Other than that he dosnt bother speaking to me.

My mother never kiss'd me goodbye and i feel sceared and alone. My big brother is the only person i see now, tho i do have a fury gonk which i keep in my blazer pocket as a charm against vampires and wearwolfs. Nether-the-less i am still terroised by ghosts, teachers and my family.

For the next week there's no sign of our father and the telephones been cut off. We really are down to our last rations when, on the following tuesday, the old man finnaly shows his face.

Just when we think that we'll never see him, he rolls up in the middle of the nite. It's 12 o'clock at nite 'n' me and my big brother are sat huddl'd round the oil stove roasting a couple of chestnuts when we see him ghosting past the big window. His face is all white and smudg'd on account that he's pissed drunk. What's more, he has a lady ghost in tow.

They come in thru the front door, enter the room and stair at us, like it's us who are the ghosts. As our mother is not here for our father to relay his orders and complaints thru he is force't to address us personally. I, as his youngest son who tho-by-and-large is a reject, must still be order'd about and remind'd of my ignorence, backwardsness and ineptitude.

Why, he wishes to know, did i break into the house in his absence and not awaight the return of my elder brother, who has been issu'd with a key?

"Co's he doesn't get in till 6 'n' sometimes 9."

My father turns to his lady friend. "Do you see Muriel? This article here? - the one with the big feet? This is what i have to put up with!" He reaches out his white hand and feels her boney arse under her dress, then speaks at me again. "Then why don't you play in the garden untill Nichollas arrives home from skool?"

I shrug my shoulders. "I dunno."

"Not 'i dunno' , i do not know, pah-pah!"

I look at him. 'Pah-pah?' Who's 'pah-pah?' Ive never here'd that one before.

My father looks at me dumbfound'd.

"Muriel, this child has no panache. Take him away, i don't want him in my site, he lacks all style! Look at his feet. You are a yob, Gustov, a common yob! Well i wash my hands of him. No! I can't get on with him! Maybe in 10 years ile get on with him even better than i do now with Nichollas. But now? Just get him out of my site!"

It's not just the coucil estate 'yobs' that my father holds in contempt, as far as he is consern'd we are all of us refuse: Me, Crowsfeet, our mother and anyone else who is not posses'd of what he calls 'a certain panache'.

"Come along now, chop-chop! It's time for the pair of you boys to grow up! To become young gentlemen. Stop expecting life to give you evereything on a plate. Smarten yourselfs up, for christs sake! You won't get anywhere without the correct presentation. Isnt that so, Muriel? It is the presintation that counts!"

Mureil smiles her mask at us. "Your father has a lovly

presentation. Do you boys have large penises? Your father has a lovely large penis!"

'Pah-pah' then smiles, walks over to the drinks cabbnet and pours a bottle of gin into 2 glasses, one for Mureil and an extra large one for himself.

"Nichollas, what will you drink, Scotch or brandy? Gustov, you can have lemonade or beer. On 2nd thoughts, off to bed with you! I don't want you in my site, you lack all panache! Don't you think your brother lacks pernach, Nichollas? Off to bed you Smell, and maybe his new mummy will come and tuck you in. Do you want to tuck Smell in, Darling?" And he turns and grins at Muriel, who's face is paint'd up like a fiend out of a horror show.

All of them snigger as i cross the room and go up the stairs to my bed. I barakad the door and lie under the covers listening to their loud voices banging about all nite laughing and pissed.

Finnaly, just near dawn i drop off to sleep, Normans devils crucifix on my bedside table. In the morning they are all of them gone.

38

A hate'd backwater

WHY MUST children go to skool? And if we have to go why can't we at least have the afternoons off? Many of the 5th years don't bother coming in at all and when they do they are liable to spark up a fag and blow the smoke in the teachers face. Soon we will be as free as men.

Our teachers job is to trim and cajole us. To help us have small expectations of life and expect nothing. In short - they treet us like weeds rather than flowers and make sure that none of us bloom.

It is almost as if they have grown angry. That because they themselves have met none of their own expectations they somehow resent that they have end'd up teaching such a bunch of useless retards as us.

Already life in this place is missrable but what they do only exasperates our mutual sufferings. Yes, their dreams have wither'd on the vine and they go about bitterly snipping off any bud that might have the audasity of expressing it's nature in spring time.

Like clockwerk, i nip through Rollingpins hedge in the mornings then break back into the house again in the evenings. Whilst waiting for my big brother to return i make paintings in my skool exersice books and wait for my supper. If im lucky, he pours some boiling water over the instant mash potatoes and i can eat.

Back before my mother went onto the TB ward, she used to make me drink a pint of ici cold milk each and every morning, and stood there whatching over me with her arms cross't, making sure that i down'd every last drop. It's ici nature made my eye ache. For me to finish it in one go became a matter of honour, tho in many ways it disgust'd me.

"I'm building you up" she spoke "we've got to put some meat on those bones!"

At dinner times she gave me beer and cheese sandwiches, which also help't make me have a headache. Now i eat nothing and have turned into even more of a skellington.

My big brother dosnt always come home in the evenings because he to has a girlfriend. Other times he brings her round to the house. Compaired to my fathers friend Muriel, she is very calm and friendly but really i mean nothing to her.

It seams that for me to have sex with a girl will always be impossible. Girls faces are hard and jutting and always sneering at me. This is why i have been sneeking my stray dog into the bathroom. This is not a laughing matter and it is doubly sad that i don't even notice my own loneliness.

My big brother tell's me that due to my unatractive face and body, no girl will ever want me or sleep with me. Also he say's that i will have hiddious achny in my teens, i still stink of piss and his girlfriend also calls me Smell.

Is this why i lie and have become a pervert? As well as letting the dog lick me, i have also dress'd in my mothers cloths and knock't on old ma Rollingpins door, under the pretext of selling her my fathers skool boy bible.

I also told old ma Rollingpin that my mother only has 6 months to live and she believ'd me. I want'd to laugh when i saw her worri'd expression but couldn't. Instead i felt sad, for who knows, maybe it is true and my mother is going to die befor the years out and then i will be left all alone in the world. It is after this that i went out onto the street and expos'd myself.

After our bowl of mash potatos my big brother tells me that our father is coming down to the house on friday to take us to London, which i personally don't believe.

"Well he's coming! There's no clean bowls left, so tidy up the house and stop pissing the bed."

So my skoolboy life goes on, gradually playing out to end

wherever it ends.

I must wonder if my mother will ever return from the hospital or weather she will die there on the TB ward, as is my fathers wish.

Friday comes round and the old man dosnt show up just as i predict'd. My big brother sits there staring up the garden path thru the venetian blinds, doing his best impression of our mother. I ask him if he thinks our mother will ever get better and he yells at me to 'fucking shut up!'

There's no heating on so i go up to my room and climb under the covers to keep warm.

I'm still in bed Saterday dinner time when i hear a car pull up below my window. It's a taxi with the old man in it.

The reason our father has to spend all his money on taxis is on account that he's a drunkerd and has smash'd up too many cars and too many miles of crash barrier and the police took away his licence. Acording to our mother, the only reason that he hasn't been sent to prison befor now is becouse he's a Mason and give's the Judge a funny handshake.

39

We visit the mother

NEXT, WE go visit my mother in hospital. Crowsfeet, who is on day release from Borstal, bangs on the window and signal's me to meet him in the bush's. Outside he tells me that he needs some ciggerts, that im to steel some money for him from my father and that he's coming with us to the hospital. He said nothing else but his egg white eyes threaten'd violence.

Another reason Crowsfeet must come with us is to get the results of his TB test.

It is left to me to try to lift some notes from the old mans brief case and explain why Crowsfeet has to visit our mother. My father looks at me as if i am talking gibberish, then tell's me that i am a child who understands nothing and to shut up.

Actually, Crowsfeet will beat me if he isn't allow'd to come. Really, i would preffer that they all die, Crowsfeet, my father and my big brother, or that i die, one or the other. Basicly, the old man is not interested if i get beaten up or if a grown man is fiddling with me. His main concern is that i look presentable and talk the Queens English.

"No, your friend canot come with us, we are visiting your mother in hospital, not going on a pic-nic."

"But he's got to get his test results."

"Well he can catch the bus."

"Bus's don't go there, not all the way."

"This house is an utter tip. It looks like a bludy bomb's hit it! Look at it."

"Can he come though?"

"Tidy up and i may considor your requst. Nichollas, you too, get this place tidy and correct!"

We survay the room. The problem is the way that the instant mash has form'd an inpentrable crust over everything. The kitchen, espershery, is alive with fungus. Acording to our father the whole house is 'all shitt'd up!'

"It is not ship-shape!" he shouts. Don't mess up the pot's and pans for Gods sake, dine out at a restruant!"

We have to explain that we haven't any money, that we are skool children and that our mother has got TB, but he dismisses our arguments with a wave of his bony hand, and tells us that it is about time that we made our own way in the world and that we can't carry on relying on him for charity.

"Life isnt a matter of money, it is a matter of presentation and panache! Now, i don't want to hear any more of your whinging and complaining, go out and earn a living or shut up!"

I look up at his beard. "But what about skool?"

"No buts - get out there and make it happen!"

I turn and look at my big brother, who is nodding furiously, but as far as i see it our father is insain.

As well as tiedying up, me and my big brother have to put on our skool uniforms as my father says that we are going to the hospital, not a tramps tea party and need to dress and behave acordingly. Im just putting my tie on when i see Crowsfeet lopping up the garden path.

The old man peers at Crowsfeet like he is something that he's pick'd up on the sole of his shoe. It's Crowsfeet's half open mouth and gormless eyes that put him off. The old man chews the ends of his mustash, points his eyes at the taxi and we all have to troop off.

It is strange that Crowsfeet should be here at all, this boy who mercilessly bullys me, steels my faimly's money and hates me. Yet i stand up for him and champion him thru fear.

My father checks our feet as we get in the car then sits down in the front himself still bristling.

The taxi driver is a Canadian with a head and face like a walnut, you can see every type of groove and crease in it. He's name is

Bernard and he tells me that he stole a Tommy Gun during the war but had to dismantle it and chuck it in the river becouse the Military Police were onto him. It's him who drives us to London.

I look at his mash'd up old face, his story is plausible but i for one can't belive that anyone in there rite mind would throw a perfictly good Tommy Gun into a river.

The old man calls Bernard his 'choffer' and makes him take down his little sign off the roof and wear a peak'd cap.

We pull out of the drivway and onto the main road. Im not used to cars and have to clamp my mouth shut as we swing round the bends to stop myself from puking up. It's not so much the movement but on account of the stench of the upholstry. I hold onto the armrest and have to breath thru my mouth. My father turns his yellow beard and tells me to stop catching flys.

The Canadian taxi driver grows very quite and tells us nothing more of his time fighting the entire German Army single handed. In fact no one says anything as we drive thru that desolate countryside to my mothers sanitorium. I ask my father what causes T.B. but he chooses not to answer.

The taxi drops us at the main gate and the driver goes to find some place to park up and wait for us. The old man climbs out, looks up at the sun and checks his pocket watch and instructs his 'choffer' what time to pick us up. He checks his onion again and shakes it by his ear. I watch it as it snakes back into his pocket a link at a time.

Bernard motors off and we walk over to the main building. Crowsfeet trys to make me go into the bushs and smoke a fag with him but the old man won't let me wander off. Crowsfeet shows me his fist, makes angry eye's at me and signels me to steal some money off my father or he'll kill me.

I try to keep my father and big brother between us but Crowsfeet swoops in at me. My father tells me to get out from under his bludy legs. He has a piece of paper with the name of my mothers ward ritten on it in pencil.

Theres acres of corridors in that place but we find the rite ward and the sister leads us to my mother's bed.

I see my mother rite aways, way off in the distance. At 1st im not sure if it's really her, but it is. As we come closer i see that she is very gray looking, wearing an orange nite dress, that ive never seen before, and chewing at her dry looking lips.

I am scear'd seeing her lying there like that in a foreign nite gown and i'm not allow'd to kiss her, on account of the TB, and have to stand back.

My father, on the other hand, seems to be unfazz'd and is completely at home with her new condition. He speaks to her in a very brassy way, telling her to stop moping about and to smarten herself up.

The olds girl try's to smile and says hello to Crowsfeet in a strange croacky voice. Crowsfeet, who being a steeler of her cigeretts and money, only inclines his head slitely. My big brother stands next to my father with his hands clasped infront of him.

Despite my grown-upness, I'm only a skool kid. Really, i am still only so young and it doesn't seam fair that a childs mother should be lying there dying in front of him like that, or that his father should be so hartless, or that he should be bullyd from piller to post . . . that the world should be so harsh and cruel . . . that my father doesn't love me . . . and my big brother is only a boy-man and dosn't protect me in any way . . . and Crowfeet stood there as well, ready to knife me.

When i was still very, very little, i saw a film were a hurd of wilderbrests were being stamped'd across the African planes by a pride of lions and one calf, still only half born with just his tiny hoofs sticking out his mother, was stalk'd, hunt'd down then ripp'd from his mothers womb and eaten.

"The children are nicely dressed. How are you getting on at skooll, Gustov?" my mother croaks like the devil.

"S'all rite" i answer.

My father turns to me and tells me to take my hands out of my pockets, stand up straight, stop chewing on my tounge - like a wretch'd imbercial - and for hevens sake speak properly!

I can tell that he has cheer'd up.

The nurse brings my father a cup of tea and we get to have some soapy tasting orange squash. My father starts chating up the nurse then the doctor comes and leads him behind a green screen and explains things to him in a monotone whisper.

There's a chair by my mothers bed, my big brother doesn't want to sit and Crowsfeet go's outside to see if he can scrounge up a cigi, so i am allow'd to sit down.

I rummige thru my pockets, find my Luftwaffe ring, polish it on my cuff and pass it to my mother as a get well present. She smiles weakly and asks me to put it on her bedside cabernet. It says' 'Against England' only in German.

I sit there and whatch the lady in the next bed doing a bit of knitting. Actualy, if i strain my ears i can here what the doctor is saying to my father behind the screen. He is telling my father that our mother has been very serriously ill and needs a break in the warmth and sunshine for recooperation.

After the hospital we have to drop Crowsfeet off at his probation office and me 'n' my big brother are told that we are going up to

London with our father.

It takes another hour and a 1/2 to do that. We go up the motorway then pass big buildings and disappar into a sea of traffic and lites. Bernard has to go park the car so we get out and me and my big brother are allow'd to go up to our fathers office.

So he really does werk in London afterall. We go up all these stairs into the mysterius world of our father. I smoke a marowana cigarette with some men who say they are my fathers dogsbodys. They joke with me and tease me and and my brother runs and reports me to our father.

"Father, Gustov's been smoking drugs upstairs."

Our father sit's staring out the window with spitel in his bear'd.

"What? ... pardon? ... what?"

"Gustov's been smoking drugs upstairs."

"Did he enjoy it?" he answers in an abstract'd kind of way.

I stand to attention, my hart is bursting with pride.

Next, Muriel shows up and induces me to drink half a bottle of red wine, also with my father's blessing, and then we have to go out for a meal at a resturant.

My favorite food, bar none, is chocklet. Next, i like egg and chips, but only the yellow of the egg. Mash'd potatoes are good, as are saussages and lamb chops, but without the fat. Basically, i refuse to eat anything green colour'd, accept raw peas. Also, i won't eat cellery of any kind, nor bacon rinds. Burnt toast is good but i won't eat butter. If i am eating dry biscuits in the bath i will sometimes drink bathwater.

Some people will say that all this is an expression of my sensitive nature, others will say that i am overindulg'd and was never quite smash'd enough as a young child; but however the vote goes, it makes me feel good to know that i alone am in charge of what i will and will not allow into my mouth.

After the food, none of which i can eat, we walk down the bissy streets, benieth lots of flashing lites to a theater, where they have the actual crusifixion of Jesus Christ live on stage.

The seats are all in red, there's plaster cherubs flying about painted up in gold, then the music starts. I watch the proceedings thru a small pair of red plastic benocculours. You have to put a shilling in a little slot and they unclip from the seat in front of you.

Rite off the stage is all covered in smoke, aluminated by revoling coloured lites and there are a lot of long hair'd people singing and all sorts of strange harnesses and ropes. Jesus, the main one, is tall and muscular. He has the longist hair and also wears a beard, just like in the paintings of him. In the end the Romans cruscify him, rite there in front of us.

Afterwards the lites go up and everyone is banging their seats, stuffing their faces and bundling for the door, just like in skool.

No, there is no reverance or understanding of Christ suffering, just a lot of empty talk. Tho my father tell's Muriel that it was excepshinal and my big brother says that he liked it, really it was as if nothing much had really happened at all.

You're suppos'd to replace the binoculars and get your shilling back but i decide to keep mine as a soverneer. My father says nothing.

It's quite something to see the crusifiction of Christ and to be speeding in a taxi thru London at nite; to overtake a black man on his Honda 50 outside Buckingham Palice and be studying his black face thru my red binoculars and to wave at him and for him to wave back. London really is the most friendly place.

Then i have to ask my father to stop the car so's i can chuck up in the gutter. I feel it rising in me. I try to fight it but suddenly there's a big surge from my stomach as we round a bend. Bernard swerves into the curb and it goes across my lap. I fumble with the door handle and fall out on my knees onto the pavement. The wine comes out just the same as it went in, the same colour, the same stink, everything.

All the way back my father try's to disgrace me, telling me that i can't take my liquior, that i am still a little baby, that i smell and asking if 'i enjoyed my teckni-coloured yawn.'

40

Old Ma Cooper

When i wake up in the morning the house is in silence and everyone has left. The clock downstairs has stopped but i can here the kids out in the playground so it must be 1st break.

Theres a letter on the door mat from my skool, addressed to my father. I take it into the toilet with me. It is a report of some discription. I can't read most of it but it is defiantly from Shawd and he mentions the word 'lack' several times.

The whole letter is hard to define but Shawds signiture alone eminates a damning pridiction. One thing that i do understand, is a line ritten in bold capitols, that say's i am a hopeless case and have wast'd my childhood. I tear the letter up on the way into skool. I scatter the pieces in Mr's Moffits bushes.

Even when i was walking along the road i new it was going to happen. All of my bile and anger that had been festering within me was bubling away and was finally ready to spew up.

I cross the field, regardless of the prefects, march straight into class and swear in the presence of old ma Cooper, our new form teacher. Actualy, i shout the 'F' word in her face.

In many ways i have been planning just such an outburst for months 'i will show them something that will really make them shake their noses!' that was my feeling. It all happen'd like this: i came into class late, and im not making it up when i tell you that just the way that my eye's fit into my face makes old ma Cooper hate me.

"You are late, Claudius now sit down!" barks old ma Cooper, but i don't sit down and decide to re-tie my sholace instead. I peek up at her, crouched on my knees tying a knot.

Her jowls wobble with rage and she screams at me.

"I said sit down, Claudius! I will not have you disrespecting me, this class or this skool!" Next, it seams to me that i should blow my nose and i start to take out my handcachief.

"Put that handkerchif away, this instant! This," she say's, waving a pigs foot at me and turning to the other children, "is how a moron behaves!"

I wipe my nose and do as im told.

"Let me tell you something class, this boy scored 15 percent in his biology paper for his mock exams. 15 percent out of 100 that is! I read his answers out to the 1st year children in 1A3 and they laugh't till they where fit to burst. It would be funny ifit wasn't tragic and pathetic! My word, the answers he gave. My youngest daughter, who is just 6 years old - and an excilent horse woman, i may add - could come into this class and read better than this ignorant boy! She could wipe the floor with the lot of you. And she is butiful and can speak french with a perfict accent!"

"Fuck off!" i say, under my breath, then walk to my desk and throw myself into my chair. I force myself to look nonchlent and stair out the window, over the empty tarmac and playing fields beyond. I can here the rest of the class sniggering over the pounding of blud in my brain.

"I beg your pardon! – What did you just say?"

"You heard me" i mutter.

As my big brother has sworn at my mother, so i in turn have sworn at this unspeakable bitch. Afterall, it's far more thrilling to be evil than invissable. The skin on my face is taught and i can here a ringing noise in my ears.

Quick as you like, old ma Cooper comes out from behind her desk, waddles up the ile and stands there in front of me with her riding britches pulled rite up tight into her cunt.

"I will not tolerate you or your foul mouth in my class for one second longer, now get out!"

Tiredly i get up, pick my bag from the floor and walk towards the door.

"And where do you think your going?"

"Out" i answer flatly.

"Sit down this instant! I never gave you permission to leave your desk!" And she points her small trotter at my chair.

I shrug and sit down again.

Old ma Cooper sends Cowsfroth to Mister Shawd with a note and rite after registration 2 prefects come to collect me and ascort me across the playground to Shawd's office.

Now it's all in the lap of the gods. Maybe Shawd will decide to throw me out the skool on the spot, or perhaps he will postpone my expulsion till after the Easter break.

The 2 Judases walk either side of me, the Vicas son twisting my arm just as if i am their prisioner. It takes a special kind of creep to become a prefect and these 2 fit the bill perfectly. They even wait on guard with me outside Shawds office, goading me; till they are call'd away to arrest some inocent 1st year for being beaten up, or perhaps for forgetting to tie the knot in his tie properly.

I watch the vicas son's brown hair dissapearing down the stairwell and his mate, who's a ginger nut, clutching his arse. I walk over and lean on to the rail, their heads march out thru the swing doors, the door bangs behind them and the skool is in silence.

I play hop-scotch back up the corridor, stepping only on the black tiles, then check the coast is clear and place my ear to Shawds door. I can't hear anybody in there.

I stand around for another 5 minits clearing the wax out of my ears then walk down the stairs and out thru the main entrance. I pass one of the secretarys on the way, but she doesn't try and stop me, push open the front door and walk quickly away across the front field.

I have ritten a new story for my English homework. This is how it goes:

The Messerschmitt pilots sever'd hand
Gustove Claudius Form 4B1

A young skool boy walks down the street thru rain that spatters his face like cold spunk, it's wettness finding his delicate throat and neck. A horrible green bus descends on him and he has to run like the clappers to catch it. His legs kicking out like a hang'd man's, and he knows that he is only a skeleton cloth'd in flesh and he gasps and wish's that he was dying of some terminal desease, or could at least cough up a liitle blud.

He catch's up with the bus at the corner and has real tears crying down his face. The skool boy wipes his snotty cheeks on his sleeve, haul's himself on board and smiles at the bus driver.

A lady, known as old ma Rollingpin, is sat up the back with her grown up daughter, who resembles some kind of cookoo. Plus Raffles, her lap dog, is sat there peering out of his small scull like a mad monkey.

The skool boy swings himself down behind the 3 of them and old ma Rollingpin grimices her spongy lips at him (in truth the skool boy has been climbing thru her hedge on the way to skool and the skool boy knows that althou she pretends to be freindly, really old ma Rollingpin wishes to stop his childhood with Christ.

"So what if i was a Messerschmitt pilot during the last war, that doesnt necessarily make me a Natzi, does it?" the skool boy suddenly speaks, "or mean that ive been crawling thru anyones hedge! Being a member of the Luftwaffe dose not automaticaly mean that someone is any less of a human, or mean that they should necessarily march around barking like an infernal goose!"

Old ma Rollingpin dosnt look at the skool boy and keeps her face resolutly to the front, tho tilt'd slitely to one side. Her grown-up cookoo goes to speak but the mother yanks violently at it's sleeve, forcing it to turn back round and also ignor him. The skool boy feels the mussels in his jaw clentching and unclentching.

"Even if i was the ghost of a Messershmitt pilot i could still, don't you agree, be my country's greatest living artist?" the skool boy asks the back of old ma Rollingpins head, which is wrapp'd in a purple, chiffon scarf. Then, leaning round to the side so as to be able to peer at her man-like nose. "I would paint marvalois crusifixion scenes," he tease's her, "my friends dubing me The Rembrandt of the Skies."

The Skool boy then sits back and looks out of the window at the passing houses. It is certainly rong of him to steel and drink his fathers whisky, but also swashbuckling and devil-may-care.

They pass an old woman struggling along the road pushing a wheel chair with a crippl'd child sat in it. The child in turn is holding a pet rabbit on his lap with a bandaged paw, and then they are left behind as the bus speeds off down W-works hill.

"Did you see that poor child and his rabbit? Isn't anyone going to stop and cure him?" The skool boy stands to get off the bus but already the little cripple boy is miles back and the chance of rescueing him hopeless. Regretfully the skool boy sits himself back down, force's himself to think of himself as the little cripple child and make himself cry.

Blowing his nose, he sits up. "Naturaly, it wouldn't nessisarally follow that i would fly only Messerschmitts and might well even be happier flying a Heinkel 111, tho that of course would be just plain ridiculous!" The skool boy trys to gain old ma Rollingpin's attention, but the cantanckerious Christain dosnt seam to have an oppion either way.

"Ile proberbly never see that cripple child again till the day it dies but if i ever become rich and famous i shall buy pomigranits for all the crippl'd children in the parish and distribute them for free!"

Old ma Rollingpin turns ever so slitely, looking at him out of the tail of her eye, and the skool boy knows that he's hook'd her with his Christ like revelation.

"In our mess it would be well agreed that 'God was with us' in our war against England.

"Of course, some of our leaders what not so near to God themselves, our esteem'd leader, Hermann Göering, for example was a well known 'perfum'd gentleman', or as fritz so delicately put it, 'Ein grosser fetter Schwuler!' Which is impolite of him and i apologise on his uncouth behalf, God rest his soul! But what if, like my good friend Fritz, i too was knock't clean out of the skies by one of those sly island monkeys (the English); my little sky horse in flames round my waist and my hand sever'd at the wrist as i bail'd out into that strange empty sky; my poor hand falling away from me as my parachute blossomd above my head like a great white Lilly?

"Or wouldnt it be more likely that i'd be flying too low to bail out and would have to instead crash-land in some smelly Kentish duck pond? Then maybe a band of gay gypsies would come running to my rescue, dragging my smouldering corpse from the flaming fuselage and dress my burns in felt and fat. And wouldn't it just be my luck if one of their wretch'd hounds took a spiteful nip at my poor, burn'd hand and ripp'd it clean off, like as if it was nothing more than an old leather glove? Then in my delirium i would have to watch as that beast haired off across the fields with it's gory prize clamp'd in it's vile jaws."

The skool boy finishs his speach and glares roguishly at old ma

Rollingpin, letting himself dribble slightly down his chin.

Old ma Rollingpin turns her face sharply away and her puffy hands fiddle with her purple, chiffon scarf.

Her grown up cuckoo child coo's some kind of agreement but other than that there is only silence and the noise of the engin.

The skool boy peers into the chrome rail on the back of the seat, his face made distort'd and ridiculous. Looking up he pulls a face and Raffles, (old ma Rollingpins lap dog) snarls up at him from her vast lap.

Aparently, this riculiously minture dog thinks that it is a 6 inch high human being with roving, grape-like eyes. It licks it's chops and bars it's sharp little fangs at the skool boy.

"Little dog, it is hardly my fault if an ex-German prisoner of war, known as Stüker Joe happen'd to fall in with some notoruis good time sally and set up home in a wretch'd shack where my fathers house now presently stands."

"No dear," snaps old ma Rollingpin, "knowbody suggest it was your fault."

"Well you impli'd it with your sarcastic scarf!" shouts the skool boy and Raffles snaps at him. The skool boy is forc'd to withdraw slitely over the back of the seat.

"It is not as if a son can be blamn'd for the way his father wears his parting!" he add's, holding all 3 of them with his quick, skool boy eyes.

Old ma Rollingpin, who hasn't both'd shaving, lets out a deep sigh and peers out of the dirty rain speck'd window at heaven-only-knows what. Which is rude of her and pretty well proves that she is wrong.

Meanwhile, her grown up cookoo child turns her head and

smiles impudently at the skool boy. She has one normal eye which looks at you and one boggly eye, which studies the cealing.

"I think it's a miracle the pilot surviv'd at all," he tells the boggle eye, "if those gypsies hadn't smother'd his legs in goose fat and bound them in felt, who knows what would have been the outcome."

"Goose fat? . . . what sort of felt?" the boggle eye asks.

The skool boy smiles back at her. "I suppose that you know that the pilots severed hand is still looking for him," he says excitdly, "for the pilot, i mean. The hand crawl'd all the way from G- town centre to the top of W- hill, on it's bare fingers! That's 6 miles, all-but. Thru town and cross country, and all under the cover of darkness!"

The skool boy studys the cookoo child's face and she nods. Her head is held a little to one side her mouth hanging slightly open, in fact just like a cookoo.

"The hand rest'd up in bushes during the daytime, frighten'd out of it's wits by marauding crows. A red fox nearly ate it alive but the hand scurr'd off down a rabbit hole just in time, were a nursing mother rabbit reviv'd it with milk."

The grown-up cookoo turns to it's mother and pulls at her blue coat sleeve imploringly, "Do you hear that, mother? Those crows are such breastly creatures, aren't they?" But old ma Rollingpin just fixes her jaw, runs her pudgy fingers thru the sparse belly hairs on Raffles pink tummy and grunts.

The bus conductor comes past and the skool boy is forced to buy a ticket, which is doubly unlucky. Actually, he slip the conductor a foreign coin and pretends to be so deep in conversation that he hasent notic'd his error.

The skool boy looks down as his feet as the conductor cranks out the ticket, and Raffles sticks out his toungue, makes a little bark and threatens to split on the skool boy. Quick as you like the skool boy butts in and cuts the dirty dog dead.

"Of course, even travelling by nite isn't entirely free of obstacles and dangers, least of all for a completely unaccompani'd hand. Badgers, for example, are natorousey inquisitive and can be quite vicious."

Raffles stairs dumbfounded at the skool boy, shock'd that he understood his crafty, doggy mind.

At this point in our story the elderly lady, known as old ma Rollingpin, lets out a loud and undignifi'd "humph!" and her espesherly doughy fingers, adorn'd with all manner of cheap trinkets, sneak surreptitiously beneath Raffles belly, and appear to be now caressing it's doggy breasts.

The skool boy grips onto the chrome rail of his seat and lean's his face boldly into Raffels territory and shouts "This isn't just any run of the mill old mitt we're talking about here, Madam! We're talking about the hand of one of the century's greatest living artists! The hand that thumb'd it's nose at Picasso, punch't Vladimir Mayakovsky between the eyes, pull'd André Breton's ears, and wrote a rude and unpublishable letter to the Belgian pretender René Magritte! The very same hand that finally got itself unceremoniously chew'd off by the gypsy dog, Bishop's Finger!"

"Bishop who?" mutters old ma Rollingpin haughterly.

"Finger!" shouts the skool boy, and a stern looking gentlman at the front of the bus turns his head and holds the skool boy with a penetrating gaze.

The skool boy lowers his voice to a hard wisper, "as to whether or not that canine thief was fully aware of the great werks of art once undertaken by the apparently lifeless hand now held in it's vice-like jaws, no one knows. But one thing is for certain: Bishop's Finger was galloping like the clappers towards an encounter."

The skool boy surveys the 3 of them cearfully befor continuing.

"After Bishop's Finger's merraculus theft of the hand, he was chas'd across stile and country by a gang of screaming gypsy children. On and on they ran, miles passed until finally they reached the outskirts of G-.

"There, 2 of the smaller children gave up the chase but the others follow'd the dog rite into G- town centre, where Bishops Finger nipp'd across L– Circus and a van carrying cut glass slammed on his breaks and the driver was sliced up like lunchon meat.

"Seeing the children were disstracted, Bishops Finger dashed up an alleyway and manag'd to throw the last of them off his sent. Unfortunaly, no sooner had the dog jump'd clear of one sauspan then he land'd smack-bang into the fire: at the end of the alleyway he was intersept'd by the mangy bitch, known simply as 'Nun's Delite'. There then ensu'd a most ferocious dog-fight over the ownership of the hand.

"The dogs raged like beasts possessed. Just as it seam'd that Bishops Finger would become it's ritefull owner, Nun's Delight would get hold of an index finger and give it a good shaking. It seamed that the poor hand would be torn completely assunder then the local butcher, known by all for his love and simple kindness, embedd'd his meat cleaver in his cutting-block, march'd out of his shop, across the pavement and chuck'd a kettle of scalding water over the 2 warring hounds.

"In the yapping bedlam that follow'd the hand manag'd to scurry out of harm's way up a drainpipe and onto the butcher's windowsill, where it nestl'd fearfully. Needless to say, one finger was badly maul'd, it's index nail turning quite black - in short, the hands once imaculatly manicur'd nails were now chew'd and blud'd.

"The hand lay there motionless, seriously traumatis'd by it's recent experiences in the mouths of Christendom's most fearsome hounds: Bishops Finger and Nuns Delite, respectively.

"The hand wait'd until the hubbub had died down then slowly roll'd over onto it's side and press'd a cold thumb up against the plate glass window, as if wishing to make love to a tray of pig trotters that lay there in sea of greecy brine.

"Being thus absorb'd, the hand didnt notice the approaching feet of the gypsy children and before it knew what was what, it was snatch'd up and flung to the ground. Whereupon the children desend'd on it and proceed'd to kick it around the street like a rag football."

The skool boy jumps up in his seat miming the scene out in front of them.

"The hand jerks across the cobble stones! The hand rolls lazily in the grit! The hand scores a goal! The children scream and shout, stamping their feet and dashing at the hand wildly! The hand twists and spins thru the evening air, the feeling slipping from it's fingertips! The hand opens and clenches it's yellowing fist! It seam'd that at last the hand was beaten but summoning up the last of it's strength, it flexes it's scuff'd fingers and jump's up at a passing skool girl's knee, deftly caress'ng her thigh, just above the sock."

"How perfectly horrible." gasps the cuckoo daughter.

"Horrible, my foot! Ive never heard such a lot of hooey in all my life!" pronounces old ma Rollingpin.

"But what about Stuka Joe's parents, mother, don't they care what happens to their own son's hand?"

The skool boy nod's his head in agreement but old ma Rollingpin holds him with her dust color'd eyes then turns tiredly on her bewilder'd daughter.

"But you know perfectly well what happen'd, dear" she says witheringly, "Stüker Joe's parents came and took him, and those poor, dear, children back to Germany and left Sally-what's-her-name, to stew in her own juice!"

"I know but what happen'd to Stüker Joe's hand, mother?"

"What happen'd to his hand, indeed! I suppose that if this silly boy told you that it went on holiday to Margate and bought itself a stick of rock and a funny hat you'd believe him!

"Really, Constance! I don't know... they buri'd it... or burn'd it... or whatever it is they do with such disgusting things!"

Old ma Rollingpin sighs tiredly and, holding onto Raffles, lifts her vast behind, fiddles with her underwear and re-seats herself. Raffels also gets up, turns several circles on her lap, before springing up at her gargantuan breasts.

"Now look what you've done, you've gone and upset Waffles with all this silly talk. it's all a lot of silly nonsense, isn't it Waffels? Yes." She pats Raffle's small, rat-like head.

"Don't take any notice of the silly boy! You're a good doggy, aren't you, den's? Yes!" And she feeds Raffles a small sweety from out of her handbag.

The skool boy leans over and whispers loudly into the Cuckoo daughter's ear.

"After scearing off the gypsy children the hand just lay there in the gutter, pathetically trying to crawl under an empty cigarette packet before losing consciousness. Later that same evening, when the butcher clos'd up shop, the butcher swept grit and sawdust down onto the poor lifeless hand but it could at last reast and start to recopperate."

"Aah, the poor thing!" sighs the cookoo daughter.

"Oh shut up the pair of you!" snaps old ma Rollingpin, "I won't sit here and listen to any more of this tommy-rot!"

"Madam, wouldn't it be quite likely that the butcher would mistake the hand for some discard'd pigs trotter, or some other nameless piece of offal?" The skool boy really does try to reason most politely with her but old ma Rollingpin is belligerent to the last.

"He'd pick it up and bung it in the saussage bin as soon as look at it!" she sneers angrily.

"Oh no, mother! Not a man's hand, surely!" The cookoo daughter wrinkles her large nose and sniffs the air like an oversized sea-gull.

"Why, Constance, you poor dear, you really were born yesterday weren't you! Im telling you there never was such a hand!"

"But what about Stüker Joe?" simpers Constance.

"Yes, Madam, as your good daughter quite ritely asks, what about Stüker Joe? And come to that, what about the 2 Sea-Cadets who happen'd across the injur'd hand later that nite - at approximately 11.30 p.m to be precise; and bending over, as if to read it's bludy'd palm, saw the sever'd hand pointing an eerie, milky-white finger towards a bush, underneath which, quite unbeknownst to it, lay a slither of Heinkel pilot's left foot, glistening in the moonlite."

"Close your ears dear, i refuse to listen to any more of this pithel!" and old ma Rollingpin really does put her fingers in her hairy lug holes.

The skool boy ignores her and standing back on his seat, raises his voice, so that the whole bus can here, and proclaims:

"There was a Band-Aid plaster protecting a painful blister on the expos'd heel of that slither of Hinkle pilots foot, identifying it as the foot of none other than Straffle Furer Paul Stimetze! Yes, ladys and gentlemen, and it can now be reveal'd that those 2 patriotic Sea-Cadets then stood bravely forth, pick'd up the hand between 2 broken sticks and boldly toss'd it over the railings into the 1st Avenue allotments.

"Apparently, the hand flew thru the air like a great white spider, spinning dizzily, grasping for a twig before landing with a dull thud, palm up, in a clump of damp smelling stinging nettles."

With a look of utter disgust old ma Rollingpin stands and clasping her spiteful lap-dog under her arm, jerks the communication cord with her free hand. The bus judders to a halt and the skool boy's knock't to the floor, as if he is of no more significane than a sever'd hand himself.

The skool boy stairs up from amongst dust and discarded bus tickets as old ma Rollingpin towers over him, her great legs encas'd in flesh-toned surgical stockings.

Raffles bulges his grape-like eyes, licking his chops and generally galloping like a fiendish little demon that can scarsly wait to sink it's sharp, needle-like fangs into the skool boy's soft, delicate hand.

"So what if i am a sever'd and abussed hand, Madam? Does that make me any less human than you?" he calls up to her. "I still have rites, no matter how much you might try to deny me them and hush me up!"

With that the skool boy is thrown from the bus. He struggles and manages to hold on to the handrail, but old ma Rollingpin simply rap's him across the knuckles with her furl'd umbrella and he is forc'd to relinquish his hold.

The hand clings by it's fingertips to a bus stop in the back of beyond as the bus pulls away into the twilite. After several minutes the hand lets go it's aching fingers and drops soundlessly to the ground.

Staring about it the hand see's it has been cast out into a den peopl'd by ravens, stoats and all manner of vicious cut throats. A world that on the whole can be quite a dangerous place for a sever'd hand to be.

Afterword.

Some readers will ask why our tail couldn't of had a happyer or more realisic ending. Prehaps the sever'd hand could of been reuntit'd with it's pilot owner, Stuker Joe? Or maybe the sever'd hand could have found a companion in the slither of Heinkel pilot's left foot and the pair of them set off together in search of their master's smouldering body.

However, we can assure the esteem'd reader that any such hopes were ill-found'd, as later research suggests that the slither of Heinkel pilot's left foot was not even in possession of it's own toes and was therefore in no condition to go tramping about the Kentish countryside in search of burn'd pilots, imaginary or otherwise.

Some unoriginal thinkers might be sceptical about the accuracy of a story purportedly ritten by the sever'd hand of a Messerschmitt pilot in the 1st place, no matter how great an artist in life it apparently was. To these dissbelivers we can only point to other similer accounts of 'living limbs' that have been reported in the Soviets.

Still others may ask why the sever'd hand, if so talented, didn't find employment painting a beautiful portrait of a sexual society lady, or perhaps draw a detail'd map of it's travels and smuggle them back to Luftwaffe Headquaters in Natzi Germany? Wouldn't this have been more sensible, more patriotic and more credible than scaring innocent people with groundless stories of burning pilots, mad English dogs and deprav'd skool children?

It is our conjector that the answer to this, and the miriade of other questions, lies in the traumatis'd condition of the sever'd hand. Or even as some psychiatrists have suggest'd, in the sever'd hands belligerent and reactionary nature. This would certenly go some ways to explainging why the hand chose to rite and publish'd such a crude and defamitry commentry. In the end the reasons for a sever'd hand setting out on the road to literary fame must, like the motives of all such flambouyant ambition, remain cloud'd in mystery.

Finally, and most importantly, it must be ask't if it is rite that the ritings of a sever'd hand (and the hand of a possible Nazi at that) be allow'd into print at all? What will the Russians think? And for that matter, the Flemish and the French too?

Book the
3rd

A naked oddicy

41

Snow ball

SOMEHOW MY father has been trick'd into taking our mother on a holliday so's to help her recouperate. Must be that her doctors gang'd up on him, cos there's no other way he'd of fallen for it.

Straight off they let her out the sanitorium and our father has to go down there in a taxi and pick her up. Befor he heads off he sumons me 'n' my big brother into the kitchen and reminds us that the house is all shitte'd up and needs to be ship-shape-and-Bristol-fashion on his return, or we'er for the high jump.

He then puts on a strange theatrical voice, raise's one hand and like an old bard intones that 'without the benefit of a warm, dry climet and benificence of rest, our mothers tebeculocess is sure to resurface, only this time in an even more villerent strain that will surly kill her stone dead.' Above all else, he enfersises, 'she must have peace and quite and no more stress from lifes woes.'

My big brother jumps to it and goes outside to start mowing the lawn and i go to the bathroom and try to comb some of the knots out of my hair. So, my mother is alive and well after all and all she needs is some rest and sleep in a warm climate.

With her needs in mind my father has book'd a yaching trip thru the Bay of Biscay, up past Gibralta and across the

Mediteranian to the land of homer. The old man is to be the comidorr, naturally, and me and my big brother will make up the crew. Our mother can do the cooking, cleaning and general chores bellow decks, all that remains is to set sail.

My mother emerges from the back of the taxi, looking tied and drawn. Our father, on the other hand, looks the very picture of health and contentment. Tho his face is a little puffy and the sacks under his eyes rather full, at least his wiskers are freshly brushed and his shoes polished to perfection.

The old man even offers to carry my mothers bags for her and mussels them into the house, as pleas'd as punch with his brave and heroic efforts. The world falls befor me and i step into it, but i am not fool'd into beliving a single thing, ile swallow this holiday when i actually see it.

My mother comes into the kitchen and drops into a chair. Her skin is grayish and her lips bloodless and dry looking. She says that she no longer smokes ciggaretts.

"He's kill'd my mother and now thinks that he's going to kill me. Well, his got another thing coming if he thinks that." Then she has a coughing fit.

As soon as shes regained her breath she gets up and starts fussing about, cleaning the cooker and packing stuff for our holiday. She feeds the cat, which along with Here Boy, hasnt had any grub for the last 3 monthes. They have been running wild and have turn'd quite ferril.

I too have packed some things in my duffel bag. Mainly stuff that will fit and that i don't want nick't. I wonder what will be stollen by Crowsfeet in my absence? As my mother worries, so she has taught me worry. In this respect my mother considers me to be her comrade in suffering. As my father bullies her, so Crowsfeet bullies me. I am company for her if you like.

One thing is for certain, the 1st weeken'd Crowsfeet gets parole he'll be round here ransacking the joint and anything that isn't nail'd down will be flogg'd off down the local flea market.

Ive done my best to hide my most priz'd possessions but all i can do to protect my Victorian Royal West Kents Colour Sargents jacket is try to baracade my bedroom door. But i know that all my best efforts will proove hopless, Crowsfeet will take from me whatever he so wishes and no one will help me or stop him, ever.

It is true that my childhood, by and large, has been ruin'd by my familys neglect and the fists of bullies. Some may view this observation as a dramatical overstatement, but if they had been on the receiving end of sistamatic bullying and mental abuse for there entire childhood then maybe they would shut their fat, over-stuff'd mouths for 5 minits and apologise.

Once everythings packe't in the taxi we climb abord. As usual the old man sits in the front seat next to his 'choffer' and me 'n' my big brother sit in the back waighting for our mother to emerge from the house. The car viberates in little shudders and i start to feel sick. I ask my father if i can get out and stand in the drive way to get some air, which he say's i cant.

"We are leaving now, Gustov, you should of thort of it earlier."

"Can i wind the window down?"

"No you cant. I don't want a draft on my kneck as we drive along."

I explain to him that the reason i want air is because i can't breath and i feel ill. My father tells me to 'shush!' and turns his blond bear'd sharply away from me.

Its the stench of upholstery in this taxi that makes me want to throw up. It really is the worse mixture of sacacrin perfume and old leather. I hold my nose and try to breath thru my mouth and we carry on sitting in silence.

Everything is turn'd towards my mother; everything is waighting just for her: the engin ticking over: me 'n' my big brother: the driver and our angry father.

15 mints tick by and the old mans neck starts colouring up. It really is turning pinker and pinker. Soon his skin will start flaking off his face and blind boils start springing up in his bear'd again.

He lifts his dark glasses from his nose and his bludshot eyes sqwint painfully at the sun. He checks his pocket watch and turns slitely. I see his cheek in the rear-view mirror, his face already puffy and broken into pastry-like layers, has started erupting on account that he has had an allergic reaction to the peroxid in his 'Born Blond' hair shampoo.

The story is this: when my father was a kid he had white/blond hair and all the nabourhood kids call'd him 'snowball'. Now once more my father wish's to be the special blond boy of his childhood and to be held in glory by his mother again. That's why his face is scortch'd: his need to be 'snowball' has resurfac'd and taken over his life.

Finnaly, my mother comes out round the side of the house, tottering backwards towards us on her high heels. It really does seam that shes going to get into the car and we will be able to drive away and leave, when suddenly she turns and doubles back under the porch.

She opens her purse, takes out her key, opens the front door and slames it with all her might. She hangs there with her mouth open, pulling on it with all her mite, her whole body waight dangling from brass door catch: to make sure that it is really, truly shut.

She was so close that you could'v almost reach't out and touch't her and now we have to watch her clinging there again, almost dragging her own arm off.

"Damn that woman!" and our father puts his sunglasses back on his nose, winds down his window and shouts at our mother to 'bludy hurry up and get in the bludy car!' his hands also now are peeling and raw.

"For Christs sake, Juny, it's shut. We are waighting, now get in and let's go! We'll be late for the plane. For God's sake, it's shut!"

My mother turns her ashen face towards him, stairing blindly thru the summer air.

"What about the cooker" she shrills, "did i turn the cooker off?" And befor he can stop her shes got her keys out her purse and is leting her self back in again.

I see her go out thru the kitchen and start checking the hot plates with her bare hand, then she disapears into the bog.

Shes in there a good 5 minits and still we sit here, the smell of upholstery filling my head. Suddenly, the old man flings the car door open and is really about to go into the house and drag her out by her legs when she reappears, her mouth hanging open like a ghost, her lips all freshly paint'd shocking pink. She is now wearing a different dress and shoes.

She pulls the door shut behind her then hangs there again, pulling and pulling at the handle. The old man jumps out of his seat and steps towards her and she cowers away, scurrying around the off side of the car and climbs in beside me 'n' my big brother.

The old man gets back in, slames his door, and we really are leaving.

The taxi creeps down the allyway. I just have time to look frearfully up at my naked bedroom window and say goodbye to my tresur'd belongings: my military cap badges and Royal West Kents Scarlet jacket. This very evening Crowsfeet will be trying to flog my priz'd scarlet jacket to Goldfish on the council estate green.

We pull out onto the road, my mother siting there clutching her handbag.

"Did i lock the back door? . . . what about the cooker? Did you see me turn off the cooker?"

I shrug my shoulder's.

"Mary's looking in every day. Shes coming in to feed the cat and Here Boy."

"Damn the fucking cat!" the old man mutters.

"I beg your pardon?" Our mother has anserw'd him back, possably becouse she is embaric'd at beiing sworn at in front of our fathers driver.

I look at my big brother, but he never really makes eye contact and dosnt even bat an eye lid. The old girl asks the old man again what he said but our father just stairs drunkenly out of the windsreen, his jaw mussels clentching and unclentching.

My mothers face shrinks a little further back onto her scull and our father lowers the sun visor and cheques his whiskers in the vanity mirror. He licks his fingers then brushes his mustash with his finger tips. He feels the spungy mass of his face then snaps the visor back up.

We can't be sure we really heard him swear or if we diddn't just make the whole thing up.

No body talks to each other, it is only me who is optimistic and friendly and i am despis'd for it.

We drive on in silence. Everything is passing, hedgerows, children playing cricket, houses and then the river. I can smell my mothers lipstick mixed in with the uphollstry, which helps me want to puke even more. That smell means my mother is going out on the town.

42

Imaculatly manicured finger nails

WE GET to the airfield just in time. My father's 'choffer' drops us off outside the ticket office. My big brother grabs a luggage trolly and we follow the old man up the runway, passed the customs shed and show our passports. There is a duty free shop and my father takes us inside and buys us alchole.

"What would you like to drink on board ship, Gustov?"

I look at him. Is he talking to me?

"Don't stand there catching flys, what would you like to drink?"

"I don't know" i reply catiously, in case it's a trick. "Nichollas is drinking scotch. I will drink gin, and you . . . what will you drink, Gustov?"

"I can't drink gin," whispers my mother, "it makes me depress'd." My father ignores her. "So whats it to be, Vodka?

Absyinth? Mothers ruin? Come along, chop-chop, we haven't got all day!"

Of course it has to be rum. I am after all an expert on all things naval. "Rum." i say.

"Rum it is." And he lifts a heavey black bottle from the shelf and drops it clanking into the baskit. I watch it rolling there next to it's 4 green brothers.

"Is it alrite to bring that much thru customs?" my mother asks timidly, "i think thers'a limit on what each persons allowed."

"Ile do what i bludy well like, woman! Ive got a bludy Rolls Royce park'd in the gararge at home."

This is perfectly true, tho of course he is not allow'd to drive it on account of him having his license revoked for drunk driving.

My brother chooses whiskey and my mother already has a bottle of guiness in her handbag. Yes, once more, as in the oldern days, we are to pretend to be family.

The plane is an old 3 engin job with black crosses drawn on the wings and propellers, it comes rolling out across the lawn. We walk up the steps at the back and climb into the cabin, just like hair Hitler.

There's a girl sat in front of us who draps her arms over the head rest and strokes the back of her seat. My father points out that unlike me she has perfectly manicur'd fingernails.

"Now that is a pefict set of manicured finger nails. Juny, look at those nails. Your nails are filthy and distgusting, Gustov, where as that girls fingers are pefictly splend'd."

I watch her nails, painted blud red, then she takes her hands back and gets up to go to the toilet. I stair after her, mesmeris'd.

She is perhaps a year older than me. Her nails may well be

'splend'd' but her hair is unkempt and sticking up in little sprouts just like mine, which is something my father has failed to point out. I watch her legs move and i would like to lie with her and feel her naked body press't against mine, tho of course i would not shear this thort with anyone. It is a feeling that i feel mainly in my ears, neck and throat and thighs.

After letting me know that my nails are sub-stander'd my father opens a cheep magazine, occasionaly peers around the cabin and pulls little bits of skin of his nose.

Next we're told to buckle our selfs in, then rite away we start belting down the runway. Everything is banging about like billy-o. The sign over the door gets dissloged and comes crashing down into the gangway. We stay like that for hours, our fillings almost being rattled out of our heads then with a leap we jump into the air.

1stly, it feels like we going to fall back down on our arse, but we keep going, the engins whining like angry flys.

The old man adjusts his reading lite then presses a little buzzer and the stewedess trots out from behind a green curtain. He asks her to bring him a large GNT and some nuts. He says it in a manner'd, drooling voice that he learn'd from somwhere other than a terric'd house in G- , which is where he actually comes from.

"Hello my darling. You couldnt possably fetch Johnathon a large GNT, could you?" He looks around and smiles to himself pleased as punch "GNT - Gin and tonic!"

The stewardess brings 2 small bottles on a silver tray and pours them for him. The old man knocks them back in front of her and instantly orders 2 more. He looks over to my big brother to make sure that he is also getting sozzeled.

"Its time to be a man, Niccollas. Come along, drink up!" I too am offer'd alchole.

"As we are going to sea it is high time for these young gentleman to learn to drink. And i expect you both to have a girl in every port!" The stewerdess smiles thinly at him and we are made to get drunk.

Naturaly i drink navi rum so as to become hard and iron like; to understand the ways of men; to not be a child; to stop being soft; to stop being hurt and trodden on.

I force myself to knock it back and all the while our mother is sat quietly by the little porthole, peering out at the impossible clouds.

All the trip she says nothing, except to console me over the fact that i can't eat any of the food as im 'too fussy'. I hate my mother to make any comments about my eating habits, my complextion, my bed wetting or any of my health problems, espesherly when as it is only done to humiliate me in public.

Over hearing that i won't eat the boil'd vegetables my father mocks me and my big brother immediately chimes in. My mother joins in by telling the stewerdess that as a baby i wouldn't be wean'd and that i will only eat chips and chocolate.

"His teeth are appalling," my father informs her, "worse than his mothers."

"He wouldn't stop crying as a baby" adds my mother.

"And he still wets the bed, don't you, Smell!" my big brother adds triumphantly.

"Oh, and last year he had a terrible abbsess, diddn't you, Gustov? It was on his front teeth. Show the lady which teeth, Gustov." I clamp my jaw and sqeese my eyes tight shut.

"The antibiotics wouldn't werk so we had to take him to the hospital. Well i did. His father was . . . away, wern't you, darling." My mother looks to my father, who holds her with his cold, angry blue stair. My mother drops her gaze and looks down at her hands, pulling at her weding ring and gnawing at her bottom lip.

I dig my nails into the flesh of my palms, just to see if i can draw blud. The stewardess smiles her face tightly and pours my father another large 'GNT'. At last my mother shuts her big, stupid, fat gob and my father continues to get drunk as we carreen thru the sky.

By the time we come into land the old man is completely blotto. He sits there drooling, then suddenly there's this violent shuddering, follow'd by a load roaring noise and we drop from the skys like a stone.

My stomack is left in the clouds. I cling to the arms of my seat and look friegtendly about me but no one else is the least bit concern'd and my father mearly stairs mesmeris'd into his empity glass of gin and tonic, swilling the ice around in his gob.

"Don't be a baby, Gustov, drink up! You should have a whore in every port, shouldn't he Juny!" He grins his face at her. "And you too Nichollas! You are sons of mine and must have a whore in evey port!"

The stewedess comes out from behind her curtain with her little bottles to top him up one last time.

"Exilent my child, exilent! Have you another? And for my son, Nichollas? He will have whisky. And my youngest son . . . Gustov, - he will drink . . . rum! . . . And for you, Juny? . . . a GNT?" My mother stares out of the window ignoring him. My mother only drinks Guinness, if she drinks gin she will cry.

The reason the plane dropp't so violently is that we needed to lose hight to land. We were too high and the pilot lowe'd all the flaps so as to slow our air speed. Apparently, this was not normal pratice, so it apears that i was not a coward after all but rather the only one who was fully awake.

We skim in over the blue waves and i peer out, past my mothers head, of the cabin window. You can actually see the little people paddling about on the wet rocks and leaping into the dark water. Next, there's a furry little brown man waring red bathing trunks, stood there with his hands on his hips, whatching us as we wizz by, for all the world like a bear.

Theres another big bang as we hit the deck and then bounce rite back up into the air again. The pilot trys this several times till he is satisfied with the effect. Finnaly the plain glues itself onto the ground then swurvs from side to side as the pilot slings the anchors on, jamming the propellers into reverse.

"Plains don't as such 'land'," my father shout's over the screaming engines, "but have a 'controll'd crash'. A good friend of mine is a senior airline pilot!" He smiles smugly and nods.

Even before we touch down people are climbing all over each other to get to the exits. The chief steward orders everybody to shut up, sit down and remain belt'd in their seats but no one takes a blind bit of notice.

One man, with a large black mustashe, smashes his way down the gangway using his suitcases as battering rams. He gets rite the way down to the pilots cabin then stands there with one hand on the door and his elbow jutting out, refusing to let anyone pass or dislodge him from the door. There is not an ounce of malice in his actions, only a natural desire to get off the plain as quickly as possible and to hell with everyone else.

Then the plane judders to a halt and everybody jumps up and gets stuck in. Teeth and knees are used as weapons. Anyone who stands to get their stuff from out of the over-head lockers is liable to get a good fisting in the ribs. Basicly, it's a free-for-all.

Once the chimpanzees are off it's everyone elses turn. My mother is the meekest of them all and my father tells her that she is milling about like an old hen.

"For Christs sake Juny, stop fussing! Just pick up your damnd bag and get off!"

Naturally, our familys last out.

1st thing you notice when you put your nose out the cabin is the stinking heat bouncing rite off the concreat into your face.

43

Bludless crickets

WE WALK down the steps then over to their custums shed. There are little gangs of policemen stood about, some of them clasping real machine guns.

My father hands over our passports to a tall man wearing a giant cap which flops rite down over his ears. There's a huge glinting badge stuck rite smack bang in the centre and speggetti hanging off the peek in fastoons. My big brother is given his passport to hold but i am not alow'd to hold mine.

After stamping our passports we have to march across a lot of waste ground, which the police tell us is the quickest way to the port. Actually, they don't so much tell us but point with their machine guns.

Theres piles of rubble 'n' bits of old iron sticking up out of the ground with big wedges of concreat stll hanging on the ends.

My father, still wearing his wool 3 piece suit, starch't collar and Edwardian drape, leads the way across that desert, us dragging our bags behind him.

"I am an English gentleman and as such will dress like one, until we reach the true tropics."

Finally we make it to the sea. We have to wait for a train to pass, then we nip across the railtrack and there we are.

There's some crains and a gasomiter, but no sign of any ships and all the while the sun is pounding down on our heads, trying to fry our brains out.

The old man is just about to make us do a rout march back to the air field when our mother spots a girl standing by a little wayside awning. She has black hair and is wearing a short mini dress, a black piller box hat and is holding up a little sign with arrows drawn on it.

My father goes over and shmooses with her and she tells him that we must wait here for a bus. Her English is good and my mother points out to my big brother that she has 'very sexy legs'.

"In hospital they showed us this film where the black ladys were dancing naked with their breasts out."

Sure enough an old horse-drawn tram comes trundeling along and we climb on boad. There are several family's already taking up the seats so me an my big brother have to stand.

We head off thru the waist ground and after only about an hour or so arrive back at the airport. All the other passangers are waiting there, sipping drinks under a shady canopy. The locals all get off and the girl with the perfictly manicur'd nails sits down with her mother and father and starts reading a book. I try to will her to notice me but she loves her book more than me.

Becouse im the youngest i have to stand all the way and let everybody else sit down. There is no air on that bus and no water to drink either. We go crawling thru the back streets of the city, only pausing every 6 or 7 yards to roast in the sun. Apart from that it's perfictly comfy standing there without anywhere to rest your legs.

After 4 traffic jams and about 30 stops we finnaly turn off the main road and start draging ourselves up this big winding hill. Just as our horse is fit to drop the conductor comes round, checks our tickets and chucks us off.

We'er stranded half way up a mountain side, on some kind of road side dump and no one speaks any English. There's some tables and chairs slung under the trees, the grown ups sit down there and order some drinks from an open air bar.

I beg a glass of lemonade and sit down to drink it. Rite away i can feel the enamel on my teeth burning off. All around is the noise of singing crickets blasting away. My mother and big brother both try a glass of the local gut rot and the old man downs a large glass of whisky and a watery looking beer.

"Why are there so many crickets?" i ask.

"They are not crickets they are cicardas." My father corrects me.

"What's a cicarder?" My father looks at me, then turns away to spy at something in the far distance. "A large cricket" he says silently, his beard wet with froth.

Imaculatly Manicured Nails is sitting over under a giant cypress tree with her mother and father, still reading her book. Ocassionaly she sips at a miniture cup of black coffee. She then puts down her book and goes to werk with a pice of cloth, buffing up her perfict nails.

Theres a little comotion when her father jumps up and points excitadly at a pile of old rocks glinting away in the sun on the opposite hill side, some of the other holliday makers get up and take photographs. I wonder off into the bushes to see some of these famouse crickets of theirs.

You can hear them kicking up a racket in every direction but once you go into the bushes you can't find a single one. Judging by the noise you'd imagin there's got to be millions of them. Everytime you think that you finally got one corner'd it stops singing, and disappears into thin air. You hunt around, rite where the noise was coming from, then all of a sudden it starts up singing again 15 feet away in a completely new bush.

I follow several of the fellows rite round the wood, stumbling about in the braken, but there's not even a grasshopper to shake hands with.

By and by i have the feeling that im lost and have to stop to take my bearings. I think i can hear voices coming from over the way so i start retracing my steps. Yes, it's definatly my father advising someone about the proticol of wearing of 'socks and sandles in foregn climes'. Im just going to double back into the jungle when i find a little pile of empty 'cricket husks' pil'd up beneath a giant spyders web. There nothing left inside them at all. It would seam that there are some very large spyders round abouts who have suck'd the blud out of these once fat and juicy crickets. I brush the dirt from my knees, get up and run back out onto the terrice.

That nite we sleep in a concreat bunker in the hart of the city, not unlike a carpark. In the morning we'er woken by several loud explosions. I open the window and check outside. There's a police car below and a lot of smoke coming out of a shop front. An ambulence also rolls up and they chuck sand on some big pools of black stuff and put some packages in the back, but it's hard to tell exactly what's happening.

The fire alarm goes off in the hotel and me 'n' my big brother leave our room and cross the hall to wake our parents up. Our mother is just getting ready and will be down in a moment. There's no sign of the old man and she doesn't know where he is. Apparently he went out for a drink and hasn't been back all nite.

We go down to the the lobby, the fire alarm still banging away. We have to stand out in the street for a while, then we'er allowed back in.

Theres a small café attached to the bar and the old man's sat at the table wearing dark glasses and eating a hard boiled egg. He tell's us that we have to eat breakfast imedetly.

"We have no time for dilly-dallying. The ferry out to the islands leaves at 10. We get off at H-, where we will rondevious with the flotilla at 4.30, sharp! Eat up now or go without."

I, for one, decide to go without. My mother and big brother stuff their faces and my father keeps taking out his pocket watch, studying it and telling them to 'chop-chop'.

"What sort of boat is it?" i ask.

"1stly, young man, it isnt a boat it is a ship, or more precisely, a yacht." I look to him and then to my big brother, who kicks me violently under the table and i almost fall off my chair.

44

In the land of homer and the greeks

THERE'S NOT a lot to say about the sea's of Jason and the Argonaughts, except that on the ferry i saw a manter ray and a sea turtle smil'd up at me; and when you look directly down into it, the water is blue black, disapearing into nite. Only when you look at it from an obleek angle do the wavelites glint into your eyes like knives.

Also the land is very rocky and you can smell pine needles even when you're far out to sea, then as soon as you come within a mile of land you here those cicarders kicking up their din again.

That's what it's like: suddenly the land closes in around us and we pass lots of American war ships all ready to open fire, then the crickets start clacking away.

Next, we see a Great War Battleship moor'd at anchor. I point this out to my father, who nods sternly. It is his job to see things, not mine.

When we get there i can see why the old man has been keeping schtum about this boat of his: the 'yacht' has been borrow'd from some Royal Naval Leutenant he claims to know.

This 'yacht' is not strickly brand new, but neither can it be describ'd as totally derilict either. No one could argue that it doesn't float, but it could do with a little lick of paint here and there, and some tingles on the hull might help keep the water out. Other than that the old bath tub is really quite sea worthy. Yes, all in all we were ready for my father's magnicificent adventure.

Basicly, we jump on the ferry just as it's about to leave the docks. We catch it by the skin of our teeth. All our luggage is chucked on boad and i watch the brave salors stowing the gang plank and putting up the guard rail.

I don't feel ill once, owing to the sea being extreamly flat. There is a bad stench of deseil oil spewing out of the air vents and a lot of men with fury arms are still chucking roaps about but i get up wind of the fumes and then im fine.

I climb some steps to the upper deck to get a better view of the mainland and i see Manicur'd Fingernails again. She's sitting there with her sour looking mother and apologetic looking father, who is nursing his wrists.

Manicur'd-nails hasn't got cloaths on anymore and is wearing a scarlet bakini with most of her body out on display. Her thighs are already brown and bursting with vigour.

I quickly duck back down the ladder and blush. Later, i sneek round the long way then stop behind a bulkhead and peer at them without being seen.

There is little or no food to talk of on that ferry. I refuse to eat the small pastries they offer up as it is impossible to distingash the nuts on them from the flys. Apart from siting the turtle and the manter ray there's nothing much else to report. It takes about 2 hours to cross, then we go in thru the harbour entrance backwards and dock. We still have to hang around for ages as the salors net up our baggage and swing it out over the sea on a little derrick. Finnaly they dump our baggage on the quay side.

What you notice in this port is the stink of singe'd rubber floating over the harbour. That and the noies of small scooters, bibbing and reving their tiny wasp-like motors. Naturaly, the sun glints off the water straight into your eyes and the hot ground blasts at you like an open oven.

Apparently in the winter time the temperature is quite bearable.

The old man paces back and forth examining his onion.

"Where the hell is anyone when you need them. Can't these niggars do anything rite?"

I go over and look in a wooden crate at some dead chickens. There's no water in there and one of them looks like it might just still be alive.

At last a great brute of a man starts stackin our stuff onto a niffty little wooden wagon. Our father stands there pretending to direct him but the fellow just stakes the suitcases anyway he pleases.

The old man motions to the porter in sign langawige, acting out how he must tow the trollie along the quay to the far jetty. The great brute dose just as my father directs and the old man strikes out in front, very proud to be leading a savage along the water front like a tame kitten.

Its quite clear that he is roasting in his Edwardian wool suit and he puts his brollie up, trying to gain a little shade. This, he explains to us, is how a true English gentleman goes on holliday.

"I will not be wearing shorts, sandles, or any other inapropreate casual wear until the holiday formally begins." He announces, pulling out his time piece "And it begins tommorow morning at . . . sun rise! That is, once we are on bored ship, fully ensconc'd, ship shape and Bristol fashion! And not a single second before!"

He nods to himself, entirly satisfi'd that this is a completely rashional decission.

The old man turns and waves his brollie at the muscley porter, who is actually limping slightly, but still pushing the overladen trollie in front of him like he was Samson.

I don't need the porter because i have all my belongings on my shoulder, tuck'd in my old duffel bag. On the top is my pith helmet, which i now take out and wear.

We keep moving imperceptibley along the harbour wall, like a little caravan of misery. Along the way, every 50 yards or so, there are these little brazziers with octopuss legs sizzling on them. So that is where the stench of burning rubber comes from.

My big brother borrows some Drackma off the old man and comes back with a packet full of char'd legs. You can still see the suckers on them. I bite into one but my teeth bounce rite off and i spit it into the drink. Before it even sinks it's attack'd by a whole army of small fry, their little mouths nipping away, making the leg dart about like as if it was somehow still alive and kicking.

I watch them swarm out of the darkness benieth the oil scum and start noshing. Above are the boats, all of which are gaily colour'd, many of them with guady eyes paint'd on the bows.

I have to run and catch the others up. After one last heroic effort we come to a wooden jetty which jutts out into the natural harbour, and rite out at it's end lies an old moldering hulk.

Theres a few strings dangling in the drink and a moth-eaten

bit of canvas insolently plapping from the mast. This, apparently, is our ship.

Whilst we are still soaking in the full affect, a hatch opens amidships and a man jumps out on deck. His hands and face are black with oil, in contrast to his hair, which is golden blond; and he wears very short denim shorts with great big golden brown calfs and thighs showing. In fact his whole body is muscular and tann'd.

Our father smiles his capp't white teeth and gapes at him in open admeration. Regaining his composure he hails out across the water.

"Jonathon Claudius, how do you do, sir? I am the skipper of this vessel and this is my sorry crew." And he motions at us stood behind him like scarecrows.

"A lovely day for sailing, is it not!" And he laughs his wretch'd false laugh that he lerned somewhere.

The man with the golden legs is called Dave, and really my fathers name is Reginald, not Jonathon. It turns out the engin is totally bust'd. Old golden legs recons that he might be able to fix it, he's just off into town to see if a part has been shipp'd from the mainland, but quite frankly, he is dubious.

"Between you me and the post, this yachet isnt sea worthy. If i wasn't being paid good money to fix it i'd send her straight to the breakers yard. As it is, the 1st storm will send her to the bottom!"

Me 'n' my big brother haul on the mooring roaps and our gay little ship drifts across the water and clunks into the jetty. We climb on board. It's true, the covers are off the engin and you can see past the rustin mottor rite down into the bilges and the sea bed beyond.

"Ile be back if the new carbaretta has been shipp'd, otherwise it will be next week." And with that Dave vaults onto the quay side and saunters off, swaying his hips. The old mans head and eyes follow Dave like his a woman.

"Imagin seeing that chap walking up Regents Street, Juny! With a tan like that! My word, he'd certanly turn a few heads." My father is in love with blond, tann'd men. I look down at my thin white legs.

"Your legs are like bludy maggots!" he say's, "come along now, chop–chop, lets get this place ship-shape. Come along look lively!" and he turns and ducks below decks. "Bring those bags aboard you boys. Nichollas, Gustov, jump to it!"

I pass a bag to our mother in the sturn and she drags it bellow decks, weezing on acount of her lungs. In the end the old man gets his 'nigger' to chuck the rest of the gear on bord then pays him off with a handful of shrapnel.

In short - we all clamber aboard that woodworm'd hulk and sit below decks in it's hot, airless cabin.

Evereybody is compleatly bushed, except the old man who's in a kind of estercy, arranging all the roaps and anchors and stuff.

Our mother creeps around behind him, putting bits of luggage into pidgion holes and cleaning out the cupboads. There's no air down here and i go back out on deck so's i can at least breath.

The whole place is swarming with people, everbody shouting and waving; kids buzzing up and down on their little scooters, bibbing their horns and almost knocking any old souls into the oggin.

A string of donkys come past carrying barrels of booz on their backs. Already it's dark out. You see the sun go down fast as a stone and that's it - nite time. The taverners lite up the prom with fairy lites and thats all reflected in black water. Meanwhile, all the little octopuss braziers are blazing away like torches in the nite, the stench of chard flesh rising into the distence.

I lean over the sturn and dangle my arm over the side. The water is full of phospherious and you can here fish jumping about too, out there in the darkness. I here my parents arguing bellow then there's a thump and i look up just in time to see my big brother jump onto the jetty and slope off into the crowds.

Rite away i grab my hat and run after him. He trys to shake me off but i catch him easy-peasy.

He snarles at me to get lost but i dont, i stay rite on his tail and follow him up some back streets - where theres no lites at all - and then your on the open road and walking thru nothing but dust. The crickets are still going 19 to the dozon and the sent of pine trees is like an overcoat.

There's a boozer up amongst those trees. My big brother sits down at an empty table and waights to be served. I sit down at the table opposite and watch him.

After a while a man in a white coat approaches. He brings a bottle of clear liqued and pours my big brother a glass. My big brother gives him a small pile of shrapnel and gulps it down in one go and almost chockes. The waiter pours him another then comes over and pours me a glass of the same.

We stay there drinking all nite. The stuff costs next to nothing but tastes very foul. The trick to make it more barable is to mix it with water, it clouds up and then your ment to just sip at it.

I pull a sour face. Really, you can't sip at that stuff, you just have to knock it back in big draughts or you chuck up.

The main trouble is that every time you manage to get one glass down, the waiter automaticly tops it up again. No matter how much you shake your head or try to cover your glass with your hand, he still just keeps pouring. To tell the truth, we get pretty well slaughter'd up there amongst the pines.

In a lot of ways it's highly amusing that me 'n' my big brother were never properly look't after as kids and had to make every rong turn in life on our own; reliving every one of our fathers ham-fist'd mistakes. The trouble is, i find it very difficult to walk.

When we finally get back to the ship it's gone 2. The Greeks are still getting saused up and racing up and down the promenade on their mopeds but it is time for us to die.

The hulk is in compleate darkness. We meander up the jetty; i can just read her name, riiten in peeling green paint, rite across the sturn: THE STYX.

Our parents have quit arguing and you can here the old man sawing wood bellow deck. There's only the one cabin so me 'n' my big brother have to sleep outside in the stern sheets.

Once the locals shut up and go to bed, and all the lites are switch't off, the sky goes compleatly black. I lie there staring up into that never ending nite.

Ive seen stars before but not like these fellows: great clusters of them all over the shop - the hot, brite stars of infinity.

Its true: i look untill everything goes topsy-turvy and it seams that im not staring into the hevens but instead pinned to the earth over a bottomless pit of stars. Suddenly i jump up with vertigo and chuck up over the side: hot jests of anasseed flavor'd sick.

I lie back down on the hard bench, holding my poor stomach and my big brother starts talking to me about a donky.

"What donky?" i ask him.

"The donky!" he crys "the little donky is talking!" He pouts, almost on the edge of tears.

I sit up and look across to where his head should be: a shadow in darkness, just benieth the bulkhead.

"What donky, Nick?"

He grunts and i here him roll over. I listen to him sobbing. He really is crying in his sleep about a talking donky. I look at the sky a bit more. The stars definetly dissapear into infinity.

45

Benjamin Horatio Claudius

THE SUN here is very sharp in that meridian and it wakes me about 5 o'clock, luckerly i have my pith helmet with me. I put it on and walk around the deck, peering from benieth the brim.

The water has rainbows on it and the sunlite flashes all sorts of colours. If someone wasn't wearing the correct type of head wear it would be quite easy for them to develop heat strok, trip over the little wires that act as a gaurd rail, fall in the oggin and never be seen again.

I walk back to the stern of the boat and jump ashore. All ready i feel a little sea sick from the gental rocking of the ship moor'd here in harbour.

I go for a march along the prom, looking to see what the local fishing boats have brought in. All the fishermen have bristling mustashes and arms like rusty old cabels.

Some of the men smile at me as i walk down to the end of the large groin, others ignore me, or turn their shoulders.

I shade my eyes and look out at the old battle ship. I try to memorise it's shape and the number of guns so's that i can tell my grandfather. It's quite possible that he had to fire shells at this very cruzer in the Battle of the Jutland Sea.

Sitting above the great smoke stacks, high on the opersite hillside, is an ancient twist'd fort, strung out between the red coulourd rocks. The ramparts and towers jut up into the blue sky like rows of rotting teeth.

It's impossible to know what such a fort was built to defend, except maybe some fish, the pine trees and the rattling cicardas.

I walk back down the groin, along to the end of the harbour and follow a little dirt track which cuts acroos some dirty sand dunes. After about a hundred yards the path opens up onto a sandy shoreline. Actually, they are building wooden ships along there, so really this little strip of beach counts as a shipyard.

Underneath the giant ribs are some of the most raggedy old cats, which you can't coax out for nothing.

I hardly mosey about down there for no more than 5 minits, co's i get bored easily and can scarcely look at the world if im on my own. I just make one circuit till i figure it must be time for the old man to set sail.

On the way back to the ship i run into old Golden legs. He's wash't his oily old face and is walking towards me in his leopard skin bathing trunks.

I slow down so as to talk to him about manly things, such as broken engines and woman and the like, but even tho he can see that i am just a boy and wish only to be friendly and jocular, he chooses to shout that he personally doesnn't find a broken engine in the least bit funny and strydes past me with his gleaming brown body. I stand and whatch as he quickens his pace then leaps to the air like a golden God before smashing down into the blue waters.

When I get back to our hulk the rest of them are all up and about. My mother has been ashore and brought some Greek yougurt, which she gobbles up whilst my father looks on in disgust.

"I don't eat woggy food" pronouses my father.

I personally would not call black people 'wogs', or Greek people 'dagoes' for that mater but my father is not me. I sit down by the tiller and my mother hands me a cup of tea.

"It's not got real milk in it!" She says apologeticly.

"Do you want rum in there?" asks my father.

I look to him and can see that our gay captain has already 'splis'd the main brace'. Before I can shake my head, he un-corks my bottle and glugs a large trebble in there.

"You want to be a salor, don't you? You're the expert on the Napolonic Navy? - Well lap it up, dear boy, like your grandfather befor you! And remember what he said: Whatch out for the wog's! They'll swim out to your ship at nite, climb in thru the port holes, slit your throat and rob you blind!" he tilts his head critickly at my pith helmet. "You shouldn't be wearing that, it isn't nautical" he says levelly.

Once the old girls lick'd up her yogurt, she goes back bellow and starts rustling up egg 'n' bacon on the calor gas, for my father and big brother.

All the ingredients have been brought in from England in suitcases. Once shes cook'd it up she has to call them to the table. The sun is already blasting down and my father is stripp'd to his g-string.

My big brother too, is in his bathing trunks, roasting his flesh and gently getting piss'd.

My mother calls out in her high pitched voice, which she usually uses for the cat, and they both saunter bellow.

I am not particularly concern'd about my grandfathers tails of theifs swimming out to rob me, because by now all of my possetiens have already been ransack'd by Crowsfeet back in England. Apart from my pith helmet, which i am wearing, i own nothing.

My mother calls me as well but i don't want to eat anything and go sit on the front deck beneath the awning to rite my book.

I am werking on a story about a sea captin during the Napolonic Wars. His name is Benjamin Horatio Claudius. Claudius is a personal friend of Nelson and has been sent on a special mission to intersept a renigade Turkish galley intent on breaking thru the Aegan sea to join the French and Spanish combined fleets at Cadiz. My father calls me regularly, every 1/2 hour, ordering me to have another glass of rum.

I finish a whole page before we have to set sale. The gist of it is this – Nelsons eye, which he lost at Corcica, has since washed up from the other side of the Mediteranian and is guiding Claudius in his battle plans; advising him of tactics and making predictions about the weather.

The old man shouts at me to 'bludy chop-chop' so i have to put down my pencil and jump to it.

There are a dozen other yatchts in our flotilla, all with werking engines, who smartly motor out of the harbour then set sale for the next island on the itinery. We alone have to zig-zag out of port under sale with our drunken father as our gay captain. Me and my big brother are put to werk pulling on roaps that are call'd 'sheets' and running sales up and down the masts, even tho i feel like pukeing up.

Meanwhile our mother is below decks in the heaving gally, supposedly recuperating, in between cooking up full English breakfasts and doing the washing up.

Up on deck the old man's body is being kiss'd by the miterain sun, his chest, shoulders and nose already ravag'd. Heavy, blister'd sacks of skin hang from his forehead, matching the bags under his eyes. I look to him stood there at the tiller, chewing on his bear'd and studying the bergee at the top of the mast.

The 2nd leg of our oddessy is pretty uneventfull as the wind is with us all the way. We get to the port in the late afternoon, moor up and then have to listen to our father telling us what an expert helmsman he is.

Before we go ashore we al have to have another drink, then im sent below to help my mother pump the bilges out. The truth is that even on a clam day The Styx leaks like a sieve in a gale.

The following day is much the same story: it takes all morning to get out of harbour, most of the afternoon to catch the rest of the flotiller up and when we come to getting into port in the evening we still have to hobble into port entirely under sail. We dodge a couple of collisions, just miss the harbor wall and drop anchor.

The old man tells us to tidy away the sheets and stoe the spiniker. "I want those ropes coiled perfectly you understand?" And our gay captain goes bellow to dress for supper. 20 minits later, he emerges wearing his 4 button, Edwardian blazer, starch'd coller, stud and tie.

"An Englishman must still dress like a gentleman even when on holliday, but espesherly amongst the wogs!" And he leaps ashore.

"Im taking Ma-ma out for supper" he calls back, "you boys stay here and swab the decks. We'll be back befor 2." He consults his onion "Gustov, it's your whatch!"

Our mother trys to climb back on boared to put on her lipstick but he has hold of her wrist.

"But i havent anything to wear" she pleads.

"Nonsence, woman. Wear what you've got on." She almost struggles free but he grabs her round the waist and lifts her onto the gangway.

"But i need to check that i turn'd the stove off."

"Its damnd well off. You already check'd it, you silly cow! Now come along!" And he leads her away.

We whatch them go, him in his white linen trouser and Royal Yacht Club tie and her in some old rags that she brought knock't down in some sale on C - High Street.

The sun is espersherly low and fat this evening, it's orange rays turning the clouds quite pink. There are a few black clouds appearing and a strange chill in the air.

That is the very 1st time i have ever herd our mother call'd 'Mama' before.

46

A punch in the mothers eye

ME 'N' my big brother sit out in the setting sun not talking. There is a silence that comes over the world and even the cicadas shut up for 5 minits. Suddenly my big brother stands and announces that he is going ashore to get pissed. He ducks bellow, rumages thru the old mans bags then he comes back on deck with a small roll of Greek notes in his fist. He looks down at me and sneers.

"Are you coming or not, Smell?"

I follow him ashore. We wait for a fraight train to pass then cross the tracks and into the shade of the buildings oppersite. There's a dive next to the police station with palm trees growing all round it. We find a table, the waiter comes over and my big brother orders ozo and a bottle of domestica.

All in all there is not a lot you can say about my big brother, apart from if you speak to him about anything he just 'shushes' you. Or on the other hand, if you reply to one of his observations, either in the positive, or to disagree with him he becomes aggressive, or plainly ignores you. On the whole he is fearfull, arrogant, miserly and considers himself to be altogether marvolious.

Next, Manicur'd Fingernails passes by with her mother, who is quite small and stoop't. Manicur'd Fingernails is still wearing her scarlet bekini top and some smallish shorts. I am ashamed to say that my big brother smiles at her and whats wurse, Manicur'd Fingernails aknollages his rude stair. I clamp my jaws together and stair into my glass.

Other than sit here lost and alone, watching this world go by, there is nothing to do. Except of course get drunk on this horrible liquor. Tommorow we will set to sea again and i will be sea sick again.

The waiter fills our glasses and i take out my notebook and start to rite some more of my novel.

There is a very big naval battle, which took place earlier in

Claudius's carreer, in which he captured a Spanish 3 deck ship of the line with nothing more than his tiny, under-gunn'd Sloop, HMS Hucking.

I put in all the details and by the end of the engagement there's blud pouring from the gunnels and the deck is plow'd over like a field. But still Claudius stands there completely at ease amongst the blud and carnage, cassualy taking a sun sighting on his sextent.

Even when the finnal shot of the Spanish Man 'o' war decapitates his 1st officer rite in front of him, Claudius meerly takes a pinch of snuff and orders his cabin boy to fetch him a glass of medira.

My big brother is highly critcal of my sitting here ritting in front of him and demands that i stop at once. One thing he can't abide is my face, another is my company, and a 3rd is me ritting. Espesherly, he points out, 'as i can't even spell.'

He snatches the pages from my hand, stairs at them for a brief moment, before flinging them to the ground. I stoop to pick them up and am just about to give his chair a shove when i spy the old man coming along the prom.

I have to look twise. It's not so much that he's drunk, rather that he's drench't from head to foot, leaving a trail of sea water behind him. A pack of stray dogs follow in his wake, one of the braver hounds suddenly dashing forward and nipping at the old mans shirt tails.

My big brother stands, bent in the middle and calls out, but our father completely ignores us. Looking neither to his left nor rite he just keeps on marching, his wet footprints being sniff't at by his new friends.

I wonder weather to put away my pencil and note book and go

after him but then the old girl comes trotting round the corner. She see's us, comes over and wearily plunks herself down at our table.

"My God that was awful" she says in a broken whisper, her hands shaking as she lites up a cigeret. She is wearing a nifty new pair of sunglasses. Undernieth you can see the edges of a puffy, purple eye. Also, you can see that shes been crying.

"He wouldn't go into any of the restrants, none of them were good enough. Well you no what he's like about 'woggy' food. But then we met this really nice French couple at a bar. They spoke perfict English and they took us to this restrant that this mans brother own'd.

"Well, we found the restrant and the chef agreed to cook your father a stake, just the way he likes it - very well done. You know - burnt to a crisp. But your father was already drunk and showing off. He kept trying to make the man have a drink with him, but he was an alcoholic and his wife said that he'd been on the wagon for 6 years and wasn't allowed to touch a drop, but your father just kept on and on and his wife got angrier and angrier.

"In the end the man snapp't and they down'd a whole bottle of Pair William between them. So when they brought the food, your father wouldn't even touch it. He said it was 'wog food, fit only for the wogs!' Then the wife stormed out and the mans brother dragg'd her husband out of there and your father shouted at him 'if you want to have a decent cup of tea in this world, you have to go to the Savoy, not a dago's dust-bin!' It was awful.

"This couple on the oppersite table kept looking over and the lady had really large bossoms and your father start'd shouting about his Rolls Royce and his yachet and about how much money he earns a year. Then he orderd a plate of oysters 'for the lady with the large bossoms' but she didn't even like oysters.

"That stake was a compleat waist of money! I ate mine, it was lovely, and i would have had his as well but then we had to leave because your father had been insulting the mans wife. He said that she look'd like the Michalin man, then he buys the husband a cigar. Oh it was awful. I couldn't get him out of there.

"In the end they threw us out. They said they were closing and made us leave. I didnt know which way to look.

"Of course, your father thinks that he's clever and that everybody else is 'bludy thick!' but it's him who's ignorant. He offer'd to buy everybody Champagne but of course they didnt sell 'real Champagne'. He thinks that every one was impressed but they wern't, they were disgusted.

"Anyway, we were walking back along the front when your father said suddenly he was going for a swim and he jump't off the harbour, still wearing his hat, suit, socks, shoes and everything, straight into the water! His cloths will be completely ruin'd. That's another waste of money.

"There were lots of people stood on the quay side watching and then he wouldn't come out."

She dabs at her black eye, "and then he punch't me, and that's all."

I feel my hart racing. I look to my big brother, who just sits there and says nothing, examining his drink.

"Why did he punch you?" i ask.

"Becouse i thort i'd lost my purse, but i haddn't. I found it. I went back and seache't everywhere but it was in my bag all the time. Anyway, it doesn't matter, he brought me these glasses. They were quite expencive."

I try to see thru them into my mothers eyes but it really is to dark. Then my big brother throws his chair back and storms off into the nite.

I whatch him go.

I would love to walk away too, but i don't have anywhere to go.

Personaly, if i see my father punch my mother, i will kill him.

47

A mad man at the helm

NEXT MORNING, at 8.30 on the dot, the floatilla motors out of the port in perfict line asturn. All except us, as our engin is still bust'd. Besides, the old man would rather make us hobble about under sale even if we were about to be driven onto the rocks and destroyd.

The old man stands there at the tiller shouting into the gale and me and my big brother have to scurry about like a couple of rats just to keep up with his list of orders.

At no cost will he accept a line from another yacht. Even when we lerch leeward into the path of an American war ship he just smiles and tell's us to hang over the side and fend off with our bare feet.

Meanwhile the old girl stays bellow recouperating from her TB. She still does all the cooking and the tiedying up, just like in the olden day's back home, only now it's bellow decks in a keeling boat with the tempriture soring in the 100's.

After nearly staving in the hull and just grazing an ancoured lite-ship we eventually make it out into open water, but by that time the floatila has clear'd off. We can just see their little red sales disapearing over the horizon, but it's hopless.

The old man piles on the canvas and we beat out to sea. Once we clear the headland a great swale starts rolling in and i begin to feel sea sick. I crawl into the bottom of the boat and lie there, huddl'd in some blankets, my head wrapp'd in a towel, unable to move.

My illness amusses my father greatly. I grimice up at him and he makes sarcastic comments about my 'infusastic look.' In truth, i am hung over, hate this holliday, the sea, my fathers face and the whole idiotic race of the Greeks.

"Any one for GNT?" he trills. "Juny, pop bellow and mix us all drinks and i fancy a little snacky-wacky. How about eggy-bak'e? What about you Gustov, would you like a nice sausage? Or how about a greecy pork yougurt?"

The old man opens his mouth and looks around the horizon, thoughrly amus'd with himself. My big brother obliges him by laughing in his false, hollow way.

"Nichollas, i want every scrap of canvas up that yard-arm, sharp! Bung up everything she can carry. If we don't have an engin we must out sale these other yachets by superiouor seamanship! You see those 2 islets? We'll cut in between them and head the flotilla off at the straights. That will save us a good hour. If we play our cards rite we can beat them to port and be sitting there drinking cocktails when they come in - My god, i'd like to see their faces - then they'll know who they'er up against! Aim as close in to these foaming rocks as possable."

The old man stands there with the tiller jam'd between his legs like a giant wooden cock, a large gin in his hand, his bear'd damp and bristling.

I roll over on the hard narrow bench. This is not a restfull family holliday to help my mother recouperate, this is just an excuse for the old man to kill us all.

"Take that sheet in, Nichollas! Chop-chop, they've tack'd and we haven't. By jove - now we've got them!"

There is a sudden, tremendus blast of wind and we heal hard over. The water rushes up at us and a scream comes from below as the old girl gets chuck'd up against the cooker. Everything in the gallie goes crashing to the decks. Pot's, pans, boiling water – the lot.

I lie amongst the debris, clinging onto the halliards, the waves lashing against my face. We've got so much canvas up that the Styx is held flat against the waves. The old girl cries out from below as another roller washes in and fills the gally.

My brother begs our father to let the foresale fly but the old man is oblivious.

"Come along, Nichollas, your not frighten'd of a little breeze are you!"

Finnaly the sales spill the wind of their own accord and we slowly begin to rite again, drifting off amongst the jagg'd rocks, then another great blast pins us hard over.

When it seams that we must for sure sink for good, only then does our father grin in ecstisy.

48

Fair weather saliors

LATE AFTERNOON, the Styx crawls into harbour, her sales flapping like old dishrags. We are still bailing as we pass the rest of the floatilla already smartly at anchor.

Their captains and crews hail us hartily, boading their dingys, heading ashore for drinks and friendly family get togethers.

We alone are sepret because we are special. The most important thing, as far as my father is concern'd, is that we have 'panash' that we 'have style' and that we win.

Even as we limp into port, the old man is planning the downfall of the other ships and new glorys which awaite him.

He points to verrious vessels and tell's us about the short fallings and the inadiquetess of the other, lesser captains. His main anger tho is reserv'd for the wind, which is tottaly dissobedioant.

After the wind, it's me and my mother who get it. Me, for my 'lack of enfusasim' and my mother for 'fussing about like an old hen'. My big brother on the other hand, who is tanning rather well, is consider'd an excellent crewman.

My father stairs darkly at the neat little row of ships moored benith the towering cliffs.

"We, at least are true seamen – this lot are nothing but a bunch of fair weather sailors - they were motor-crusing and that gentlmen, dosen't count!"

Yes, whilest all the other crews are relaxing themselves we alone have to dash about – rowing out the dingy and chucking the anchor in and out of the drink. And no matter what, refusing all help from any 'motor assist'd vessels'.

"Nichollas, Gustov, look lively, jump to it, we'er going in under sale! Shorten that sheet! Ile show them what real seamanship is all about - the British don't have the blud of Nelson in them for nothing! Mind your damn'd head woman!" and the spar swings wildly thru the air - just missing the old girls neb by a fraction - before slamming over to larboard.

The deck slants away, every plank of the Styx juddering in protest. Finnaly we go about, face up wind and my father shouts at me to let go the anchor. The chain rushes thru my fingers, nearly taking me with it, then there's a mighty splash and the rope breaks.

Its about midnite before we can rustle up a spair and finnaly drop sale and relax.

We go belting about like that, island hopping in the footsteps of the Argonuts, just so's that the old man can order us about, impress the other captains with what a dashing figure he cuts and hopfully kill of our mother in the prossess.

Day time's he sling's every ounce of canvas he can up the bean pole, nite times, we struggle into port and he gets totally sozzel'd in one of the tavernas, bullies our mother and harangs some innocent tourist for wearing socks and sandles, having thick, trunk-like legs, or perhaps having a wife that looks like a wing'd harpy.

49

A lee shore

AT THE next island, S-, it's blowing a force 6 so we can't get in at the main harbour and we all have to drop down the coast to an open ancorage halfways round the island. There's a lot of fannying to and frow and by the time the old man gets our bathtub to sail in a straight line im ready to puke again.

Naturally everybody else motors down there and the achorage is full by the time we get there. We tack back and forth looking for a gap till the old man actually manages to find the wurst possible spot to pitch tent: rite on the windward side of the whole flotilla, where we'er expos'd to the full brunt of the storm.

What with no engin we go belting in there under full sail and plough up half a dozen bow lines. Me 'n' my big brother have to try and hang over the side and untangle that mess and all the while the waves are bowling in from the Crimea, doing their upmost to capsize us.

The old man grins like Ahab, the spray splashing his burnt face. He flashes his bludshot eyes and barks contradictory orders.

Eventually we pick ourselves from the cat's cradle get in the row boat, row the anchor out and sling it over the side. After that we'er allowed to go ashore.

As im fit to puke i jump out into the bracking waves, fall to my knees and crawl up the little beach, my plimsouls full of shingle. I feel my stomach heave and nibble at a bit of seaweed that i find lying there, trusting in it's madicenel qualitys.

The truth is, when you go to stand you feel just as sick as you did sitting out there on the oggin, bobbing up and down for all eternity. It really is as if the streets are bucking and rearing under my feet, trying to throw me off their backs into some horrible ditch. I squat down in the dust and hold onto an old rusty cannon theyve got sunk into the concreat and concentrate on my breathing, swallowing my excess spit.

It turns out that we'er strand'd on that out-crop for the whole of the next week, waiting for that gale to blow out.

The main thing is to escape from the hell of the Styx: the heat and stench of the bilges in there is something quite special; and being trapp'd at anchor on that lee shore isn't a joke either. The only means of escape is our little row boat. If you get left on board any time, that's it - till someone comes along and resques you.

And even if you stay ashore all day, come nite time you know that at some time you have to return to that stinking coffin and try to sleep without chucking up. So this then is the land of the Gods.

50

Observations in relation to the riting of our novel

As I have already plan'd, for my novel im going to have the hero, Benjamin Horatio Claudius, sent to the Mediterainian where he acts as a 'special agent' for Lord Nelson's missing eye. The gist of it is this: Captain Claudius has to blast away at some Otterman renigaids who've got too big for their boots and are intent on joining forces with Napolian's combin'd French and Spanish fleets. Now unless Claudius can settle the Ottermans hash before their gallies arrive off Toulon then the chances of Nelson stopping the break out of the French and Spanish will be scupper'd and the invasion of England become a certainty, thus altering Europian history for ever.

I don't know why ive decid'd to rite a novel, it's certainly not because i enjoy it and i have no ambition to become a ritter. In fact, just one look at a blank page is enough to give me the collywobbles.

Besides, who ever hear'd of a boy from the 'B' stream of The W- Secondery Skool for Boys setting out on the road to lituary fame? It wouldn't be allow'd!

No, the powers that be will be up in arms, and our otherwise 'liberal thinkers' make some very snyde comments about the authors 'low' background, the uselessness of his grammer and the lack of any real sentences.

To top it all off they will no doubt vomit at the appalling spellings and my audatiousness be sited as a reason to ignore my honest efforts compleatly and forever.

"Give it no air, don't even aford it the dignity of a bad review!"

"Stiffel it sir, and kill it like a kitten!"

Yes, all in all, they will feel justifi'd joining arms with my teachers and all the tracherious 'yes men' of the world in judging me and my honest and truthfull testerment to hell.

51

Death under a horse

JUST SO as to be able to eat and drink i learn to nick some of my fathers coins and maybe buy myself a small fish to fry up.

The trick is, to wait till he's on the bog with an attack of 'Greek arse' then sneek into his cabin and lift the dosh from his wallet. It's not stealing as such: just beer money to make sure i have a little something to rattle in my pockets: to not starve and be penniless.

Theres no cars as such on this island, just donkeys, bikes and the occasional horse. The rest of the time you have to use shanks's poney.

On the 3rd day of the gale, the old man hails down a gee-gee and takes our mother out on a gallop round the coast to the new harbour. There's only room for 2 in the carrage so me 'n' my big brother have to walk it. That's a couple of miles, round the unmade cliff road, then another 1/2 mile to the town.

The horse clips off at a good trot. We see it's arse winding round the cliffs then one more view of it's tail and it's gone - just a woosh of dust. You could see the old mans blond hair as he wav'd his hat in the air. Just the arse end of the horse then nothing: the sea and the sky.

We plod off after them, my big brother one side of the track, me on the other. 1/2 ways along i spot a lizard crawling up a crack in the wall. I call to my big brother but it dashes under a rock when it feels his fat feet clumping towards it. It had pinkish colour'd hands and only half a tail.

Next up an older boy buzzes by on his moped. He comes wizzing round the corner, that close that some little stones get flicked up in my face. The trouble is, there's another cart coming down the track and he smacks rite into the horse. He skids off his mop'd into a cloud of dust and the horse start's screaming it's head off.

I honestly think that the horse did his best not to stamp on him but he still caught one in the head, then the wheels of the carrage went over his tummy. The driver jumps down and the passangers help him drag the kid onto the side of the track. His black, shining hair gone all inky with the blud. Really, it's as if his face has collaps'd or something.

They've got no hospital on the island so someone has to go and radio up a helicopter to come in from the mainland.

I stand a ways off, high up on a rock watching the blud creeping thru the dust, the horse meanwhile has cut it's leg.

The helicopter comes quicker than you'd think and rite away they wrap the older boy in a red blanket, belt him onto a stretcher and whisk him off into the sky. There's wires and tubes and a man flying next to him, holding up a bottle of clear fluid.

The helicopter goes out over the ocean kicking up little wavelets. We watch until it becomes just a speck in the distance, the boy still dangling below, then it vanishes for good. My big brother says that they were too late and that the kid was already dead.

After that it takes us another good 20 minits or so to get to town. We follow the cliffs path till the track opens up and you come to these little dust color'd houses.

They don't really have what you'd call roads on the islands, more like donkey tracks mainly, then there's some tourist shops and we start seeing some white faces.

It get's more and more crowded the nearer we get to the harbour. Must be a boats in, co's the place is teaming with fat Americans dress't in flowery shirts. Another thing, the further we walk into the town, the brighter the shirts get.

Everyone is trying to buy something but there isn't really anything to buy, except for belts, sandles and bags, all made of the same cheep, stinking, goats leather. Also, there's these little statues of a man carv'd out of green marble, with a pair of giant balls and massive cock as tall as his nose.

One thing i do get: a man hawking his junk on the streets sells me a liter for my clay pipe. It has a flint and strike, which is attach'd by a hook to the end of a coil of slow burning rope, just like the solders used in the Great War.

"They us'd 'em so they wouldn't get spy'd by snipers and shot"

I tell my big brother, who just grunts.

I lite up my clay pipe and puff out a big lungful of brown colour'd smoke. My brother stares at me with real hatred and contempt and tell's me to bludy well put it out. He then turns and storms off down a hidden alleyway.

I call after him but he really has legged it. I have to put my pipe in my pocket and run after him. I too cut thru a small cover'd way and try to head him off between the church and the sea. It's pitch black in there and i can't tell which direction im heading. When i come out im on the harbour wall.

There's 100's of people milling about, eating and drinking and generally filling their faces. Then across the way i see Manicur'd Nails sat under a palm tree, reading her book and walking rite up to her is my big brother. By the time i fight my way thru the crowds they'er already deep in conversation.

I stand to the side and look at her face. Her name is Raquel, shes 15 years old and comes from 'up the north'. It's my big brother who chats her up, i just watch from under my pith helmet, take my pipe out my pocket and practice blowing smoke rings.

According to Raquel, her holliday is a disarster as well. Apparently her father has terrible arthritis in both his hands and can't tie a knot, pull up the anchor or even comb his own hair. Then, on the 1st day he slipp'd and sprain'd his ankle as well and Raquel and her mother have to do all the hard graft, everything!

I let out some little puffs of smoke and nod as if i understand, tho she isn't really speaking to me at all.

Also, Raquel's mother never want'd to come to Greece in the 1st place, on account that she can't stand the food or the heat. Other than that their yachet is pretty dandy, not some clapp'd out old bathtub like the Styx. The engin werks, theyve got an echo sounder, comfy bunks and a werking fridge. Nevertheless, Raquel says that she is sick of the sun, hates boats and is bored stiff on the island because there's nothing for young people to do.

This is what happenes: my big brother gets down on his hands and knees in the dust before her and does some press up's. He counts's up to 20, he's voice sounding very strained and then they go off into the bushes and have sex.

Im left sitting smoking my pipe, which tasts hot and bitter and is burning the inside of my mouth. I give it a good suck but somethings jamm'd in the stem and it won't go. I poke at the mouth-peice with my pen knife but whatever's in there is jammed solid. In the end i bang it on the heal of my shoe and the bowl breaks off.

I look to the bushes but they'er not coming back out yet.

I throw the stem of my pipe away open out my note book and take some notes. It is hard for me to rite my novel in any real kind of style, especially when my big brother is lying in the bushes with a girl who to all intesive purposes belongs to me. And to rite a novel for the English, a people who by their nature prefer pomposity and lies, is next to impossible.

What im trying to say is that i am not cock-sure and boastful about my talents but shy and retiring. If i sometimes come across as outspoken and opinionat'd, well that's just an effect of youth, but you would be rong to asume me as anything other than a fragile skool boy who hates the riten word.

Eventually they come out of the bush's. Of course, it should have been me who went with Raquel, not my big brother, and i can't help but hate her a little for making a slut of herself in front of me. I think she must notice because she avoids my eyes and trys to be nice to me, even complementing me on my pith helmet.

Everything is unfair in life because tho my big brother couldn't cear less about Raquel, he has used her body and i who am in love with her must stand aside and say nothing.

We go look for the old man to see if we can scrounge up a couple of notes for some booze. After wandering up and down the harbour 6 times over we finnaly run into them sitting outside on a terrice over looking the sea. The old man is 3 sheets to the wind and our mother is feeding scraps of fish off her plate to a whole hor'd of 3 legg'd, 1 ey'd, tailless cats.

My father hails my brother drunkenly and insists that he pulls up a chair and 'sups an ale'. " Ah Nichollas, i see that you've brought one of your sluts along … would you like a little drink my darling?" He puts his arm around and trys to kiss her but Raquel stands and goes round to the other side of the table.

Just then one of the cats jumps up onto my fathers plate and my father bangs his glass down and yells at it like a mad man. No sooner has that cat been vanquish't and my father congratulat'd himself on his historic victory than another cat leaps at his beard, pawing after a piece of fish.

The old man shoo's it away then challenges my brother to an arm wrestling compertion. They have to move all the glasses and bottles to do that, but still there isn't enough room for their mighty biceps. They square up but then my father complains that my big brother is using his free arm to gain extra purchase against the table. After exchanging accusations they agree to get down on their knees in the dust and wrestle amongst the pussycats.

My father eyes my brother molevenantly, then turns to Raquel.

"Nichollas is not fit, young lady. I am twise his age yet fit as a fiddle!"

He then downs a huge draft of ozzo and starts to get undress'd making a pile of his cloaths.

"Forget arm wrestling, i will race you back to the ship. Man to man!"

The old girl gets wind of something, stops fussing over the stray moggys and looks up ansiously.

"You can't swim out there, not in the dark" she says. "You won't be able to find your way to the ship. Your'll both drown!"

"Nonsence, Juny, im perfectly capable."

"But Nichollas?"

"If Nichollas is afraid then he dose not need to compeat. Are you afraid, Nichollas? Are you afraid that you will loose to your old man? Then you better walk home with your new lady friend and mummy. But i am swimming back to the ship round the headland and i will see you all later!"

And with this he dives off the harbour wall into the blackness bellow. We see his torso disappearing into the gloom followed by a loud splash. A wave of phospherious flys up, glowing green-white and then silence. We wait a moment, peering into the dark waves.

Then there's a call from way out to sea and we see his white head floating by the harbour entrance.

"Come along Nichollas, if your coming. Or are you a bludy mummys boy?"

My brother looks to Raquel, disrobes and walks down the harboure steps and into the sea, my mother shrieking histerically after him.

52

The fathers speech

ME 'N' my mother walk back round the coast road, picking our way thru the darkness and Raquel tags along holding my mothers hand.

"There sure to drown. It's stupid! Stupid! Stupid! They will have to swim rite out to sea and your fathers completely drunk. He can't walk, let alone swim. I don't mind him killing himself but his own son!"

Raquel agrees in her northen way but i say nothing. I know that they'er all nuts.

All the way back the old girl keeps harping on about what a low-down-scoundrel my father is, and she never calls him her husband but simply refers to him as 'Gustov's father'; and then she expects me to agree with her and back her up in everything she embroders.

When we get back to the beach i have to row them both out to the floattila. 1st i take Raquel to her ship, which is pretty straight forward as it has a lite on and is nearest the shore. Then me and my mother have to search around in the darkness for the Styx.

There are hundreds of little black waves battling against us, pushing against our prow and flinging their white tops into my eyes.

We pass rite thru the flottila 3 times, ducking under the anchor lines, befor the Styx finnaly looms out of the darkness and there's 2 ghosts sat on the poop deck.

I tie up and help my mother onto the yachet. My big brother's lying there gasping his lungs out and my father is boasting that he is quite prepaired to swim back round to the harbour and do it all over again.

"If Nickollas is capable of it then so be it. I will race him."

The following morning there's a flottila meeting called and we all have to meet at the local tavernna. Everyone has to attend and im made to comb my hair and put a clean shirt on.

Our father wears his skippers cap and the old girl draws on some eyebrows.

My big brother is the only one who doesn't have to come because he's still laid up on his bunk.

The taverna has grape vines growing all up the outsides and there's a little banqueting hall outback, which is where the meeting takes place.

Theres a whole gander of Yachting types there, all wearing sailor's caps and competeing with each other for supremacy.

The meeting is called to order and rite off it's decid'd that the floattila should waigh anchor directly the wind drops, or at least when it veers round to the South East a little, which everybody new already.

Its then point'd out by Golden Legs that the Styx has no chance of beating round the headland unassist'd and will require a tow. My father, who has not been drown'd, shakes his head dissmissivly and stands.

"I am a member of The Royal Yacht Club, Juny" he says loudly, showing my mother his tie "and i do not accept tow lines from speed boats!" and with that he bows, curtly, and sits down. So it seams that for the time being we are to stay put.

Meanwhile, it is revieal'd that the Turks and the Greeks have declair'd war on each other and that all the local men have been conscript'd and all fuel not for military use has been put on ration. Consequently their is no disel oil for the local fishing boats, much less the yachets of English holliday makers.

At this point my father stands again, bang's on his glass with his spoon and makes a speech.

1st off, there's no way that he will submit to the ignominy of having the Styx towed round the headlands by a bunch of fair-weather sailors, particularly by the likes of Arthritis Sprained Ankle, 'a man who couldn't even raise his own bludy anchor without injury to the afore mentioned ankle!'

2ndly, my father points out, the vast majority of the 'captains' are, in his estermation, 'meer children' where as he has class, 'impecable taste and panache!'

Next, he talks about a man of science who went to sea in a wet suit.

"The afore mentioned gentleman was subsqently attack'd by sharks and the injurys he sustained were such that it was inpractable to remove him from his wet suit as the doctor said it was the only thing that was stopping him falling apart.

"Now that man had guts, he had courage and he had panash and determination. Take Captain Cook, another example – a map maker of supream excellence, bar none! Lady's and gentleman, charge your glasses, i give you, Captain Cook!" Finaly he shuts up and sits down and starts picking over a bit of lamb that's been serv'd up to him.

"This isn't roast lamb, Juny, it's positively raw! For christs sake, you can't get a decent meal in the whole damn'd place! I met these Budhist monks, only little fellows brown as berrys, but by God, they march't clean over the Himalayas and start'd to feast. Those Budhists know how to stuff down a banquit – incredible! But this? it's red raw!"

Everything my father speaks of is either exhault'd to the hevens or trodden into the dust like worthless garbage. His favorite are the rich and his least favorite, the poor. And then he mocks 'the blacks'.

Why then dose he want to have a sun tan?

Raquels father, who has been hiding behind a potted plant, now stands and trys to explain to my father that no one is offering to tow the Styx anywhere, as no one has any diesel oil and that to all extent and purposes we are all in the same boat. The old man dismisses Raquels father as a half wit and a man without panache.

"You, sir, your crew and your yacht, are not capable! Your wife is ugly and if my son wasn't bedding your daughter then i would! Waiter! Yes, you! Buy this man, who lacks all panache, a drink! Yes, buy this 'insolent puppy' a bottle of your finest champage!"

"Oh shut up!" snaps our mother.

The old man waves his hand in her face "you are a woman, Juny and therefore understand nothing!"

My mother turns her body away from him and sits there showing the world that she is not with him. My father stairs into back of her scull, but as yet she has not drop'd dead.

It's about 4 in the afternoon when we finally drag the old man onboad. He trys to take a piss in the wardrobe and the old girl has to hold him up and walk his feet into the cabin. He rolls onto the bunk and the old girl undresses him.

He lies there on his back snoring his head off for the reast of the day and dosnt wake up till morning.

Just about sunrise he makes an extra loud sucking noise and suddenly jumps in the loo. He's in there a good 1/2 houre, cranking the shit handle and groaning, then the door fling's open and he steps into the cabin fixing his wiskers. Next, he pours himself a large GNT and chucks himself out on the fore deck to begin roasting his flesh for the day.

Really, of course, he is far more refin'd and steps into the sun like a retiring English gentleman. He calls for our mother to bring him a 'GNT'. How he loves to use that phase. He looks cocketishly around as he says it, checking who's watching, then chuckles to himself. No doubt he hear'd some top exectutive, or perhaps a government minister, reel that one off in some London whorehouse.

"Presentation is what counts' Juny! Prention and panache!"

After swiggin his gin he lies back down in the sun and tell's us that he is going to be 'as brown as a bludy nigger before the end of the holiday.' But he will not, he will still just be red and peeling, his drinkers nose is espesherly puffy and tender looking.

All morning he has to dash bellow with what he calls a dose of Greek arse! I listen out for him down there pebble dashing the pan. There's a cry of pain followed by heavy breathing, then pause before he lets fly again, then he starts cranking, pumping his shit into the butiful, blue Mediterainan. And all the while he's swearing under his breath, cursing the wogs, their food, their drinking water and he's useless family.

When he comes back on deck he's got a real sweat on and is looking for trouble.

"I was perfictley well back in England, Juny. It's only sinse you started posioning me with this damn'd woggy food that ive had a tummy upset."

By the afternoon the winds finnaly dropp't and it's possible to sit up on deck without feeling totally sea-sick. I peer over the side into the depths below. A shoal of silver, rocket shap't fish passes over the bottom followed by a large, black jellyfish, which you can see clear as you like. My big brother says that it is over 6 fathoms deep here – that's 30 odd feet, rite to the bottom.

The old girl comes up from the gally wringing her dish rag. She checks the wind and chucks a bowl of water over the side. Then, feeling rather dairing, tells us that she mite go in for a little dip.

1st, she checks that i have some sun cream on my shoulders then sits herself down on the sturn and dangles her feet over the side. There's a little ladder there and after a while, she climbs on and lowers herself into the tepid water.

"Oh, it's really warm" she calls, and we watch as she slips in up to her arm-pits then pushes off from the side and timidly starts practicing her breast stroke.

She really warms to it and does 2 whole circuits of the yachet. She is just comeing in for a 3rd lap when the old man darshes below holding his guts.

I listen out as he lets rip an almighty wet fart, crys out in pain and starts cranking the shit handle like crazy. He really is emptying his arse into the pot and giving the leaver a good jerking.

Our mother, now on her final circit, smiles up at us just as a great bloom of orange shit jets into her face. Great clouds of the stuff clogging the cristal clear waters and catching in her hair.

Presently the small fry come darting in to nibble at the half chew'd peanuts and strings of rotting lamb.

53

Ouzo with Theresa

AT TEA time it is decided that the floattila will sale at 1st lite.

"If you require anything ashore, then sort it out today because i want no late comers, or whinging, when we're at sea!" And my father gives me and my big brother a meaningfull look.

I, for one will be happy to leave. One more nite and we'll be out of this dump and can at last set sale for the land of the golden fleece.

Evening time, my parents stay aboad and me 'n' my big brother go ashore alone. My big brother makes me row. Usualy im not allowed to row but the day i spercificly don't want to he makes me.

Actually, it is impossible for me to sit and pull on those oars because a rash of hot boils has sprung up across my arse and everytime my bottom comes into contact with the rubber seat it feels like i've got red ants burrowing onto my flesh and squirting hot acid.

I pull on the oars and wince, my big brother siting in the sturn sheets flexing his arm muscles and calling 'In! – Out! In! – Out!'

and i have to look at his stupid face and grit my teeth.

Before we even hit the shingle my big brother jumps into the surf, wades up the beach and stryds off into the bushes. I don't even get a chance to stow the oars and he's gone. He puts a real sprint on.

He goes one way and i have to wander off on my jacksie.

Theres a small path that leads over the rocks.

After the little beach you come to the old harboure. Skeletons of part-built ships jut up into the nite sky, like the ribs of dead whales.

I drag my feet thru all the wood shavings then the sun goes down. It's gone in a second and straight away it's properly dark, no dusk at all. You have to mind where you place your feet. I walk along with my hands out front guarding my face. By and by my eyes grow accustom'd and there's plenty of starlite to see by.

I pick my way along the desert'd dockside, bravely walking very close to the crumbling edge. The reek of diesel oil and shark attacks comes up to me.

There's an old tary rope dangling into the drink with something heavy on the end of it. I haul it up over the side but there's no shark, just an old rubber tyre. I examine it for wear before letting it splash back into the inky-black. The sound of it hitting the water startles me and i turn and run, smashing into a rusty winch handle and cutting my shin quite badly.

I realise that im dangeriously near the edge, only now i'm bleeding. I get up and i stagger on whimpering quietly to myself.

Next, the sexual scent of pine needles fills my nostrils and the nite ciccadas start banging out their wretch'd song. If i could just get hold of one of those insolent beasts, i'd teach it to rattle it's hiddious legs at people all day and nite.

I set off into the bushes to capture one of those beasts, but it's impossible to corner those inflated grasshoppers. They always keep one bush ahead of you.

Then i remember the bludless husks i found on our 1st day in this strange land, suck'd dry by some large and heavily poisonus spider and quickly i jump from the bushes and brush myself down. I will wait till day lite to get my revenge.

A manky, stray cat hisses at me from underneath one of the freshly laid keels but i walk on tottaly unpeterb'd, marveling at my new found fearlessness.

No, darkness no longer bothers Gustov Claudius. It seams that i am at last becoming a man.

I pass rite beneath another ship, the limbs of sawn timber making great arcs thru the nite sky and then i notice music and laughter floating across from the other side of the creek. There's a little lite glowing, it's reflection playing on the oily waters. I pass by a row of derricks, cross via a small pontoon, cut back along the opersite quay and there i am outside an old hut, listening to the sound of girls voices on the inside.

It is not possible to tell what language they are speaking but they are defiantly not Greek. Then again, they are not English voices either. Suddenly the door bursts open and i have to jump back as a young couple come staggering out into the nite.

They twang and drawl insolently and then i know who they are: they are American skool children and they are drunk on 4 penny ouzo. They 'hic-up' at me befor dissapering, arm in arm round the back. They giggle and shout before suddenly becoming hush'd.

I stare after them in wonder. They are children, just like me only they are not children, they are tottaly different: they are happy, together and laughing.

I summon up my courage and step into the cabbin. My eyes battle with the lites. It really is impossible to make out anything other than there's a bar with a shadowy figure of a man stood behind it and the faces of about 5 children lit by candles, all sat on the floor round low tables.

The barman has silver hair and black mustashes, i approach thru the gloom. He pours me a glass and nods towards a jug of water. His gold medalion winks at me.

There are young girls in this strange waterside cabin and i can now hear by their voices they are all American.

I crouch at one of the low tables and they don't look down their noses at me, or mock me, or get up and leave. No, they don't hate a boy on account of his poor accent, or poor education but instead lord him for his Englishness, admiring of his long blond hair, gentleness and youth; and even offer him a puff on their drugs.

I pour water into the oozo, it turns chalk white and i sip at it and pull a face. At last - a drink that is more vile than whisky!

Slowly, the voices come nearer and surround me and i am enveloped by friendlyness. Let me be friends with you, American people. I will talk to you boys 1st, becouse your women scear me and can hurt me with there denial.

Besides, i am a homosexual or at least, i have been touch'd by the hand of a grown man, tho i will never utter this. So please, forgive me if i am quite and shy.

I talk to a boy with curly hair who's name is Finch. I tell Finch all about the Styx, mention to him that my big brother has an electric guitar and ask him if he is familer with the Napolonic period navi. He nods his head and seams very interest'd, so i tell him about Nelson and his most famouse battles.

Next, i risk asking him if he has ever heard of The Queens Own Royal West Kent Regiment, but he hasn't. So i can't really tell him about my Victorian colour sergeants scarlet jacket. Besides, Crowsfeet will have nicked it by now.

Finch leans over the table and asks this red hair'd girl for a puff on her ciggeret then she leans across the table and hisses at me. I don't quite understand, then she gets up, push's me in the chest and tells me to 'fuck off!'

"Go find your own boy friend, you little slut" and she slaps me.

Finch holds her by the arms and some of her friends grab hold of her from behind and pull her off me. Finch shouts at her to shut up. "He's a boy, alrite, he's a fucking boy!"

"Im sorry," she gasps, "i thort you were a girl."

And i smile like crazy, laughing and hiding my pain . . . that i should be mistaken for a girl . . . that i am not a man and never will be . . . that even a girl thinks me another girl and can smell that i have been rape't by a man.

I retreat into the shadows and stroke my stinging face. Really, it would be best if i leave this place. There is not a corner of the earth made for Gustov Claudius. But then she comes and rescues me: Theresa from Butiful Delaware. And she leads me away to a quiet corner and feeds me oozo and retsina and we smoke American cigarettes that taste of nectar.

Never before have i enjoy'd puffing on these vile things. Always i have had to pretend, but with you Theresa, they taste like love. And even the sour oozo has a special sweetness. And i smile into Theresa, from Delaware's, laughing eyes. Her wet lips part and her tongue licks quickly across her perfict teeth and i fall into her soft, welcoming bossom.

We leave the voices of the cabin behind us, swaying drunk in the heavy, nite air. So this is what i was born for, Theresa from Delaware: to be held and honour'd by women-kind, not hated and rebuff'd.

15 years old and a real woman, your breasts thrust against my boy-chest like missiles. Yes, you are built for me, Theresa from Delaware, and we lie in that towering nite on a rock above the ribs of a half-built fishing boat, the stars exploding in the sky. Stars that Vincent would have marvel'd at and would have lov'd to paint.

Oh yes, Theresa from Delaware, i am not just a skool boy but an artist. It is the only noble trade on God's earth, don't you know. To be in rapture and wonder at every leaf and bud of nature, that is my lonely path Theresa.

No, i will never become mundane or be mediocre, because i have the call of Genius pounding in my blud. I may be damn'd, laugh't at and ridicul'd, Theresa from Delaware, but i will paint on, humbly, alone. And like Vincent, i too will take a slut or a whore as my bedfellow, for i and Vincent are like brothers, Theresa, did you guess that? What he felt, i too will feel, what he suffer'd, i too will suffer, what fired his mind will, by laws of artistic nature, fire my mind also.

No, im not ordinary in any sense of the word, Theresa from Delaware, for my fingers have been kiss'd by God. Here, let me put them to your eyes like fingers in the sun. And you, in turn, touch me, Theresa. But slowly and gently, for i am afraid and have never known the secrets of a woman.

Please, if you can, be mercyfull with me Theresa, i am scar'd to hold your heavy breast and to kiss it, so i fumble slowly and painfully, my lips aching for that large, fleshy rocket to ride against my teeth. And you unbutton me and hold me in your warm palm, then lean back, ever so slitely, so's you can look down at me and see me lit by starlite in your girls hand.

So many stars, Theresa, and then shyly, i too glance down at you holding me and my breath is caught in my throat with excitement, until i must surely faint of it.

This is our island, Theresa from Delaware, our island for all eternity. This is our rock, where the impression of our young bodies will lie together for always.

One by one i unbutton you, the breath lock't in my trembling hart. There is a wonderful tuft of golden hair that springs up, and slowly i slip my timid finger into your most secret place, and every moment i might die. You too are breathless, aren't you, Theresa? You too are shy.

Its so slippery and hot in there, like a wound might be. It scears me Theresa, that your juces might be acid. In truth, being there inside you, it numbs my fingers and all the while, those devilish cicadas try and interupt me as i lie against you.

It is nite time and time for the Gods to ride forth!

Theresa lifts her arse and trys to pull her jeans down lower, to get her legs further apart. I bang my knees on the rocks and she places my hardness against her softness and i kiss you, Theresa from Delawear, and hang onto your neck and you hold my hips and ride against me. But please, don't move your hands to my buttocks and feel that rash of raw pimples that has sprung there. Please, dear God, don't!

And i have to pull away so that i won't be sham'd at this most delicate time: at the moment when Gustov Claudius, stumbles to become a man.

Please, help me be strong, Theresa from Delawear, help me to escape the terrible pounding that this world has already dish'd out to me.

People move about in the shadows that surround us and at one time i am certain that i here my father calling my name. Then a cat runs across my leg, and all the while the cicardas are laughing from the bushes.

I kiss you good nite my lov'd one. We will meet here again tomorrow, and so share many sweet kisses, you walking me to the shore and me walking you back home till it's a madness.

* * *

I walk back along the dockside as if lift'd to the arms of the gods.

When i pass across the little ridge of pine trees the sky is already liteing in the east. I follow the little path across the rocks, cut back down to the desert'd shore but the dingny is gone. I run up and down the beach looking for it but really it has been wash'd away in the nite.

Out in the bay the yatchts ride at anchor and beyond them the hulk of the Styx is just vissable in the gloom and distance. There's no way of getting aboad that death boat. I sit down on the shingle and can't belive that i am at last kiss'd.

I love you, Theresa from Delawear. No longer will this world mock me, i am no lowly homosexuel but a man, a man who has known the secrets of a woman!

All along, in my aching heart, i have known that i am special, that i have only been waighting for this moment to be anoint'd by you, Theresa from Delawear. 15 years old and already a woman.

It was you who held me in the palm of your pritty hand and shyly lookt down at me and let me know myself as God.

I look out to sea, walk back up the beach, climb into an old fishing boat, pull an old stinking net over my head and sleep the sleep of love.

54

A Merman

GOLDEN LITE fills my eyes, streaming thru the chinks in the decking above me. I blink and turn my head away. I am in the stink of tar and roap and fish and bilge and slime and i am hugging an octipuss trap. It takes the form of a pot with an old piece of hemp tied round it's neck, like a noose, and a stinking old lump of fish rotting in the bottom.

I suck on the lose strands of roap - Theresa, i love you. I will eat your hair! And i roll around in that old fishing net, my mind gone wild. Suddenly, there are voises from outside and i stand and stick my head out thru the little hatch and the world laughs with me.

The sea is as blue as ink, the little boats bobbing at anchor and a brown merman sits on the rocks bellow, a live octopuss sqirming in his fists.

He lifts it to his puckering lips, bares his teeth and sinks them into the rubbery neck, like a wild dog. And i see the startling whites of the mans eyes beneith his dark brows.

The octopuss writhes in agoney then droops limp, it's tenticels uncurling from around the merman's wrists. The merman then grimaces up at the sky, wipes a string of gray slime from his beard and cearfully tucks the lifeless body into the waist band of his swiminging trunks.

There is a whole garland of it's dead brothers and sisters already dangling there, their useless tenticels flopping against his manly thighs.

Just then he looks up too me and smiles before running to the edge of the sea and diving between the jaggedy rocks into the inky depths below. The water foams round his ankels as he disapears into the beutifull sea.

The babble of voises rises again and i look up. There's a party of people picking their way along the beach towards me. They are chanting a song, i try to catch the words but the wind carrys it away from me. They walk with their heads bow'd and are apparently seaching for something.

One of them, a man who looks a lot like my father, throws his arms up into the sky, turns full circle, puts his hands on his hips and aparently starts lectureing the small woman stood by his side. I hear snatches of their rise'd voises.

The woman, who looks a bit like my mother, yells back at him and pushes him in the chest. They are obviously having a heat'd debate about whatever it is that they have lost, the one who looks like my father jumping up and down in the white colour'd sand, his hair waving mysteriously. He shouts again in the womans face, gestickulates wildly out to sea, then turns and storms off. The little woman, who really could be my mother, stears after him gobsmak'd.

Someone else, who could be my big brother, is stood magnifsently up on the hillside, acting as some kind of lookout. I shade my eyes and peer in the direction that the man had point'd but there is nothing out there but the empty sea.

Just then there's a great tubeulence in the water bellow me and the merman comes crashing to the surfiss, a green colour'd octipuss writhing in his arms. He dives again then breaks water a little further out.

He grins in the heat of the battle, holding his adversary at arms length, admiring it's eel like ternasity. Then slowly, he pulls the reluctant beast towards his waiting jaws, drags it's gray, writhing body to his lips and bites at it's neck like a wolf.

The octopusses tentickels entwine themselfs round his wrists and neck, feeling for his ears and nose - almost sensuely stroking at his beard'd face - before stiffening in estercy. Each leg releases one by one, till the green carcassis is left hanging dead in the mermans triumphant fist.

I stand transfix'd, my head and shoulders clear of the deck, staring at the octopusses strange arms, cover'd in hundreds of little suckers.

Then i imagin something stupid. I imagin that this merman lifts his free arm and waves to me like a brother, or even perhaps like the father who i have never known. This perception only lasts a split second before i realsise that he is mearly striking out for the shore, swimming with just one arm, his broad chest pushing effortlessly thru the waves, his free hand trailing the octipuss behind him.

Shortly, he arrives at the little cove below me, springs from the water and clambers up onto the rocks. He stands there like a hero counting the trophys in his belt when suddenly, one of the octupus's comes back to life, slips from his fist and summersalts back into the sea. In one movement the merman turns and dives in after it, jack - knifing thru that air, a pefict arc into the deep blue.

I try to peer into the depths but there are dark shadows in that water and it is impossible to see his thrashing tail. Several minits pass in silence then just as i think the octipuss must have dragg'd him to his death, the merman resurfaces, spouting water from his laughing lips, the octoppus dead in his fist.

The merman tucks it's body into his belt, puts his hands behind his head and lies back, bobbing up and down in the sea like a brown seal, the little wavelets rolling across his oily belly; the tenticels of his pray splade out around his thighs like a strange skirt, washing too and frow in the purple waves.

55

Lost, fear'd drown'd

IT'S MY big brother who spots me 1st, from his look-out post on the ridge. I smile up at him. I only wish that i had my pith helmet on so's that i could salute him properly.

I really am anomously proud of my achevments of the nite befor and my hart swells with pride. After all my brother is a male too, and along with the merman we could perhaps form a gay band of gigilos, traveling the 7 seas and serviseing the poor, lonely island girls of the world. Tho of course this would be ridiclious as i am in love and would never sin aganst my sweet American girl.

My big brothers voice carrys across to me as he calls out to my pearants, waving his arms and pointing me out, stood here, waist-deep in my little fishing boat.

So the couple who look't like my mother and father really are my mother and father after all. How extraordinary life-like life sometimes is.

The pair of them stand peering stupidly out from undereneath their shad'd eyes, looking in every single direction apart from where i actually stand.

I wave to them too: my family. My father has his blue nautical swimming trunks on and his hair is dye'd the most blinding peroxide blond, but he is still unsure that his hair is truly white enough, glowing against his scarlet nose.

My big brother shouts and points to me again and my mother actually walks over and checks benith a large white rock, to see if im not hidding under there. She calls my father over to help her lift it, but he shushes her with his puffy red hands.

It really is comical to watch them in their efforts to understand where i am. In the end my brother has to run down off of the ridge and point directly at me and i climb up onto the deck and wave with both my arms.

Finally, dim realisation dawns on their faces. My mother liftes her hands to her face and calls out in a high shrill voice. She has a funny white hat on and then my father comes lickity-split over the rocks, he looks quite athletic there for a moment, with his blue bathing trunks and his blond chest hairs floating in the sea breeze.

Below, the merman pulls himself from the dark sea and starts pumeling his octopusses on the rocks. He lifts it high above his head and smashes it down again and again, tenderising it's rubbery body untill it becomes almost like gray slime in his hands.

He then takes a 2nd octopus from his belt and starts cracking that against the rocks with all his might. My father halts, looks at him, then smiling like a maniac, nods hello before he rushes on.

The octopus man lifts the grey, slimey body in his hands, hooks out both it's eyes with his thumbs and throws them to the seagulls, who dance down into the waves after them.

My father stands on the shingle bellow me shading his eyes.

"Where the bludy hell have you been, we've been searching for you all bludy nite! Get down off there, your mother's been nagging me senseless, jibbering on and on that you've drown'd! Well what am i suppos'd to do about it? If he's dead he's dead! Now go back to sleep woman and we'll look for the little bleeders body in the morning!"

"The dingy had gone so i couldn't get back to the ship!" i reply innocently.

"You should of shout'd."

"I did."

"What time was it?"

"I don't know."

"Haven't you got a watch?"

"No."

"Well get one!"

"I aint got the money."

"Ain't! What is all this 'aint'? Do you mean 'i haven't' by any chance?"

I show him my nak'd wrists. "I can't afford one."

"Well get out there and get a job!"

"Im still at skool, dad."

"Well there's no good complaining about it to me. Go out into the big wide world and make it happen!"

He glears at me, he really has got the most terfick pair of bags, the sort that you just want to puncture, just to see what monsterus type of blud would come out.

"Where did you sleep, then?"

"In there" and i nod over my shoulder to the fishing boat.

"You know that i was up half the bludy nite. Your mother has made my life a bludy missery. I told her we would be taking you home in a wooden box!"

"What for?"

"Becouse i thort you were dead! I walk't clean round that bludy harbour a dozen times!" he looks at me sideways, "there were couples in all the bushes, in the strangest postions."

Just then my big brother trots up on his athleats legs and scowls at me. I look up and sort of smile.

"Where was he?"

My father waves his bony finger thru the white colour'd air. "He says he slept in that fishing boat."

"All nite?"

"I had to, the dingy was gone."

"Why couldn't you just wait for him with the dingy, Nichollas?"

"I did, i wait'd but he never show'd up" my big brother lies. "What were you doing, you stupid little shit!"

He trys to push me over and i dance backwards and just grin.

My father shades his eyes and stairs back out to sea.

"Well hes not going ashore alone again, i can tell you that much. I'm going to chain his fucking foot to the bludy anchore in futcher!" and then he walks off.

My big brother puts his hand on my fore head and pushes me away, then follows after his lord and master.

56

Love lost

Befor we set sail and leave this land forever i just have time to sneek ashore and meet Theresa for one last time.

I am not a good swimmer and am scar'd of sharks and currents, but nether-the-less, when no one's looking i drop off the back of the boat and strike out for the headland.

It's a long way's off and there's plenty of barnacles on these rocks and a good amount of slime to match. Also, i dislike the taste of salt water and pass over some very deep and dark caverns on the sea bed.

Doing my little doggy paddle it really is as if i will never make it. The 1st jagged rocks are far to steep and have a dangerious overhang and i have to paddle back out then come back in from the other side, there's a small cove there and pull myself from the water.

I know the house where Theresa is staying and follow the path up the dusty hillside. The garden is surrounded by black cypress trees that stand there like fingers of green flame.

Between the biggest 2 there's an iron gate. I push it open and walk up the front path and knock on the door. After a while a Greek maid comes and looks me suspicously up and down. I try to explain to her that ive come for the American girl but she doesn't speak English and just shoo's me away.

I sit out front of the house for a while then go round the back and choose a window to throw a stone at. There's one with prittyer curtens than the other so i throw some little sticks up at it. Finnaly Theresa shows her face and signels for me to meet her down by the sea in 10 minits, so i pad off and wait there for her on our rock.

About 20 minits later she shows up. I stand and try to kiss her like that's normal. Then we sit and i tell her i have to sale next morning and will never see her again.

Theresa nods and looks down. We kiss a bit more but it's all a bit to sad and hard werk in the daylite. Then we go for a little walk around the shipyard and some local kids shout 'American pigs' and throw rocks at us.

We escape them and head back along the shore. My big brother is there waiting in the row boat. He tells me to get in.

"We've got to go now. The old mans pissed off with you!"

And i really have to leave. To kiss Theresa good bye on that little beach and watch her getting smaller and smaller as my big brother rows me away into the blue ocean.

It is unspeakable that, after meeting the only girl in the whole world who will ever be able to bring herself to love me, i should be forc't by my family to never see her again. And that, to my betters, and grown ups, my pain means nothing and is in fact a cause for ridicule and amusement.

But still they took me away, Theresa. Away from Greece, our island and that small rock which will always be imprint'd with our young bodies.

57

Back to skool

Everything, it seams now, is changing. The world really is like some strange, unreal dream. But also everything stays exactly the same, or rather repeats itself in strange circles.

Once again i am back here in our cursed skool, a meer skool boy trapp'd behind my desk. Once again, my father left us and return'd to his former way's.

My mother hasn't died after all, nor has she had her promis'd nervous breakdown but is still weighting nurvisly by the vernitaion blinds for our father's iminant return. In short - our father has fail'd in his mission to kill her and is in no position to present the family home to his London mistress and everything is as it was before.

Even now, just 2 weeks after our return from the land of the Greeks, it is impossible to believe that Theresa from Delawear was ever real and ever held my hand or lov'd me. It is also impossible to belive that one day i will be free to leave this place and sale to

America to be with her, and all these days that stack up in front of me, for ever and ever, will finally have slipp'd away and vanish'd for good.

Soon, this life will only be a hat'd memory and it really will be time to pretend to be a grown up and walk the streets of men, jostling for position, unsure of ourselves and full of bluster. Yes, we will become just like the grown ups who have built this world and bulli'd us into oblivion.

Rather than cutting over the back to skool as usual, i instead walk along the W- road. There is no need to hide any longer, Crowsfeet is back in Borstal for good, convict'd for stealing an officers army revolver and trying to flog it on the estate. No, Crowsfeet will not be able to bullie me now, or ever, for his spell has been broken.

Anyways, i have to buy some sweets from Smelly Al's for breakfast. Of course, i keep a weather eye open, just in case Crowsfeet has per chance escap't and is again on the lose, robbing, lying, thieving and punching; but overall, the atmosphere is damp and decent, the streets and gardens bath'd in gentle wet fog.

There's some twitterings in the bushes and 2 blue tits flitt anxiously at Mr's Moffets ancient cat, Basil, who tip-toes along the garden wall. Soon everything will be over for you too, you, raggedy old beast, and even you little blue tits will be pushing up the daisys before the years out.

They tell us cartloads of rules in our skool but no one tells us anything that will ever help us or is really true.

Everything they utter is 2nd hand and here say. They talk about God but know nothing of God, or love, or charity or death for that matter. It is not a good day for buying sweets as i only manag'd to lift 10 pence from the old girls purce.

When i arrive out side Smelly Al's, a boy they call Dogend is being beaten up. It isn't the type of fight where 2 boys square up to each other, but rather one where the victim has his arms pinn'd to the wall behind him by 2 big boys, whilest a 3rd smaller, meaner boy punch's him repeatedly about the ribs.

Dogend goes boggle eyed, lets out a gasping scream and crumples to the floor. The mean kid then kicks him as he rolls away into the gutter.

Dogend lies there growning, aparently at deaths door, then suddenly springs up grinning from ear to ear - he's found an almost un-smok'd Number 6!

Still half twist'd over and rubbing his guts, Dogend carrys his prize to he's trumphant attackers. The leader of which takes a bit o' strike from his pocket, sparks up and shears some puffs with he's comrades. Yes, today seams a friendly day.

I cut back from Smelly Al's and slip in unnotic'd thru the skool gate. Even the classrooms seam less full of anger today. Prehaps it is the fog that makes the world more subdued, or maybe it is just that our season in hell is drawing to it's natural close.

I walk over the grass and becouse of the fog escape being nabb'd by the prefects.

Yes, everything is unusually peaceful. No one is slipper'd in registration, for instance.

We file into asembly and plant our arses amongst the small pieces of yesterdays dinner, as normal. Jump to our feet, shout out our hymns and mumble the Lords prayer, as normal; then listen to one of Shawds sermons about responsibility before being sent off to our useless lessons. Everything is as normal but somehow different. For example, no one was cain'd.

I pick my way along the path between the rotting pre-fabs with my classmates. The stench of boil'd rags floats across the playground and we don't even bother holding our noses in disgust. Inside those kitchens the most hiddious old women who ever liv'd stand over vast black cauldrons, boiling the life out of food out of utter viciousness.

Actualy, they probably have no such feeling, maybe just contempt and bordom, and really they hate their jobs only as much as the teachers hate their jobs and as much as we enjoy being there dispis'd puples.

So why can't we all just go home rite now and stop pretending? Becouse the Generals want their war, and by God they will have their war, that's why! And we, the little solders of the futcher, must be trained thoughly in it's ways of stelth, small mindedness and meanness.

But after all, even a cart horse is allow'd to express something of it's inner nature, at least part of the time. And a mouse is allow'd to be something like a mouse and insects are just insects, so why do we have to be train'd into being something so unnatural as grown ups?

Actually, assembly didn't quit go like that and one boy was servely dissaplined and most of us had already got wind that Applecakes was dead.

Even outside Smelly Al's i'd heard some kids talking about a boy who'd chuck'd himself off the motorway bridge. No one new it was Applecakes for sure, but any idiot could of geuss'd it.

All thru assembly we sat there silent, watching Shawd's guilty face, trying to see past his eyes, to see if he's soul had chang'd during the nite.

From where im sitting they still look as mean, tiny and cunning as ever, but im too far away to see if he's been crying or anything.

We listen out for his hard voice, to see if there's a slight tremour. If he really is responsible for Applecakes death then maybe he will get down on his knees and beg our forgiveness.

No, Shawd dosnt repent, he just stands there, his small hands gripping the podium, as he clears his throat twice. Actually, Shawds voice is quite normal and he doesn't mention anything about Applecakes at all, other than that he's dead and that we've all got to pray for him.

It is of course possible that Shawd really did like Applecakes and genuinely care'd for him but still hat'd him enough - as he hates all of us children - to kill him.

Marshgas lives up the same street as Applecakes, so i dig him in the back and ask him, but getting information out of Marshgas is like getting blud out of a stone.

Cowsfroth, who knows nothing about it, says that his uncle, who werks with Applecakes dad, told him that Applecakes did try to hang himself off the bridge, but when he jump't the rope took his head off instead.

I try to imagine Applecakes without his head on, but it's quite impossible. Would his eye lashes still be quite as dark? What must it feel like to have your own head ripp't clean off and how long does it take for you to notice? Then we have to sing another hymn.

Once everyone's shouting i ask Marshgas if he thinks Applecakes head is still hanging on the end of the roap or weather it fell off into the river.

Marshgas doesn't seam to know and just stairs ahead and makes a big show of mouthing the words.

"Have the police found it, or is it drifting about on the river bottom?" i whisper. But again Marshgas just ignores me.

For someone who's meant to know all the facts and details, Marshgas's knowledge of Applecakes's corpse is pretty pathetic.

I bang him on the arm but he still keeps his nose in his hymn book and tell's me to shut up because 'sir's watching.'

"Maybe it's face down in the black mud," i continue, "or being scuff'd up against some gravel bed, or maybe getting it's nose chopp'd off by a ships propeller."

I lean into Marshgas's ear but nothing i say will ever wake the likes of Marshgas up. And all the while i have to speak out the corner of my mouth and keep a weather eye for old Shawd.

"Perhaps his head's crawl'd out onto the bank and lives in a ducks nest" i add. But Marshgas still doesn't bat an eyelid.

"But what would it live on, you ask? Well, maybe it could dive back in to catch some small fish, which it gobbles up using it's ears as hands."

Still Marshgas says nothing. "You might wonder how it's ears have gotten so long?" Well that's an easy one - they have obviously stretch'd due to being soak'd in salt water."

I make my little jokes, not because im insensitive but just to amuse myself, because i am afraid of death, because i want someone to stop me. Besides, i want Marshgas to smile, for me to know that he is alive too and that i have a companion in the world.

We have to sit down and Mister Boyce reads us a parable of the Good Samaritan, then we stand again and sing The Lord is my Shepherd.

"Why do you think he killed himself?" i ask Marshgas. "Do you think old Shawd was 'seeing' him?"

Marshgas hisses at me to shut up.

Weather Applecake's death was an accident or if he was driven to it by some unwarranted teachers attentions dosen't seame to have even entr'd into Marshgas's mind.

We sit down again and Shawd tells us that the skool tuck shop is to be closed until further notice due to it's entire contents being stolen by thieves.

"If they do find his head do you think that they'll bury it in the same box as his body? Or burn it? Or just nail it up by it's ears?"

Im just asking Marshgas these simple questions when his eyebrows start wiggling and a real look of terror passes across his face.

I feel a presence behind me and just have time to duck as Shawd swipes me. I half turn and dive to the left but Shawd has me by the throat and drags me out to the front, his small fist quite throttling me.

"So, you're the comedian again, master Claudius!" He shouts, shaking me by the neck.

He has to reach up like a hideously strong dwarf. Then he swings me around by my coat and slams me up agaist the wall, as is he's way.

"Ile teach you to be disrespectful of the dead! You impertanent little shit. Now stand there with your face to the wall. Ile deal with you later!"

Shawd turns and marches back up onto the podium. He spits in his hand, palms his comb-over flat, adjusts his cuffs, then stairs menicingly around the hall.

I stand there trying to loosen my tie, which has cut into my neck quite painfully. No one could deni that Shawds anger is any less keen.

All thru the rest of assembly i try gaining Marshgas's attention. I wink at him then try flicking bits of chew'd up paper at the back of his neck. All the while i have to keep a weather eye for Shawd, in case he sneeks up and throtles me again.

Once we get to the lords prayer we know that we'er on the home run and will soon be out of there, but as we bow our heads, Shawd starts plucking at the old harp strings.

The gist of it is this: Applecakes was a brite and gift'd lad and will be sorely miss'd by all of us, which isn't exactly the whole truth. No matter what fairy tails Shawd dreams up we all know what Applecakes was like and say what you like no one like't Applecakes. Sure, now that he's suddenly dead it turns out that everybody was his best mate, but i remember the olden days when everybody's story was tottaly different. I keep my head down but stair thru my fingers, memorizing the whole sham.

I clean under my thumbnails with the clip of my biro whilest Shawd goes thru his song and dance, basically lying thru his teeth. Then we have to sing yet another hymn.

Everyone's itching to be dismiss'd and already grabbing up their bags from the deck when Shawd decides to makes 2 further announcements.

1st off, the archaic and draconian rules regarding the wearing of skool uniform and short hair, will be relax'd for those of us who have now reache't the 5th year. This comes as no surprise as we are now fully sexually mature. However, due to the fact that a certain persistent eliment within the skool still insists on behaving like children we will still not be permitt'd to walk on the grass, cut across the back fields or smoke or bring alchole into the skool.

Finnaly, Shawd reads out the punishment list. Naturaly, my name is on there, but not for talking in assembly but wearing my greatcoat in skool, which is a new offence i personally have never heard of. I put up my hand to protest.

"Put your hand down, Claudius!"

"But it's not fair, sir."

"Rules arnt made to be fair. Now turn round and face the wall!"

"Its cold out, i only step't in thru the door."

"Well every one else in this skool knows the rules, they've been pinned up on the skool notice board for the past 6 months, go out there and read them."

"I've never seen them, sir."

"Well you need to open your eye's boy! It clearly states that all outside coats must be remov'd before entering the skool building, with no exceptions. Your not an exception, are you, Master Claudius?"

"No, sir."

"No, sir! I should think not. Now belt up and face the wall! All the names that i have read out will stay behind. The rest of you, - dimiss'd."

I stand there waiting 'til all the others have fil'd out past me. Several boys from B5 make rude signs at me as they pass. The Badger for example, draws his finger across his throat and sticks his tongue out. Cowsfroth pretends to be masterbating and Dingbat merely points to his own kneecap and grins manicaly.

After sticking his papers in his briefcase, Shawd comes down off his podium and starts barking at me.

"Ah, Master Claudius, it's a pleasure to have you back. So you're the joker who thinks he can wear his outside coat into skool and think it highly amusingly that a young lad has tragicly lost his life? You must shear your joke with me, or perhaps you'd like me to call his parents so that they can come in and enjoy the merriement?"

"I wasn't joking, sir."

"Then why were you giggling like a skool girl in my assembly?"

"I wasn't, sir. I was asking Marshgas a question."

"Asking Marshgas a question? Oh, i see. Truly, this is an extraordinary new thirst for knollege you've suddenly aquir'd, Claudius. We must see if it can be put to good use. Maybe you could help me fathom out why an idiot moron from 5B3 is going to be expelled from skool at 1/2 term?"

All the while Shawd's admonishing me he's is also circling round me like a vile hyena.

"I just ask't him something, sir. That's all."

Oh, this wouldn't be the famouse professor Marshgas, you are referring to would it?"

I shrug my shoulders.

"And what question, pray, was so pressing that it couldn't waite to be saited till after assembly?"

"It was about Applecakes, sir."

"Applecakes? Do you mean Appleton, Claudius?"

"Yes, sir."

"And what about Appleton, Claudius?"

"I just wonder'd if his head came off, sir." Shawds face whitens slightly but then he continues with his bluster.

"And who gave you that information, Claudius?"

"No one, sir. Some of the boys were just talking and i wonder'd if his head came off."

"And what other gems of information did you glean from these 'skollers'?"

"That Applecakes hung himself on account of you fiddling with him, sir."

And with that Shawds famouse kneecap comes smashing up into my skool boy thigh and i fall face down onto the cool, dark colour'd, parqi flooring.

"Now, Claudius!" hisses Shawd, "all outside coats must be remov'd on entering the skool building! You know the rules as well as everybody else!"

"What rules, sir?"

"Whatever rule i deside you must obey, boy!"

"Yes, sir!"

"So why where you wearing your overcoat in my assembley?"

"I don't know, sir."

"Well, you'd better stay down there until you remember, hadn't you? Now i want to see 24 press-ups!"

Shawd points to the ground and really does expect me to perform 24 press-ups for him.

His face is comical with it's bald dome and angry, rodent-like eyes. I smirk to myself and carry on lying there. Actually, i turn my face away sarcastically and Shawd screams at me, pulls me skidding across the floor, out thru the swinging doors and along the corridor.

I manage to get to my feet but he keeps on draggin me along by the scruff, tripping me all the way up the stairs to his office. He shoulders the door open and shoves me inside.

I look round his dismal little cubbyhole. The real reason he has brought me to this place is not because i was talking during assembly, or that i ask't about Applecakes head, nor is it because i wore my outside coat in assembly then refus'd to get down on my hands and knees and perform 24 press-ups at his feet. No, the real reason i am here is because of my confiedence; becouse i am still partially intact and the fact that i haven't yet been tottaly broken.

Shawd turns the key in the lock and drops it into his top pocket.

"Rite then, Master Claudius, lets see you lose your temper now. Becouse this time the door is lock't and this time you'll have to come thru me" and with that he takes off his jacket and starts rolling up his shirtsleeves. "And as soon as you lay so much as one dirty, little, finger upon my person, Master Claudius, i can garrentee you will be down Canterbury nick before your feet touch the ground! Do you hear me, boy! You think that you're a man, do you? Well, if you're such a tough guy, come on and try some of this, you pathetic little shit!" and he hold's his fist's up ready to punch.

I look at him, this incredible idiot then look away thru the window at the gray outside.

"Come on, boy. You think that you're such a hard man. You think your so smart. Oh yes, your smarter than the rest of us all put together, arnt you! Well lets see you fight." I keep ignoring him, my face turned slighlty away. Shawd grabs hold of my face and makes me look at him.

"Well, ive got news for you, boy. You're not 1/2 as smart as you think you are, you're a blinking idiot! Your a moron! And your going to end up on the same scrap-heap with all of those other useless, good-for-nothing scum! Do you hear me?!" I blink slightly in acknowlegment.

Old Shawd drops my face and turns away in disgust. He paces up and down on his little legs, then stops short and walks rite up to me again, 'til his nose is almost touching my chin.

"You may think that the rules don't apply to you, but you are sorely rong young man. There's no room for 'stars' or 'special talents' in this skool, Claudius. Not whilst i am skool proctor, there isn't!

"Doing your silly paintings in your silly art classes with fancy, Mister bludy Catweasel. But ive got news for you - you will not be taking any art exam or going to any fancy art skool whatsoever. Because i personally am going to make sure that you don't! Do you understand me boy! Do you understand?

"You think it's us who are all stupid and your Mister bludy smartie pants, don't you! I can see it ritten all over your insolent bludy face! You're some sort of bludy genius and weer all idiots, is that it?!

"Oh yes, Claudius, i am going to make your life very miserable for you. So missrable that your life won't be worth living! So missrable that you'd rather be in hell! Oh yes, i am going to break you, Claudius. What do you think of that?"

I look pass't his left ear out the window. There's a purple colour'd wood pigion taking off from a branch, heading over towards Green Acre farm. Shortly, a 2nd wood pigion, that must be it's mate, takes off from a near by bush with a pice of straw in it's beak.

"You let that sink in, boy! Because no one is going to entertain your airs and graces out in the big bad world. No, you'll be brought up by the short and curlys in 2 shakes! In 2 seconds flat, to be presisce!

"Oh, yes, then you'll be sorry, but by then it will be too late and there'll be no time for painting your silly pictures. You'll be brought up by your boot straps, quick as a flash, no mistake!"

Shawd comes in even closer, so's that i can examin the red vains on the end of his nose. "As long as you are a pupil in this skool, you will follow all of the rules and time-table most meticulously, most meticulously. If you have a problem with that, then you know who you have to deal with, don't you! Do i make myself clear, Claudius!?"

I stand there and clear my throat.

"With respect, sir ... in my humble opinion ... sir, you run this skool like a despot, sir. As if you were a bullying lieutenant in the Royal Navy at about the time of Nelson, sir. Like as if you have no care for the lives of your crew and you hate all humanity, sir. Like as if you have kill'd one of your crew, sir, by driving him to commit suicide, because of one of the breastly acts you have perpetrat'd against him, sir." And i stand to attention.

Old Shawd picks up a pen and moves it to another place on his desk. Next, i am bang'd up against the cupboad and a small fist is push't into my face. There is white scum in the corners of Shawds mouth and he sprays me with his boil'd egg spit. His breath smells of raw meat. "Rite, Claudius, im going to leave this office for 2 minutes, and when i come back you will have complet'd those 24 press-up's of punishment i set you, or else! Do i make myself clear?"

His other mitt has me by the scruff and it really is quite difficult to breathe.

At last he wipes his mouth and releases me.

58

The Dockyard beckons

I HAVE smarten'd myself up and had all of my golden locks shorn off.

I am also wearing my father's old RAF trousers, an ancient skool blazer and one of his starch'd collars. Now that we are allowed to wear our hair long, i sport a short back and sides. Now that a blazer is no longer required dress, i wear one. The same goes for the skool tie and polising my shoes, if my father we'er here to see me perhaps he would be proud of me, but i doubt it.

It seems that i am not the only pupil at this skool to have become a man over the summer holidays. Marshgas to, says that he has had relations with a girl.

"Im surpris'd that you could fit yours in" i tease him. Marshgas blushes and looks down. "How big is it on the donk?" Marshgas looks up and grins.

"It comes up to a certan hole."

"Your mouth?"

"No, my belly button." And he looks down again.

How i love to bullie Marshgas. As i am bulli'd, so too i must bully. Marshgas is my subject. What will become of him when he leaves here? He certainly won't grow any taller.

* * *

We have all been told that we must have jobs when we leave this dump and that it will not be acceptable for us to just sign on at the Dole office.

Like Applecakes, if i gave myself the command i would hang myself.

I have decid'd what will happen to me in the future - i will be punish'd and made to suffer for my simple innocence.

Friday morning every boy in the 5th year is handed a pink slip with their name and a time ritten on it, in red pen. 15 minits before our designated time we are to que up in the corridor, outside Mister Meatons office. Meaton is the career officer. He will decide which jobs we are fit for then send us along to our respective interviews.

One at a time us kids dissaper in thru that door, then 5 minits later come out clutching a 2nd slip of paper with our futchers all sign'd stamp't and date'd.

Yes, the Dockyard is going to swallow us all up. Then it is my turn.

When i go in, Meaton is sat stuff't behind his desk, munching on a pork pie, his face like a stack of luncheon meat.

Meaton looks up out of his butchers face.

"Sit down . . . ?"

"Claudius, sir."

"Yes . . . Claudius, sit down." And he swallows a mouthful, brushes the crumbs from his plump fingers, and leafs thru his file.

"So, Claudius, im here to help you find a sutable career. A job . . . whatever . . . one that will suit your . . . qualifications." And he swallows one last crumb of pie, sticks his finger in his back tooth and re-shuffles the papers in front of him.

"Now, what would you like to do?. Youve given it some serious thought? . . . Because the time is rapidly approaching . . . when you leave this skool . . . have you any idears? Interests, perhaps?"

"No, not really, sir."

"Well you need to start thinking about it. Seriousely . . . think about it. What about the Dockyard… There are many openings for a lad in the Dockyard." And he picks up an application form and pretends to be studying it with interest, as if it's some great new idear.

"No, not really, sir."

"Look . . . Claudius, you have to consider what you are going to do with your life. There aren't that many openings for a boy with your … projected exam results. The Dockyard realy is the most sensible option."

I rock back on my chair, gnaw on my knucle and studdy the lite up on the cealing.

"I don't think you'll find any answers up there. Now come along, i haven't got all day! . . . Look, ile put down dockyard on your form, shall I? Just for the time being. It will be easyer in the long run.

"Now is there a trade your interested in? Come along, sit up straight, take your fingers out of your mouth and show some interest."

Meaton squints at me. "You wouldn't treat the furniture at home like that, now would you, so don't treat skool property like it.

"Come on lad what are you going to do with your life, boy? Come on, amaze us!"

I sit up and look Meaton in the eye. "I want to be a painter, sir!" "Yes, excellent. Painting and Decorating. That's a good start.

Im sure we can find you an opening there ... Now let me see ..." and he starts rummaging about in the Dockyard file.

"No, sir, i want to be an artist, sir, like Vincent van Gogh, sir."

Meaton looks at me dubfounded, then laughs in an uncertain way. "Of course your pulling my leg, Claudius."

And nodding to himself, dismisses my idear with a gesture of his plump hand.

"No, sir, that's really what i want to do, sir." Meaton looks at me, really for the 1st time.

"And what are you going to live on, if i may ask ... Claudius, fresh air?"

"Vincent van Gogh's brother, Theo support'd him, sir."

"I see, so now you're telling me that your brother is going to hand over his hard earn'd wage packet at the end of each week so's that you can loaf about at home painting pictures all day!" And Meaton smiles triumphantly. "And then i suppose you're going to cut your ear off as well!"

"If my brother won't support me, sir, ile go on the dole."

At this point Meaton rites the word Dockyard on the top of my form and he tells me that the interview is over.

"I'm sorry young man, but you havn't the qualifications . . . there's nothing more i can do . . . of course art skool is out of the question . . . there are minimum qualifications. It's out of my hands. Im sure the dockyard will be . . . adiquat."

I stand, go to the door and turn the handle to leave. Then, Meaton calls me back.

"You will get a sencible job, Claudius. A sencible job that suits your station and is a reflection of your exam results."

59

The Ghoul of the Motorway Bridge

HAVING RULES and lessons driven into us and naughtiness and individualism smash'd out of us is what counts at this skool. Only, for all their pathetic attempts at teaching us the rudiments of an education, we still don't seem to be able to actually read or rite yet.

No, after five years of their shouting and beating on us we have managed to learn nothing, or rather we have learned to make faces and stare out the window at nothing in particular; dreaming of a world that proberbly never existed, or ever will.

I have been told by Shawd to report to detention and rite down what i believe my destiny in the big, wide world will be.

The fact that i think that im better than everybody else and lack all humility isn't necessarily true, tho none of my ambitions, in my teacher's estimations, are anywhere near mediocre enough.

This is my essay:

The Ghoul of the Motorway Bridge
Obviously i will not live beyond the age of 17, so there is little sence in me waisting my time striveing for exam results, bothering to please my parents and teachers, or worrying about achiving any kind of station in life.

I have blond hair and unusually dark eyebrows. My eye's also are darkish, tho my mother says that their true colour is hazel.

When you see me walking or running amongst my classmates it is apparent that i am a racehorse amongst donkeys. Also, i have a snaggl'd tooth and my head has been ripp'd clean off.

I live in the River M-. My family have always live'd on or about the river but i can honestly say that i am the 1st in a long line of theifs and scoundrels to actually live 'in' the river.

By living 'in' the river, i mean that i am a ghost and not to be triffeld with. As everyone knows rivers are the places of all beginnings and all endings, and as my family began here so they will end here, with me - the ghost of all their rongdoings.

Being a ghost means that i sometimes choose to leave the river of my own free will and hover up over this dessolate motorway bridge, from the top of which i can see all the way into the wretch'd town of my birth.

The dirty smudge of the cathedral spire sticks forlornly up into the nite sky. It's when you realise that that spire isn't medevil at all but was in fact stuck on by some inflat'd Victorian that you begin to see life for the sham that it all really is.

Street lites flare up over this sad, melancholic river and a skoolboy can get quite romantic about his horrible past, takeing to walking in graveyards, mulling over childrens graves and wondering about the dust of rotting children that lie within.

In the buitiful dawn of time my ancestors hunt'd this river for food. Under the cover of darkness they pick't their way down from the high chalk hills to wait in ambush by the little brook, that ran where the old Town Hall presently stands.

Presently a herd of wolly rhinos would come to take their

morning wallowings, charging about in the reed beds like insain tracktors, only pausing now and again to take a swiff't drink, then raising their wolly heads to let out throaty rasps, before rushing off to knock one of the cheekier young rhinos into a particularly deep and muddy bog.

At this moment the top shooter would step forth and spear the animal in it's massive hart. Then the other hunters would come, clubbing the beast about the ears with their stone axes; and whilst the rhino was still in it's death throws, push fire into the death pit, scortching off it's red hair, cooking it alive. And so the feast would begin, women children and the old, bringing knives and cooking pots.

Perhaps you think that i rite this down merely to shock you, or amuse myself; or to ridicule you as i swing ghoulishly back and forth above your heads, grining on the end of this tar'y rope.

And you would be rite in thinking me a sarcastic youth, but also i am a sick and infirm youth, a shadow youth and in many ways already something of a ghost.

There are many secrets and lies i have been ask't to love, hold and protect in my short life but now it is time for me to speak: I have been favored by a person in a place of authority and it is through the inopropriate attentions of this 'teacher of sex' that i find myself sitting here contemplating the vast drop benith my feet.

This 'sex teacher' is an older man, in his late 40's, and his stern hand has touched me in unspeakable intimacy. Truly, i have alow'd this vampire to rob me of my childhood.

In my simple childish mind, i thort that this trade had been chorograph't by my mother, and that after i was broken in, this vampire would marry my mother, replace my absent father and perhaps love me as his son. But no, we still live alone.

Once, when i ask't my mother about the circumstances of my birth and young life, she confied'd in me that when she 1st found that she was pregnant she tri'd to have me abort'd. I ask't her why and she repli'd, whilst putting a piece of burnt, butter'd toast into her mouth, that all mothers consider abortion.

And of course rather than loathe my own mother for this addmission, i reason'd that it must be me who was at fault for trying to be born, therefore deserving to be terminated, cast out and abuse'd.

As i wasn't even wanted in the womb, so i am not want'd here and i sit perched over this vile river with a coarse knot tied round my throat.

The river a distant, muddy whirl at my feet, beckons to me. By my side i have my fathers tresur'd antique Napolionic decanter - half empty and chipp't - and the wind kisses me gently on my hot forehead; tasselling my skool boy hair and, like a child in sleep, i raise my hand and brush it from my eyes.

I wonder weather my mother will cry for me when she discovers that i am a ghost? And will my parents ever question their past actions and ponder if at times it would have been more natural to have lov'd me and look't after me a little; to have said a kind word to me hear and there, to occassionaly encourage me and let me live the care free life of a skool boy rather than by neglect, subjecting me to my abusers nasty passions? Should they not have been kinder to me or in some instances consider'd my welfare?

With a terrible jolt i feel my bottom slip from this cold, rain flecked rail and i swim out into the darkness, my hands clamoring. My fathers Napolonic decanter jumps from my hand, spurting a little fountain as it revolves into miniature, to be swallow'd by the nite and distance.

Slowly and painfully, i pull myself back up onto this balustrade and continue my ghostly vigile.

From 2 hundred feet below, the wisperings of a tall ship waft up between the pale columns of the bridge. Shes a 3 master, heading out into the estery and then to impossble oceans beyond.

I peer into that blackness, listing for the boombing of her white sails and i know that i am a lost youth, a sick youth and that i in many ways am nearer to death than life.

And how does a carefree child become so marri'd to death and missery? By being force't to touch the private parts of a grown man with his child's fingers and lips, that's how; by being force't to bury his most tender and trembling hart in a dustbin of filth, that's how; by being corner'd and beaten by his teachers and bullys and being force't to deni his divinity, that's how; by being pull'd from his mothers breast if he ever dare show any signs of anger or frustration, that's how, and if he should be lost, or lonely or in any way hungry for succour, to be deni'd that succour, that's how. By being set free to be pray'd upon by beasts, that's how!

If i could let out the small broken howl of a child, i would - this once butiful golden-hair'd boy, with wonder and magic churn'd to blackness in his hart.

But as it has been ingrain'd in me that to show any kind of frustration will result in the withdrawal of love, so i will remain silent and withdraw my love also. As i have been lock't out of the world, so i too will lock the world out.

Even after my leap from this butifull motorway bridge and when i am living the carefree life of a ghost down there, in the murky depths of the river - stumbling around, blindly fumbling for my decapitat'd head - well even then, i won't search for my head out of any sense of care or compassion for myself but rather just to wave it ghoulishly in the faces of the living.

How strange that i already know that riting this down means nothing and i can never change anything.

No, nothing i can ever say or do will ever make anyone see me differently, or make anyone love me or want to hold me. No one cares about my threat to end my own pathetic life and everything i utter will merly be look't upon as a lot of childish sillyness.

So i become like the purple shadows that gather benith the motorway bridge and drink to my impotence in the world of grown ups.

Of course, rather than sitting up here, goading myself into killing myself, wouldn't it show a little more 'penasche' to murder she who gave birth to me in the 1st place: namely my own mother. Which is a sinful thing to say and i retract it here and now. Yes, i hereby deni that i have ever thort or consider'd such a thing and disown the sentiments enclos'd as ever having been mine.

If, as some people have accused me, i have an over whelming sense of lack in my life, it could be possible, wouldn't you agree, that it derives from my childhood and my mother's intense belief in our impending and certain doom at the hands of my father? This, coupled with her demand that i take a meek and lowly position in life could, i imagin, succed in poisoning a young child's self confidence.

"You wouldn't be wean'd!" she accused me, "i was running out of milk. I was at my wits end! I try'd everything but you wouldn't eat a thing!" And i look down at the brown carpet and back up to her trembling hand - holding a pint of dark, black stout - and realis'd that there was never enough for me, and never could be enough for me and never can be enough for me.

One thing's for sure, i am lost and alone because i have cut out my hart and burie'd it as if in a nitemare and have no idear where to find it.

Here's something else: one nite in my babyhood, my mother pull'd at my winkle as i stood nak'd in the bath.

"What's this?" she ask't, and i hid it shamefully between my legs and didn't know how to answer her question.

As i have been touch'd by my mother i have also been touch'd by a man, which is forbidden.

But even if (though in this instance it certainly is not the case) a child's unhappiness is due entirely to the impotency inflicted on him by his own unloving mother - and through her neglect and lack of protection, he has come to be sucked and plundered by an older man - it is still unfair to infer that he takes his own life purly out of fear of coming to this realization.

It is therefore not cowardice that stops this young man from killing his own mother, but hidden secrets that he must never alowe himself to feel, nurture or contemplate in the lite of day. Besides, any with holding of love that my mother may or may not inadvertently have been guilty of, would have been done in holy, blessed ignorance, and since she is to all intense and purposes unaware of her sin against myself and my sex, i hereby forgive her unconditionally.

Skool is a sick and rotten place, where sick people do sick things to children behind blind walls and everyone has to pretend that it is not happening and to keep schtum about it.

If you belive that every person is born free to think and behave in anyway they so choose, and that no one can therefore force or induce anyone to do anything - much less destroy their own lives - that still doesn't mean that a coward can necessarily choose how he feels, dose it?

But that is exactly what i do: i force myself to feel peev'd and insult'd and even search out new tormenters, looking for ritchins men and strange, painted women to insult me and confirm my own scathing opinion of myself. And when they attack me on the grounds of my lack of character and prudence, i just smile back at them and they look away, appall'd at my lack of humility.

No, even if a young fellow is wholly responsible for his own feelings and beliefs, i still belive it possible that thru his own stupidity, or perhaps the damnation of god, he could be train'd with minimum effort into accepting the position of a slug.

So this is how i have become a nobody, and now everyone has the rite to walk rite up to me and smash me aside as if i am of no more consequence than an ant. Also their women - with breasts and arses attached - kill me with a single twitch of their sexual buttocks and force me to wank myself off.

At last, you will say, now we truly see him: the skunk has expos'd himself in all his egocentric glory!

And so you are rite and im glad. Because my secret hope is that you will hate me and resent me, because hatred and resentment is all i understand; and is the only reaction that i can possibly tolerate from fellow human beings.

Yes, all those most tender and painful revelations i have been pouring out to you over the pages of my novel were nothing but a sacrin fog to hide my nastiness behind. In short – 'the father may well be a 1st class bastard but the fruit doen't fall far from the tree!

This is a charge that i gratefully accept, it being far better after all to embrace being self pitying than to ever dare acknowledge that in some deep, dark corner of my child's mind, i dream of killing my own mother.

And so i sit here whispering silently to myself about my own violent and unwholesome life.

It is somewhat ironical, is it not, that this very arrogance of survival that help't me endure my skool day's will also enable me to destroy my own young life? Or more precisely, it is my hatr'd of my own arrogance and my fear of my own hatr'd, that will allow me to fling myself from this vile concrete motorway bridge into the muddy river below.

I finger my little knot of rope, sat here with all my feelings burried so deeply in my subconcious that i don't even know if my hartles wish to kill myself, and my fear of what that hides is true. Or if i haven't just made the whole thing up from start to finish.

But what seems certain is this: i have been so thoroughly smashed in my retche'd childhood by my mother and teachers and by their denial of my divinty, that i have been forc't to submerge all of my god-like qualities beneath the lip of consciousness, untill it has finnaly made it possible for me to terminate such a vial, ugly, stinking son as myself, and there by destroy all thoughts that i won't even allow myself to think.

But what if i have already flung myself from that disgusting motorway bridge, the rope decapitating me and sending my riggling body plumiting to the purple shadows bellow, shortly follow'd by my still screaming head? Then, surely, it is nobody's fault but my mothers, and she must be made to see that it is so; and be made to take her shear of the blame, along with all those others - my teachers, abusers and my friends, who never once honor'd me, or ever quite lov'd me enough.

Perhaps you think that i am just a sentimental, headless old corps, or wurse still, a bitter, resentfull youth, lacking even the courage to turn myself off. But i killed myself for you, sir, my lord and master. It was your hand that touche't me. And may i just remind the esteamed reader that they should be very careful what slander they do they living, much less the dead.

Sign'd, **Gustov Claudius.**
April 22nd 1976

Hear it ends.

After word

Mister Shawd, the skool proctor, has read my journal and told me that as from this afternoon i am to considor myself expelled from The W- Secondary Skool for Boys.

By the edict of this directive i will not be allow't to sit my art exams on Monday morning but must instead proce'd directly to The Old Drill Hall, C - , where i am to register myself unemploy'd. All of which is excellent news.

An unauthenticated photograph of the author, Athens 1974

Photograph by John Hamper

Readers notes